S̶T̶
MAGIC

BOOK YOUR PLACE ON OUR WEBSITE AND MAKE THE READING CONNECTION!

We've created a customized website just for our very special readers, where you can get the inside scoop on everything that's going on with Zebra, Pinnacle and Kensington books.

When you come online, you'll have the exciting opportunity to:

- View covers of upcoming books
- Read sample chapters
- Learn about our future publishing schedule (listed by publication month *and author*)
- Find out when your favorite authors will be visiting a city near you
- Search for and order backlist books from our online catalog
- Check out author bios and background information
- Send e-mail to your favorite authors
- Meet the Kensington staff online
- Join us in weekly chats with authors, readers and other guests
- Get writing guidelines
- AND MUCH MORE!

**Visit our website at
http://www.kensingtonbooks.com**

STOLEN MAGIC

ESRI ROSE

ZEBRA BOOKS
Kensington Publishing Corp.

http://www.kensingtonbooks.com

This is dedicated to the ones I love.
Angel Joe and the 'rents, Roger and Toni.

Acknowledgments

The thanks of a grateful writer go to the following: My agent, Jennifer Unter, who is great at her job and also gets my jokes. To my editor, Danielle Chiotti, who illuminates my manuscripts' trouble spots like blood on a crime scene. Thanks to my interim editor, Peter Senftleben, and all the wonderful folks at Kensington Publishing/Zebra. Thanks to Scott Gould at RLR Associates.

Big thanks to authors/blurbers Kerrelyn Sparks and Jeanne C. Stein. Thanks so much to author Lynda Hilburn for all the promotion fun! Smooches to my Noodley sisters in the Wet Noodle Posse. Thanks to my 'rents, Angel Joe's wunnerful family, Red Leather Heather and Thanksgiving Sheila, Laura Hansen, Olde Crone Amy, Musette's Uncle Dennis, neighbors Brad and Dominick, and members of the Chorale. Thanks to Musette La Plume for squeaky love.

Special thanks to my buddies Maria Mazzaferro and Amy Berliner (née Castronovo), for giving me glimpses of what it means to be Italian. You'll notice I stole some names and stuff. Thanks to Eric at the Outlook Hotel for letting me case the joint.

And finally, big squeezing thanks to all my readers, especially those who contacted me with praise for my first book! Come visit me at ElvesAmongUs.com.

Chapter One

When it comes to elves versus humans, the deck is stacked against us—*us* being elves. Yes, being an elf means always having the last word. A shot of elven hypnotism, or *glamour,* and a human thinks what you want him to think. This ability keeps us hidden among the enemy, but it only works in person. Glamour hasn't stopped humans from slowly driving us toward extinction. Elves need wilderness. Humans consume wilderness like breakfast cereal. In the end, it all comes down to real estate.

The few humans who know about elves often say we're not doing ourselves any favors by staying hidden. *How can we help you if we don't know you're there? Let us know, and we'll share.* Yeah, because that worked so well for the Native Americans, and the Australian aborigines, and the Picts. Who are the Picts, you ask? Exactly. Who *are* the Picts? You never hear about them anymore.

Humans as a group are trouble, but humans as individuals can be very . . . *attractive.* For one thing, humans generate positive life energy when having sex—and elves live on life energy. Yes, humans are often ignorant, destructive, and careless, but they're just as often clever, generous, and loving. Humans are like the cousins you're not supposed to hang out with—the distant and disdained branch of the family tree, with the cool toys, bad habits, and a twinkle in their eyes.

Take Mark Speranzi, my photography teacher. He definitely has a twinkle in his eye, and all too often it seems to be directed at me. Since I learned most of what I needed to know during the first two classes, I'd taken to drawing Mark in the margins of my notebook.

I shaded the dark circle of his eye, leaving a white glint in the pupil, then studied the result. His shaggy hair and narrow, intelligent face were just right, but there was something wrong about the mouth. It was too smiley—or maybe not smiley enough.

"Is that a drawing of me?"

I looked up to see Mark himself standing next to my chair. At the moment, his mouth was very smiley.

"It *is* me, isn't it? I should get a haircut."

Around the classroom, other members of the class craned their necks to see what our teacher was talking about. I made a quick adjustment to Mark's thoughts so he forgot the sketch, then turned my notebook's page to hide the drawing.

His brow furrowed. "I'm sorry . . . Did you have a question, Adlia?"

"No, I'm fine." I picked up the digital camera in

front of me. "Adjust for fluorescent or halogen lighting. Got it."

He nodded and resumed his lecture on the color effects of different light, walking as he talked.

Even though no one but Mark had seen the drawing, I sat in a pool of my own embarrassment during the rest of class, wondering yet again why elves associated with humans when it was so *exhausting*.

The disadvantage of sitting in the back of the room is that you can't make a run for it when class ends. As we packed up our notes and gear, the woman seated next to me said, "Can I ask where you get your hair done? That reddish-gold color is so pretty, especially with the curls."

"I don't get it done anywhere. It's just my hair." I didn't know what else to say, so I picked up my camera. "Excuse me. I need to put this away."

She pursed her mouth. "Sorry to keep you."

I didn't *mean* to be rude. It was just that my social skills weren't the greatest. To avoid further conversation, I took a long time organizing my messenger bag as people moseyed toward the door, chatting like sparrows. When the room cleared, I walked quickly toward the exit, head ducked and both arms around my bag as I passed Mark's desk.

"Adlia?"

I paused at the door, halfway out. "Uh-huh?"

He leaned over his folded arms to see me as I edged even farther out the door. The faded denim shirt he wore hung from his broad shoulders and showed a V of olive skin at his neck. "Adlia, is everything okay? You seem a little subdued today, as opposed to your normal, talkative self."

"Ha-ha. I'm impressed you managed to say that with a straight face." Were there shades to my sub-duedness? If so, did everyone notice them, or just Mark? "I'm fine." I cleared my throat. "Thanks."

He grinned, the corners of his mouth curling. "Okay, then. Let me know if you have any problems in class. Oh, and that picture you took of the tree roots going into the creek?" He gave an emphatic nod. "Really nice."

I couldn't meet his eyes anymore. The twinkle was in full effect, making me wonder if he were making fun of me. "Thanks," I muttered again, then made a sharp turn around the door frame, snagging my T-shirt on the door's hardware as I escaped into the hall. Elves . . . we're so frickin' graceful.

Outside the Photo Center, August heat radiated off the sidewalk, even though it was evening. Hipsters sat at café tables outside trendy restaurants, looking down their noses at out-of-town parents bonding with their kids before college started.

Soon the parents would go back to California and Texas, leaving their young'uns to get tattoos and learn how to smoke dope. But maybe I only thought that because I was jealous of their family happiness. Some of them probably wouldn't get tattoos.

Walking three blocks took me past the restaurant-and-boutique zone and across Canyon Boulevard, to the city park that ran along Boulder Creek.

Elves merge with our bit of *Ma'Nah*, the earth, to

recharge. While in this energetic state, we can also travel through the earth. But the grass felt so wonderful under my feet, I resisted the urge to melt into the ground and flow to my destination. Instead, I walked parallel to the concrete bike path.

The fast, catchy beat of a drum circle came from my right somewhere, punctuated by the occasional incoherent shout of a bum nesting under a tree.

No one bothered me as I walked the rest of the way to the Canyon Gallery and Theater, an annex building of the Boulder Public Library and location of our nerdy secret headquarters.

I let myself in with a key, being careful to lock the door after me. It was after-hours for everyone but elves, or it should have been. One poor human sat slogging away at her computer.

"Hey! Who are you?" she demanded, swiveling in her chair as I passed. A shot of elf glamour and she turned back to her screen, oblivious.

I wondered how many times this had happened to her tonight, and how it was affecting her spreadsheet results.

The sign on the door to our covert office said ARCHIVES: AUTHORIZED PERSONNEL ONLY, and no human had tried to come in since we'd screwed it on. Either no one cared about archives or they weren't sure if they were authorized. I closed the door behind me and turned the dead bolt, then tensed as I saw that our boss, Kutara, was the only other person in the room.

Kutara was the head honcho and supreme ruler in chief of the elves in Boulder, Colorado. She had organized the defeat of Fellseth, an elf-gone-bad who had cut a swath from New Mexico to Colorado, killing elves to take their energy and glamouring humans to put him in their wills. Dark elves weren't that common, but since we were already fighting to survive against human encroachment, they were seen as the ultimate betrayers.

With Fellseth dead, Kutara was determined to use his fortune to preserve wilderness areas and the elves who lived in them, and also to buy some kind of building that could serve as office space for us.

She looked up, giving me the same look a hawk gives a rabbit. Kutara is lovely, with violet eyes, black hair, and a heart-shaped face, but none of this makes her any less intimidating, nor does the preppie clothing style she's adopted. Today she wore tan slacks and a sleeveless pink shell. "Did you check the tree?" she asked.

The message tree was a twisted-wire sculpture that ran up the wall by the door, its branches stuck with paper reminders. We mostly used e-mail, but sometimes there wasn't a spare computer.

Once, *once*, I had forgotten to check the tree, and missed a reminder to get a new toner cartridge. I would never hear the end of it.

"I'm checking the tree." I plucked off a scrap with my name. "Get more copy paper." It was Kutara's handwriting, of course.

I sat down at one of the four desks that occupied the center of the room, across from She Who Must Be Obeyed. The desks faced each other, with a space in the middle for cords and cables. The effect was a sort of fountain of laptops, over which we stared at each other when we weren't staring at our screens. The rest of the space was taken up with a copier/fax, a couple of file cabinets, and storage boxes.

I thumped the office-supplies catalog on my desk and felt my spine slump all the way to my skull.

Once upon a time, one of us would have gone to Office Depot and glamoured the staff to ignore some sizeable thefts. Now we paid our own way, thanks to Fellseth's money. Well, except for rent on this space.

"Do we need anything besides paper?" I asked. "Because it's free delivery if I get over forty dollars worth of stuff."

Kutara gave me the smile I had come to dread. "Galan and I have talked about getting an investment-tracking program. I thought you might be the person to learn it."

Galan was Kutara's second-in-command, and one of the few people I considered a friend. Galan had created the message tree—the one pretty thing in our office, even if Kutara had turned it into yet another tool for making me feel guilty.

At her suggestion that I learn a new program, I felt the corners of my mouth turn down. Across from me, Kutara's did the same. It was like looking in a mirror. "I'm really not sure I'm the right person for that," I said.

"Why not? You're smart enough, Adlia. You're not having any trouble learning how to use the digital camera, are you?"

"No." The camera was for taking pictures of

prospective properties. I'd mastered the basics by reading the manual, but when Kutara suggested taking a photography class, I'd jumped at the excuse to get away from the office. Basking in Mark Speranzi's presence was a bonus. "It's just that numbers make my head hurt. That's more Galan's thing."

Her expression was like a black cloud now. "Numbers make all of our heads hurt," she snapped. "Galan has done it in the past because it has to be done, but Erin needs him at her store."

Erin was Galan's human mate. They had bonded when Fellseth had taken Galan's land and tried to kill him. Erin had found Galan when he was near death and had brought him home, not knowing he was an elf. Now Galan, whose elven talent was metalworking, made jewelry to sell in Erin's New Age shop.

Kutara went on. "With Erin needing Galan, I really can't rely on him as a full-time worker."

I felt a stab of alarm. Did she plan to rely on me? "Couldn't we hire someone to track investments? Rich humans have brokers, or whatever they're called. I'd be happy to look in the phone book—"

"A financial advisor would want to know where the money came from, to see tax returns and Social Security numbers."

"We're going to need those things eventually. You can't glamour the IRS—not all of them at once, anyway." My voice was getting shrill, but I couldn't seem to help it. "How do you think we're going to buy property without Social Security numbers and stuff?"

Kutara toyed with her staple remover, snapping

it like a pair of little jaws. "Those are all problems I have to solve, and to do that, I need you to help me. I didn't think this was a huge request, Adlia, but you seem determined to—" She broke off as the office door opened.

Galan came in, his expression serious. All elves are more beautiful than humans, but with his violet eyes and long, silver-blond hair, Galan was a looker even for elves.

"We were just . . ." I trailed off as a female elf followed him in. She had frightened eyes and a pinched look on her face.

Galan put a gentle hand on her back and steered her to an office chair. "This is Fia. I found her wandering by the creek. Fia, this is Kutara and Adlia."

Fia perched on the chair and looked over her shoulder at Galan. He patted her shoulder reassuringly, and I felt a flutter in my stomach. There had been a time when I would have given anything for Galan to touch me like that. He was the kindest, funniest, most affectionate elf I knew, and so amazingly in love with Erin that any jealousy on my part felt small and mean.

Kutara smiled pleasantly at Fia, then turned to Galan. "Wandering?" she asked.

"She's having some memory problems." Galan made it sound so innocuous, it had to be bad.

Kutara came around the desk and sat on the edge next to Fia. "What are you having trouble remembering?"

Fia brushed her chestnut hair from her face in a nervous gesture. "Everything but my name. I can't

remember anything but my name, and when—"
She stopped and looked over her shoulder.

"Galan," he prompted.

"When Galan asked me, I almost couldn't remember that." She clasped her hands in her lap. "I can't remember how I got here, or where I live. I can't remember *anything*."

Kutara nodded at her. "You're safe here. We'll take care of you and find out what's happened."

Galan headed toward his desk. "Should I call Erin, do you think?" Since bonding with Galan, Erin had developed certain healing abilities.

"Not at the moment." Kutara stood. "Can I examine you, Fia?"

She nodded.

Kutara pulled Fia's long chestnut hair aside, section by section, presumably looking for an injury. "Do you hurt anywhere?"

"No. I'm hungry, though."

"We'll help you get some energy. Don't eat human food. It will change you from elf to mortal."

Fia frowned slightly, as though this basic information were only vaguely familiar. "Okay."

Galan looked up from his computer. "I showed her how to take energy from the creek, but I'm not sure she was able to concentrate enough to do it well."

Functioning normally on water energy was like trying to run a marathon on an all-lettuce diet. Creek energy would keep Fia alive, but it wasn't a good substitute for energy from *Ma'Nah*, and an elf could get that energy only by merging with his own land—land to which he was bonded.

Kutara finished examining Fia's head. "I can't find any injury. Galan, put the word out on our Yahoo Group, asking if anyone has heard of a missing female."

Galan typed something in. "I'll also ask if anyone knows about memory loss."

"Good. There must be missing-persons sites for humans, but I doubt they would do much good."

Especially since humans were unlikely to have information on people over a hundred years old.

"Adlia," Kutara said.

I froze in my chair. "What?"

"Now would be a good time for you to research investment-management software."

"Don't you want me to help find out about Fia?"

"Galan has that under control."

I opened the lid of my laptop with a sigh. "I was just going to start that."

Chapter Two

Researching investment management turned out to be a lot like editing a book on nuclear physics. First step: look up all the unfamiliar words. I didn't care about investments. I didn't want to learn about investments. But I read lots of online articles on the basics of investments so I could make an informed decision on a program about them.

Concentrating wasn't made any easier by Fia wandering around with nothing to do and not much mind to do it with.

Galan periodically asked her questions. "Do you remember any landmarks on your land?"

Considering that elves cared for their land and spent long periods of time merged with it, that should have been an easy question. Fia's answer was a blank stare and a long silence before she said, "I think there were some trees."

"Does the name *Golden* sound familiar to you?" Galan asked.

"It's a . . . It's a color, isn't it? Or a type of wood?"

"Metal. It's also a town west of here. Does it sound familiar at all? No?"

As her energy got low, Fia developed wrinkles and her hair became lank. I'd never seen an elf so energy deprived, and it was seriously creepy.

When Fia really started to droop, Galan would take her outside and show her how to absorb the energy released by the flowing water of Boulder Creek.

Sometime before three in the morning, I sat back in my chair with a huge sigh. "It looks like we should get Quicken Premier."

Kutara opened a binder and flipped through the pages. "I've heard of that program."

"Yes. Quicken is so famous that even elves have heard of it, but it still took me four hours to figure out that's what we want."

"An informed decision is best. Go ahead and download it."

"I thought I'd add it to the copy-paper order, to get the free shipping." Not to mention that the hard copy would come with paper manuals, which could be taken outside for "studying."

Kutara nodded without looking up. "Fine." She moved a stack of folders from one side of her desk to the other.

I placed the order. "Galan, this will show up at Erin's house tomorrow sometime." We didn't have an official mailing address—another problem that would be solved by having our own place.

Kutara stopped rearranging the papers on

her desk and fixed me with her eagle eye. "The prospectus on Village Developments is missing."

The implication was that this was somehow my fault. "I gave it back to you yesterday."

"When?" She picked up another folder and riffled through the contents.

"I don't know exactly when. I just remember I gave it back to you."

She looked up, clearly exasperated. "I also found the dividend statement from Larimer filed under capital gains."

I bit my lip. "Is that not right?"

"Not in this case." She heaved a sigh and dropped the offending folder on her desk. "I need you to pay attention to details, Adlia."

"I'm trying!"

"Try harder. And please look on your desk again for that prospectus."

I had already forgotten the name. They all sounded the same to me. "What was it called again?"

"*Village. Developments.*" She got up and went to the file cabinet.

I glanced over at Galan, who was pretending to be on another planet. Somehow, that made it even worse. Maybe I didn't live and die by the P-and-L statement, like *some people,* but I was here. Kutara could at least try to leave me a little dignity.

By the time I found the Village Developments prospectus, Kutara and Galan were at his desk, looking at something on the monitor.

I cleared my throat theatrically to get their attention. "Is this what you were looking for, Kutara?" I waved the prospectus in the air. "This thing that I found on top of your quarterly-returns binder?"

She looked at me with absolutely no expression on her face. "Someone must have moved it. I haven't looked at those for a month." She turned to Galan. "The overseas accounts seemed to be out of order as well. I think we should start locking the file cabinets at night. Now, about this horse property. I think it could be returned to a wild state and make good elf habitat."

Galan murmured something to her.

Kutara's expression became slightly more chilly. She slowly raised her head toward me. "The importance of this work can make me rather abrupt at times, Adlia. I hope you don't take it personally."

And that was as close as I would get to an apology.

Deciding to take advantage of whatever guilt she might feel, I said, "Well, it's been a long night. I think I'll go home."

Kutara exchanged a quick look with Galan before she said, "Adlia, I want you to stay here with Fia tonight."

"Why me?"

Galan gave me a pleading look. "Erin is depending on me to make some new jewelry for the shop. Plus, if I don't spend some time with her she's going to lock me out of the house."

Kutara was already shaking her head when I turned to her. "If we're going to enter finances in a new program, I need Guy to help me with the files I have at home."

Guy was Kutara's human lover, although they

weren't bonded. Kutara was still bonded to land of her own, and she insisted she only used Guy for sex energy and his contacts in land development. But I had my suspicions that she really liked him.

"So I get to take care of Fia. I see." I saw that both of them wanted to get home for a little energy-raising sex with their human partners, while Adlia, who didn't have anyone, elf or human, got to babysit.

I looked at Fia. "What do you think, kid? Should we knock over a convenience store?"

She stared into space. "I'm hungry."

Chapter Three

There are a lot of ways you can "work" without working. Surfing the Internet counts as researching human behavior. Reading pop-culture blogs counts as finding possible new companies to invest in, like that company that makes shoes with little tubes for each individual toe. And listening to music online counts as, well, goofing off.

Every once in a while I got up and kept Fia from doing something inappropriate, like pouring paper clips down the shredder. By the time morning came, Fia looked decidedly peaky and I was done sitting in the office.

I called Lenny, one of my coworkers. He didn't answer, so I left a message. "Hey, it's Adlia. Where were you last night? Since you're such a slacker, I think you're the next person to do a little babysitting. Meet me by the creek, near the office." That ought to bring him, if only to figure out what I was talking about.

I locked all the file cabinets, put the key under a

mess of binder clips in Kutara's desk drawer, and left a message on her cell telling her where it was. If I were lucky, she wouldn't listen to it before she needed something. *Ha.*

"C'mon, Fia." I slapped my thigh and whistled. "Here, girl." I was counting on her to get better or I never would have done it.

She followed me outside and across the concrete bike path to a couple of dry boulders beside the water.

"Sit on this rock." I waved a hand at it. "Do you remember how Galan showed you to get energy?"

"No."

"Do you at least remember Galan? He's the hot one." I sighed. "There's energy coming off the creek. Humans call it negative ions, but we call it *ma'na'spira*—mother's breath." I sat next to her on the rock, squirmed until I found a spot that wasn't too pointy, and put my hands on her waist.

If I closed my eyes, the energy around us looked like swirling blue mist against my lids. I opened to it, felt it soak through my skin, then shifted my physical boundaries slightly so that it passed through the edge of Fia. "That's it. Take a big drink."

When she was doing it on her own, I stood and watched her hair regain its wave and shine, her face plump up again.

Eventually she turned and gave me a little smile.

"Better, huh?" I asked. "Do you remember your name?"

"Fia."

"That's right. And what's my name?"

"Um . . ."

I gave her the first syllable. "Aaaa . . . Aaaa . . ."

"Adlium?"

"Adlia. Very good!"

"What's wrong with me?" The lost look on her face was enough to break your heart.

I sat on the grass and opened my messenger bag. "I don't know, but Kutara's bound to figure it out. As far as I can tell, all that bitchiness just hones her intellect."

"That what?"

"Biiiiitcheccceeness." I sounded it out for her as I opened my journal and ripped out a page to give her. She held the paper uncertainly. "Kind of flimsy, huh?" I folded it in quarters, then handed it back along with a pen. "Here. Draw a picture or something."

Instead, she sat and gazed at a couple of ducks that had risen early to stake out the best sludge. Well, there were worse ways to pass the time.

I found my place in my journal and started a new entry.

> *Galan found Fia today. Is she still bonded to some land somewhere? What are we going to do with her if she doesn't regain her memory?*

Of course, Fia wasn't the only one with memory problems, although mine were limited to the past. Unlike every other elf I knew, I couldn't remember my parents.

Kutara's best guess was that I had been orphaned at an age when most elf children still drew energy from their parents and would have died from the separation. Instead, I had apparently bonded to my dead parents' land and spent the next couple of centuries merged with it.

Kutara was the one who had found me, corporeal once more and clueless about my place in the world. That was about a year ago, shortly after they had gotten rid of Fellseth.

Kutara had taught me to be an elf in the way a stern aunt would foster an unwanted relative. She wasn't maternal and I wasn't filial, but she felt I should have a purpose in life, and working at Elf Ops was all I knew. My crush on Galan used to pull me into the office, but any lingering feelings I had were merely irritating now that he was taken.

Kutara had also set me the task of learning about humans, since all elves had to deal with them. I had spent the last nine months watching movies, learning to read newspapers, and observing humans. That's when I had started keeping a journal, and I still jotted down expressions I liked and movies people talked about that sounded interesting. And then there was The List.

I flipped to the back pages of the journal. Every other elf in the universe had some artistic talent. The List showed all the talents I *didn't* have. Wood carving, ice carving, stone carving, metalworking, painting, drawing.

Oh, sure, I had picked up drawing a little faster and better than the average human, but if that were my true ability, Mark Speranzi wouldn't have asked if that was his picture I had drawn—he would have gasped at seeing his likeness leap off the page.

I jiggled my pencil over the blank page and wrote, *Is Mark Speranzi taken?* Recently I had become obsessed with his forearms, which had the most silky, luxurious hair I had ever seen on a man. Elves didn't have much in the way of body hair. Mark's animal magnetism fascinated me, as did the way he seemed to invite me to laugh at the world, including myself.

I heard scratching, and looked up to see Fia scribbling on the piece of paper I'd given her. "What are you writing, Fia?" Maybe it would give us a clue to her background.

She held it up.

"Oh, you've drawn the ducks. Very nice." That was a feeble compliment for her sketch of a duck raising itself in the water and flapping its wings. The flying drops of water she had drawn made me want to wipe my face.

My cell phone rang, and I saw it was Lenny. "Finally."

"Got your message. Are you still at the creek?"

"Yup. I'm sitting on my favorite boulder, and do I have a present for you. A sweet, shiny girl elf!"

"Are you talking about Fia? Kutara left a message about her. It sounds pretty sad, actually."

I rolled my eyes. "Of course it's *sad,* but if you can't laugh, you'd have to cry. Where were you all night, anyway?"

"Someone must have cleaned out their garage, because I had a bunch of *paint* come through in the groundwater. You haven't lived until you've spent all night corralling molecules into one clump."

"What color paint?"

"Orange, but it's gone now. I'll be right there."

"Bye." I put away my things and stood to brush off the seat of my pants. "Fia, your Uncle Lenny is coming to take care of you now. Won't that be nice?"

Most elves would have gone back to the old homestead to refresh their land bond and grab some energy, but after two hundred years underground, a girl likes to get out and see things.

I snacked on creek energy as I strolled on the grass, watching bicycle commuters whiz past on their way to work.

"Hey! Adlia!"

I looked around. Mark Speranzi was walking toward me, camera in hand and magnificent arms on display in a short-sleeved black shirt that draped like water.

My mind searched frantically for something witty to say and came up with, "Hi."

He glanced at his watch, a silver model that looked great against his olive skin. "Are you on your way to work at six thirty in the morning?"

"Actually, I'm coming back from a wild party," I said. His expression cooled slightly, so I wiped my last statement right out of his head and replaced it with something about staying up with a sick friend. We always have the last word, remember?

"That was nice of you," he said, all smiles again.

"I can be nice." If I waited for something better to say, we'd be here all day. "What about you?"

"On my way to get coffee, and taking pictures as I go. Can I buy you a cup?"

"Um, sure."

We fell into step. I was giddy with a sense of possibilities. Here I was, going for coffee with a friend. Of course, I wouldn't drink the coffee, and I'd be hypnotizing him not to notice that. My happy balloon deflated a little. Was someone still your friend if you controlled his thoughts a tiny bit? Was Mark my friend if I couldn't answer any of his questions truthfully? I decided to keep him talking about himself, to avoid the whole problem. "What are you taking pictures of?"

"Anything that says *Boulder*. One of my easiest moneymakers is a calendar of local-color shots. You don't have to be a famous photographer to sell pictures of a pretty town when it's filled with tourists and college students looking for gifts."

"Do you use digital or film for that kind of work?" Look at me! I was having a conversation!

"I do a lot of digital, but I'm using film today, just to keep my hand in."

I nodded. "So are you from Boulder?"

He laughed. "Is anyone from Boulder?"

I opened my mouth but shut it just as quickly. Boulder hadn't existed when I was born, so I probably didn't count.

"I guess I've lost most of my accent," Mark went on, "but the rest of my family lives in Boston. My parents have a wedding-cake business. I started out taking pictures of cakes, graduated to the weddings themselves, then moved out here to get a little space from my family."

"You wanted to get away from your family?"

The concept seemed bizarre to someone who'd never had a family.

He held up both hands. "It's not that we don't get along. It's just that I have two sisters and a brother, plus about a million cousins. It's a little hard to hear yourself think." He smiled wryly. "Speaking of being attention-deprived, I *will* continue to talk about myself unless you stop me. How 'bout you? Are you close to your family?"

"I don't have any family. My parents are dead, and I don't have any siblings."

"Oh, Adlia." He touched my back lightly. "I'm sorry."

Any pleasure I felt at the contact was lost in a jolt of surprise. There were strong traces of elf glamour on Mark, and they weren't mine.

"Stop," I commanded, and he halted in his tracks. I kept him still and blank while I ran my hands over his head, his chest, his hands. Only a skilled tracker could specifically identify a glamour that wasn't his own, and even then, he'd need to personally know the elf that had done it. But even *I* could tell that someone had glamoured Mark pretty heavily.

My first response was visceral and shocking. This was *my* human. I picked up his unresisting hand and stroked his arm down to his fingertips. *Warm skin, silky hair, the complicated bones of his knuckles.* Humans didn't dissolve into *Ma'Nah* until they died. This was Mark in his entirety, beneath my fingertips. Humans were so vulnerable singly, but together they changed the world.

A heavy glamour could be the innocent result of an elf trapped by unusual circumstances, or it might be a dark elf setting up shop. Kutara would expect me to find out more.

I started him walking again and released him from the glamour. "You were telling me about coming to Colorado. How long have you been here?"

"About five years. I was visiting someone and never got around to leaving. What about you?"

Lying was second nature to me, but that didn't mean I enjoyed it. "What about me? I like to listen, and you said you enjoy talking. Do you really want to mess with a winning formula?"

He didn't laugh. "I'd like to know more about you. For instance, where does the name Adlia come from?"

It's elven. "It's Czech."

He smiled. "See? That wasn't so hard."

"Most men appreciate a bit of mystery in a woman."

He shrugged, then hiked up the strap of his camera bag. "As long as the mystery doesn't include stuff like alcoholism or cutting yourself."

I stopped, and a bicyclist who had been waiting to pass narrowly missed running into me. "Is that why you asked me to have coffee? You think I'm broken and you feel sorry for me?"

"No. I asked because I'm curious about you. Also, I like the color of your hair."

"Oh." I stared at him, resisting the urge to glamour him and see if he was telling the truth. He looked like he might feel a *little* sorry for me, but that didn't prevent me from feeling a glow about the hair comment. All this time I'd thought Mark just found me amusing. Could there be more to his attentions? We slowly resumed walking. "I don't cut myself or drink. I do keep a journal, with the obligatory bad poetry."

"If you know it's bad, why don't you write something better?" He had the nerve to grin at me.

"Because recognizing goodness is not the same as having it. Sometimes all you can achieve is crap."

He nodded. "You know what I first noticed about you? Your inherent cheerfulness."

Chapter Four

We went to the Trident for coffee. When it was my turn to order, I stepped aside and said, "Actually, I don't want anything."

"Eating disorder?" Mark asked.

"Stop trying to find things that are wrong with me! I'm perfectly normal." I started to laugh. "Oh, that was funny."

Mark paid for his drink. "No artist is normal."

"I'm not an artist."

"Sure you are. Your photography shows a lot of promise, you keep a journal, and you write poetry. What part of *artist* do you not understand?"

"The part where I'm good at any of them."

He pointed his finger at me. "Low self-esteem."

"Okay, you got me on that one, although I prefer to think of low self-esteem as just another term for modesty."

Mark grated nutmeg onto his cappuccino at the condiment bar. "Did I mention that modesty is one of my many outstanding traits?"

I followed him to a table and sat. "Maybe not everyone is comfortable being as happy as you are. Have you ever thought of that?"

He raised his eyebrows. "I can honestly say that I haven't. Why did you take a picture of those tree roots in the creek?"

"Because of the paradox. Trees want water, but the water is washing that tree away. It's like a battle that can never be won."

He leaned back, cupping both hands around his coffee cup. "And you don't think you're an artist."

He smiled so sweetly at me, I wanted to touch him. Instead, I turned away and fiddled with the strap of my bag as it hung over my chair. "Besides pictures of Boulder, what else do you photograph? Wildlife?"

"God, no. Those guys are out in all weather, getting bighorn-sheep crap on their Patagonia jackets and picking up fleas from the prairie dogs. I'm a people person, so I do a lot of portraits."

"Do you have any you can show me?"

He reached toward his camera bag, then stopped. "I would, but I cleared the card last night. Wait— I do have something." He put a hand in his pocket and pulled out his wallet. "This isn't very big, but it's one of my favorites."

I took the dog-eared photo he handed me. It showed a lovely brunette, elbows propped on the floor and face cradled in her hands. Her dramatic brows arched slightly and one corner of her wide mouth curved up. "She looks—" It had to be said. "She looks kind of elfin."

He nodded, smiling. "And she didn't believe she was beautiful—can you believe it? That's Faith. She's the reason I came to Colorado."

Of course she was. The picture didn't show the woman's ears, of course, but I would bet good money this was the source of Mark's glamour traces. Actually, she looked a little familiar. "I think I've seen her around. Has she ever come to class?"

"No."

We were interrupted by a blond bear of a man, who clapped Mark on the shoulder. "Mark! How's it going, man?"

Mark made the introductions. "Adlia, this is Butch, whose only job appears to be beating me at pool. Butch, this is Adlia—one of my more promising photography students and a specialist in humorous gloom." He winked at me.

Butch engulfed my hand with his and grinned. "Right on."

"I'm not that gloomy," I said.

"Why shouldn't you be?" Butch's grin was wide enough to show his molars. "The world's going to hell, but we can have a good time on the way." He turned to Mark. "Eight-ball tournament this Saturday night at 'Round Midnight. I'm spreading the word."

"I'll see if I can make it," Mark said.

"You'd better." Butch gave me a wave and left.

I pushed back my chair. "I should go. You know how it is—things to negate, people to depress."

He looked sheepish. "I'm sorry I said that. Sometimes I try too hard to be funny."

"Can I claim you were wrong? I don't think so. Anyway, I have to go." In truth, I was feeling pretty exhausted, and needed to get to my land.

"Okay. Listen, would you like to go to the pool tournament?"

"Um, maybe. I'll think about it."

"All right. Maybe I'll see you there."

I went out the back, into the alley that ran between Pearl and Walnut. Two businesses down, I passed a Dumpster. Chunks of broken asphalt jutted from under one of the legs, where it had been set down repeatedly. A dandelion grew in the exposed patch of dirt. I put my foot down as if to crush it and instead disappeared with a shimmer that would have made George Lucas moan with envy.

I gave the metaphysical equivalent of a relieved sigh as I dissolved into the ground and focused on my destination. The molecules of my messenger bag dragged on me slightly, but everything I carried had originally come from the earth. It followed me like fog as I flowed through dirt and tree roots, dodging pipes, wires, and the occasional underground stream.

The sensation of living things—earthworms, fungus, bacteria—felt like an electric hum, with the occasional racketing buzz of larger animals, like the raccoons that ruled the storm sewers. You learned not to mess with raccoons. I was just glad they hadn't figured out how to buy guns.

Was Faith Mark's girlfriend? *She's the reason I came to Colorado.* On the other hand, he'd also said, *I like the color of your hair.* Not *her* hair, mine. And he'd invited me to the pool tournament, whatever that was. I felt up on human culture most of the time, but less than a year of intensive study meant there were gaps in my knowledge.

Maybe Mark had asked only to be polite. Of course, it was unnecessary for me to feel all this uncertainty. Kutara would point out that elves could learn anything they wanted about a human, at any time. The only things that kept me from doing it were good manners and terror. *Never eavesdrop. You might hear something about yourself.*

I reached home and felt myself relax. Kutara was always telling me not to take my land for granted, but it was sort of like humans and their skin. They wouldn't want to be without it, but they also didn't run around yelling, "My skin, my skin! I'm so grateful for my skin!"

I let myself disperse fully, expanding out between the roots of the tall pines, taking time to tweak the course of an underground stream that might destabilize a slope, and buzzing a mountain-pine beetle with negative energy that sent it flying elsewhere. Of course I loved my land. It was the one thing that had always been there for me.

When I walked into Elf Ops that evening, I was surprised to see Fia still there, being examined by Galan's human mate, Erin. Kutara solved most problems so quickly, I had assumed Fia would be fixed and home by now. I went to my desk, where the newly delivered Quicken program sat with awful precision in the exact center.

Kutara lounged in the chair across from me, watching Erin and stroking her jaw in a way that would look thoughtful to the outside observer but actually signaled unease. When Kutara was truly relaxed, she moved about as much as an Easter Island statue.

Across the room, Galan and Lenny also watched as Erin stood behind Fia with her eyes closed and her hands lightly cradling Fia's temples.

Erin had short auburn hair and was almost as tall as an elf—certainly taller than me. She was usually so energetic and outspoken, her silent examination of Fia made the situation seem even more serious.

I spoke quietly to Kutara. "No luck finding out what's wrong with Fia?"

Kutara kept her eyes on Erin as she spoke, forefinger tracing her chin over and over. "We got an e-mail today from someone who's around eight hundred years old: He remembered an elf losing his memory. The affected elf wandered off and was found dead. They never found out what caused it."

"What's Erin doing? Trying to heal her?"

Kutara shook her head. "If I couldn't heal her, Erin certainly won't be able to. But she might be able to get a feel for Fia's energy. I'd like a second opinion."

Normally, Kutara getting an opinion from a human was like a neurosurgeon asking for tips from the aide who empties the bedpans, but Erin had learned to raise energy for elves through meditation, and had developed some healing abilities after bonding to Galan. As far as we could tell, she was unique in this, but she and Galan were the only bonded elf-human couple we knew, so it was hard to know for sure.

Elves had once had a tradition of oral history, but our reduced numbers and isolation from each other meant that much of our own past was lost to us.

Erin squeezed Fia's shoulders and came over to Kutara's desk. Lenny and Galan drifted over to join us. Lenny was dressed in his usual outfit of low-slung jeans, muscle shirt, and knit cap, which hid his ears and kept his dark, wavy hair out of his face.

"Well?" Kutara asked, still staring at Fia.

Erin shook her head. "It's like she's melting inside."

Kutara's shoulders lifted in a delicate shudder. "I felt the same thing." She turned to Lenny, who had a real gift for tracking elf energy through *Ma'Nah*. "I assume there's no way to trace her back to her source?"

He shook his head. "It'd be like trying to scent the absence of something. There's a lot of absence around."

"I see. We'll have to hope that someone notices that she's missing and eventually contacts us." Kutara straightened and faced her desk, a signal for the rest of us to disperse.

I eyed the Quicken box in front of me. "Do you need me to take her out for some energy?"

"She's just been." Kutara stood, picked up a monster pile of files from her own desk and plopped it on mine. "These are some of the least complicated financial accounts. You can start by entering them."

I'd gotten through the mind-numbing Quicken tutorial when Fia said, "I'm hungry," as she wandered past my desk for the umpteenth time.

I almost leaped to my feet. "I'll take her."

Kutara looked at me from under her perfect eyebrows. "She says the same thing every seven minutes."

"I know, but I could do with a snack myself. Come on, Fia. Let's have a nosh." I took her forearm to pull her along. Under her skin, her bones felt somehow insubstantial, even though she didn't look particularly different. It was as though there was a hollowness where her personality used to be.

There were no humans in the lobby this evening, and I was relieved I didn't have to glamour anyone. I led Fia outside into the glow of the security lights and locked the door behind me.

The building opened onto a concrete square containing planters and benches, with the creek path to our right. I was turning to go that way when I saw a shape rise from one of the benches.

"*Vol'kellet!*" the figure said.

"*Vol'kellet hai!*" I answered automatically. It was the formal greeting between elves, and one of the first things Kutara had drilled into me.

I stood still as the elf approached. It was a male, and he was a big 'un. My head went up and up as he came near, and I saw Fia do the same out of the corner of my eye. We must have looked like we were watching a hot-air balloon launch. A new elf in town was a rarity, but I had been one once. At least I knew he wasn't a dark elf. You could sense those—something about taking in death energy changed them.

This elf looked like a Viking, with thick, wheat-colored hair, blue eyes, and one of those manly chins with a little pad of muscle on the front. And whereas the Boulder elves dressed blend in with humans, he wore a traditional elven outfit of close-fitting brown pants, boots, and a loose shirt.

"I'm looking for the headquarters of the Boulder elves." His voice was so resonant, I could practically feel it in my feet.

I pointed at the building next to us. "You've found it."

His mouth had been turned down, but now he smiled with such charm that I found myself smiling back. "Your *ka'chil* is named Kutara, right?" he asked.

Ka'chil meant *hero* but could also mean *leader*. The second meaning was less common, since elves were territorial and often didn't play well with others. "Kutara heads up the office," I said.

"Is there any possibility I could speak with her?"

"Unless she's lost her voice in the last five minutes, I think you can hardly avoid it. I'm Adlia, by the way."

"Dagovar." He looked at Fia, but she didn't say anything.

"This is Fia," I offered. "She's a little under the weather right now."

"I'm sorry to hear that."

I led the way back to the door. "Do you live around here, Dagovar?"

"No, I'm from Texas." He followed me inside the lobby, looking around with interest as we passed into the offices beyond. "I heard about the organization and came here hoping to help."

That was a first. After Fellseth's death, Kutara had traveled along the path he had taken, getting in touch with other elves and telling them how to get organized. Although one group had dealt with a dark elf since then, and a few had e-mailed to thank Kutara for getting rid of Fellseth, no one had shown up in person.

"Well, you are in luck, Dagovar, because we need all the help we can get." I tugged a stapler out of Fia's hand and returned it to the desk we had just passed.

Galan and Erin had gone, but Lenny and Kutara were still in the office. I pushed open the door and said, "Hey, guys, we have a fan! This is Dagovar."

There were more *vol'kellets*, and Kutara came around her desk to greet the newcomer.

Dagovar inclined his head toward her. "*Ka'chil.* It's an honor to finally meet you. You defeated Fellseth. He killed my mother."

"I'm sorry for your loss, Dagovar." Kutara pulled a desk chair out for him.

He sat, looking slightly less enormous. "I heard about your work. If you can use my services, I would like to help."

Lenny raised his eyebrows at me, and I shrugged slightly. As eager as I was to have other people help with the drudgery, this put us in a slightly awkward position. We'd made it our business to understand humans and use their technology. Dagovar sounded a little provincial in his speech.

"Dagovar," I said, "are you familiar with computers at all?"

He nodded. "I lived with a human woman for several months, to gain energy. She worked with computers, and I learned from her."

Kutara looked interested. "What was her occupation?"

"She was an accountant."

Ka-ching! I gave Dagovar my biggest, bestest smile ever. "Have you ever heard of Quicken Premier?"

Chapter Five

It turned out that Dagovar's human lover hadn't asked him to massage her spreadsheets, but he was fairly conversant with the basics of menu navigation. He was also a whiz at e-mail.

"What is this project you're working on?" he asked, when I'd gone over the basics of how our office worked.

"Right now we're looking for a piece of property where we can have real headquarters, instead of having to hide out here."

"In addition to dealing with money, do you also seek out other dark elves and destroy them?"

"Luckily, dark elves turn out to be pretty rare. Since Kutara's speaking tour, some elves in Nebraska got together and took care of one, but that's the only incident we've heard about so far. But news spreads pretty slowly. Last week someone from Idaho joined the Yahoo Group. That was pretty exciting."

"Word of mouth is your main weapon, then."

"Yeah. It's not like we can advertise on TV."

I thought for a moment. "Well, I suppose we could, but it might raise inconvenient questions in the public sector."

Dagovar looked around the office and sighed. "I came here hoping to fight dark elves hand to hand, but if this is what needs to be done, I'll do it."

I dropped my voice. "Office work isn't what I saw as my life goal, either."

"It must be particularly hard for you, after the excitement of battling Fellseth."

I shook my head. "I wasn't involved in that. My only skills are number crunching and research."

"Still a valuable contribution." He smiled gravely. "If working in an office is not your life's goal, what is?"

"I don't know. My parents died when I was too young to remember, and I don't have a talent, so I'm a little confused about life in general." Apparently I was lonelier than I had realized, or I wouldn't be showering Dagovar with personal information. But he had a serious quality that invited confidences. You got the impression he thought deep thoughts.

"Both my parents are dead as well," he said, his voice a low rumble.

"It's hard, isn't it?" I whispered. "I mean, even though most elves aren't that close to their parents, you like to know they're there."

"It is hard."

We stared at each other a moment.

"So what are your goals?" I asked. "Maybe I can steal one of them."

He gazed across the room. "To get my due—

freedom, a mate, perhaps even children. To live without oppression."

"Wow." My natural cynicism slunk away from the strength of Dagovar's conviction. He was like a big, blond, elven superhero. "Well, I don't know if we can stop human oppression in an afternoon, but I guess we can get started."

I took Dagovar through the Quicken tutorial, which helped me learn it a lot better, and then we started on the simple accounts Kutara had given me. Dagovar had a better head for the big picture than I did, and working with another person took all of the dread and most of the boredom out of the process.

We'd gotten a good start on the stack of folders when Kutara asked for the spreadsheet of Fellseth's commercial properties.

"I already e-mailed it to you," I said. "I knew that was important, so I did it first."

She almost smiled. "Good."

A few minutes later, I heard her heave one of her extra deep, *someone has failed me* sighs.

I looked up. "The file name is PVC.xls. I sent it."

"Yes. I'm looking at it, and it doesn't have the field for how long the property has been owned."

I found the original paper file and brought it around to her desk. "Look. Here's the sheet you gave me, with the fields you wanted, and that's not on here."

She flipped the stack of paper-clipped documents closed and stabbed her finger at a sticky note on the first page. "What does this say?"

"Add a field for years the property has been owned," I read. "Why didn't you put it on the sheet?"

"Because I ran out of room. I thought a bright-yellow note on the first page might be sufficient." The look on her face was killing me. *I'm angry, yes,* it seemed to say. *But mostly I'm disappointed that you are such an idiot.*

I flipped the file closed and picked it up. "I'll add it. It won't take that long."

"How long?"

"I don't know. Maybe an hour."

Another sigh. "I had hoped to sell the least productive of these properties to a Hong Kong buyer, but he's leaving his office in half an hour. Let's hope he doesn't change his mind before I get back to him."

The guilt she was capable of generating was unbelievable. "I'm sorry, okay? Maybe you shouldn't have left it until the last minute."

She glared at me. "There were equally important things I had to do until this moment, Adlia. I shouldn't have to double-check every piece of your work."

"And I shouldn't have to put up with this crap." The horrible urge to throw something at her almost overcame me. I threw the file on my desk instead.

"Adlia!" she barked, but I was already out the door. The night air pressed on me, warm and close, and for a brief moment I considered going home. At least Galan hadn't been there, so he wouldn't be coming outside to talk to me. I couldn't take his pity.

To my surprise, I saw Dagovar appear in the glass

lobby. He pushed open the door and came out to join me.

As he approached, I said, "Don't you know better than to get involved in office politics on your first day?"

He didn't respond, just stood beside me, his head raised as if he were sniffing the air.

"What was she doing when you left?" I asked.

"Talking to her second-in-command."

"You mean Lenny? He's not second-in-command. Galan is, even though we don't have commands, or rules, or paychecks." I shook my head in frustration. "We're just making it up as we go along, and driving each other crazy in the process."

Dagovar sat on the concrete wall of the raised planter behind us. "You should never insult someone who has power over you."

"I didn't insult her!"

He gave me a pointed look.

"Okay, maybe 'this crap' is *obliquely* insulting." I sat down next to him.

He looked away from me, toward the creek. "On the other hand, she should not have treated you in that condescending manner."

"*Thank* you!"

"Perhaps she is not *ka'chil*, after all."

"Absolutely not," I said with fervor. "A real leader would treat people with more respect. Mistakes are going to happen. You can't go around making the mistake-makers feel even worse about their mistakes."

"She should be punished." His brows lowered, hiding his eyes in a band of shadow.

I gaped at him, unable to conceive of such a thing. In the world of spankers and spankees, Kutara would always be wielding the hairbrush. "You're joking, right?"

He turned to face me, his expression very serious. "Yes."

I gave a little huff of surprised laughter. "That's good, Dagovar. You're very funny."

He chuckled a little, then patted my knee. "You can call me Dag."

We sat in silence for a little longer, my mind running over phrases and crafting what I would say to Kutara. Finally I stood. "What was that goal of yours—to live without oppression? I'm going to give it a shot."

When I went back inside, Kutara glanced at me briefly, coldly, then turned back to her computer. If only the tips of her ears would turn pink—*anything* to show that she felt embarrassment or regret of any kind.

I sat down, still seething. "Kutara, I'm sorry I lost my temper and said *this crap*, but you need to—"

"I need to *what*? Tell you it's all right and give you a cookie?" Her violet eyes blazed with anger. "Everything we do here is important, Adlia. *You* are important. Are you so sensitive that I'm not allowed to express disappointment when something I counted on doesn't happen?"

"If I'm sensitive, it's only because you *always* seem disappointed."

"I have already said that this work makes me abrupt sometimes. I advised you not to take it personally. I am what I am, Adlia. No one is making you come here."

And she was right, of course. No one was making me come, yet I continued to show up. It was all I knew, and gave my life some sense of meaning. Still, that didn't mean she could treat me like a doormat. I looked her straight in the eye. "I will try to do better, and I'll try not to be bothered by what you are." I pushed at the papers on my desk. "Where's that folder? I'll add the field."

"I gave it to Lenny when you left."

I extended my hand over the top of our grouped desks, toward Lenny. "Give me the folder. I've already worked with that stuff once. It'll take you longer to figure it out."

Lenny glanced at Kutara.

She passed him a stack of papers. "Work on these instead."

He took them and handed me my folder.

Dag approached us, Fia trailing after him.

She looked at Kutara and me, her face anxious. "Are you done being angry?"

"We're done for now." I glanced at Dag, but his face was completely serious. "Are you hungry, Fia? Maybe Dag would like to take you out to get some energy from the creek."

"I *am* hungry."

I tapped Dag's arm. "You know how to take water energy, right? You have to do it yourself and then draw her in."

"I understand. Come on, Fia."

She went to him a little hesitantly. "Why are you so *big*?"

Chapter Six

I went home at around five in the morning, exhausted from dealing with Kutara, working with numbers, and being on my best behavior around Dag. My land welcomed me with unconditional support, and I thought once more that it had been my truest parent. If only it could talk, a lot of my loneliness would go away.

When I rematerialized, I felt rested but restless. Humans would still be hanging around the office, so it was too early to go to work.

I thought of Mark and remembered his invitation to a pool tournament at 'Round Midnight, wherever that was. What exactly was *pool*? I sank into the ground and traveled to the library, where one of the free Internet terminals answered all my questions. Pool did not involve water, but a green table, some balls, and long sticks.

Just for fun, I looked up the origins of the word. The online *Etymology Dictionary* said the name might have evolved from the French term for a Middle

Ages game. Players threw rocks at a chicken, or *poule*, and the one who hit the chicken got to keep it. Those wacky humans.

MapQuest showed that 'Round Midnight was a short walk away. I wasn't going to kid myself— I wanted to see Mark again. He might have a girlfriend, but he had complimented my hair and said I was an artist. Of course, Kutara believed that making friends with humans was slumming, even though she had a human lover. She insisted that he was strictly to serve her energy needs.

Maybe I should think about getting friendly with Dag. He was intriguing, although his elf-on-a-quest vibe was a little serious for my taste.

I sighed. Somewhere out there, people were having *fun*. I wanted some for myself.

Leaving the computers, I walked toward one of the automated sliding doors that led into the library's vaulted, glass lobby. A woman passed me going the other way, and my head swiveled like a cap being unscrewed. Wasn't that the woman in Mark's picture? I turned abruptly and followed her back into the main building.

She walked through the large-print and movie sections and headed up the ramp that led to fiction. I could only see the back of her head. The area we were passing through was too narrow for me to get beside her without being obvious.

We passed mysteries and entered general fiction. She didn't stop to look, but continued into the enclosed flyover that connected the new library building to what had been the original library. The original building now housed art exhibits and a movie theater/auditorium. And Elf Ops, of course.

Still in the glass-enclosed tunnel, she stopped at the small espresso bar and picked out a wrapped brownie.

I walked past her into the original building and paused to study a painting.

When she appeared in my peripheral vision, brownie in hand, I turned and got a good look at her face. The wide mouth and eyes were the same, although her dark hair was longer than in the photo.

She sat on a bench with a tired plop, unwrapped her brownie, and took a bite.

She wasn't an elf, anyway, not with that mouthful of brownie. Someone else had glamoured Mark. As she chewed, she gazed at a giant canvas depicting a dog diving into the water after a fortune cookie.

Interesting. While Mark was in a bar, poking symbolic chickens with a stick, his possible girlfriend looked at paintings of dogs. Maybe it was their interest in animals that brought them together. Or maybe they *weren't* together.

Outside, the streets were full of dressed-up people. I found 'Round Midnight and then walked past. Mark might not be there. Mark might be there. Why was this so hard?

The bar sat below street level, down a flight of stairs, and through a door framed by pink and blue neon. I went down the stairs on my second pass and entered beneath a sign showing a man's hands playing a guitar.

A few guys caught my eye and smiled as I walked

past the bar and into the room beyond, where I spotted the pool tables. People conversed in a near shout, punctuated by the occasional, "Oh!" or "Nice shot!"

I didn't see Mark, but Butch was plenty obvious as he leaned over the table, cursed, and slapped fellow players on the back. I had just taken a seat on a stool when he spotted me.

"Hey! Mark's cute friend!" he called, waving.

I brightened. That was a much better description than *gloomy.*

He took five more shots, then came over. His cue stick was black, I noticed, instead of the light wood of the other players.

"What's your name again?" he asked.

"Adlia. And you're Butch."

"Good memory! What are you drinking?"

"Oh, I don't need anything," I began, but he was already walking away.

"Pretty girls must have drinks," he shouted back. "It's the law."

He was back in a few minutes, carrying a pint glass of something gold-colored. "Hard cider. I never met a chick yet who didn't love it."

"Thanks." I wouldn't drink it, of course, but I was saved from having to make him think I was by the shouts of the men around the table.

"Butch! Come put us out of our misery!" one of them yelled.

As Butch walked back to the table, Mark appeared from farther back in the club. Butch said something and jerked his thumb over his shoulder in my direction.

Mark caught my eye, grinned, and came over. "Hey, there! Can I get you something to drink?"

What was it with men and beverages? I pointed to the glass on the ledge beside me. "Butch already did."

"If you've never had cider before, be careful. It tastes like soda, but it can sit you on your ass."

What did that mean? "I'm already sitting on my ass."

He laughed. "Do you want to play pool?"

"I don't know. I just thought I'd drop by and watch for a little, since you mentioned it." I was proud of how smooth and casual that sounded.

"Well, I'm glad you did." He smiled and touched the side of my knee briefly.

Again I felt the trace of glamour on him, although it seemed fainter. "Hey, I saw Faith at the library today."

"You did?" He frowned slightly.

"Yeah. I recognized her from your picture, although she looked kind of tired."

His frown deepened. "I have got to see that woman. She has a habit of getting involved with the wrong guys."

"Does that include you?"

"Me?" He chuckled. "No. She's my cousin, but it's more like she's another sister. That's why I first came to Colorado. She was having trouble with a stalker." He leaned against the bar on the wall behind us. "She hasn't been returning my calls, and when I go to her apartment she's always out. I'm starting to wonder if she's gotten involved with a cult."

"She wasn't with anyone when I saw her. She was just sitting, eating a brownie."

"At least it's not an anti-brownie cult. Good to know." He shifted, then turned when his arm hit something with a small clunk. "Your drink is still back here."

"I tasted it. It's not really my thing."

"A woman who doesn't like cider. Butch will be shocked."

"You can have it if you want."

Mark picked it up. "Trying to get me drunk so you can take advantage of me?" He smiled and took a sip, dark eyes looking at me over the edge of the glass.

There was probably some recognized response I could make to that statement, a code phrase, but I didn't know it. I cursed myself for not knowing how to flirt. "Um, are you going to play some more pool?"

He put the glass back on the ledge. "Not tonight. I made it through about a third of the players before I got shot down, though, which is an improvement. Butch will probably win. He usually does."

I leaned back to hook my elbows on the bar, my shoulder resting lightly against his. Should I move? Should I stay put? I could feel his body heat through my shirt. Perversely, it made me want to shiver.

He leaned toward me, resting his fingers on my upper arm and speaking close to my ear. "See that guy in the red T-shirt? That's the only real competition. Butch has been calling him Red Shirt all night to psych him out, but I don't think it fazes him."

I turned my head toward his slightly. "How do you play this game, anyway?"

"It's straight eight ball tonight."

"And that means . . ." I waved a hand vaguely.

He leaned forward so he could look me in the eye. "You really don't know?"

"I was homeschooled." A standard elf excuse. It seemed to work for a lot of things. Mark explained the basics of pool to me, his voice intimate, his breath smelling of apples. I told him about the chicken-game antecedent, and he thought that was hysterical. We were laughing together over some nonsense when a roar went up from the pool table.

Butch shook his opponent's hand and clapped him on the back.

"I guess they're finished," I said.

"I guess so."

Butch came over, took the glass out of Mark's hand, and downed the last of the cider. He looked at the empty glass, then at me. "Was this yours?"

"It's possible."

He grinned at me. "How about a kiss for the loser?"

"Um . . ."

"Forget the loser. He doesn't deserve it. How about a kiss for me?" He leaned over and gave me a smacking kiss on the cheek.

"You won again?" Mark asked.

"So much for counting on you to cheer me on." Butch shook his head sadly. "Why do I even ask you

to these things?" He took a wad of cash out of his
jeans pocket and flicked it against his fingers.
"Dinner, anyone? Sushi's on me."

Mark looked at me. "I was just thinking I might—"

"I should probably go home," I said, not wanting to spend the next few hours pretending to eat
raw fish.

". . . teach Adlia to play pool," Mark finished.
"But if you need to go, I can walk you to your car."

"Teach me to play pool?" I asked, and then remembered I was supposed to be at work now.

Butch winked at me. "Mark can't play worth shit,
but he's a good teacher—very conscientious about
making sure you bend over the table just right."

"Don't listen to him," Mark said, smacking Butch
in the ribs. "I play fine."

"Maybe some other time," I said. "I really should
get going."

Butch gave his money a last fondle and put it
away. "You two kids do what you want, but I'm finishing the night with a mouthful of raw octopus."

Mark lifted his hand in a brief wave. "I'll catch
you later."

Butch disappeared into the crowded bar, and we
got up.

"So where are you parked?" Mark asked, holding
the door open for me.

"I walked."

"Then I'll walk you home." He smiled and tilted
his head. "Or I could, you know, get you a cab, if
you're not in the mood for company."

"No, I like company."

We stared at each other. I felt the impulse to lean toward him, to touch, and wondered if he felt it, too. Mark was so friendly in general, it was hard to tell if he liked me in particular.

"Okay, then. Let's go," I said abruptly, and started walking.

The air was still balmy outside, with even more people around than before. As we reached the sidewalk, I heard the sound of a band from the nearby Pearl Street Mall.

"So where do you live?" Mark asked.

I needed to get to work, so I gestured vaguely south. "I'm just a little past the library." We walked in silence for a while before I asked, "How long have you and Butch been friends?"

"A year? Maybe a year and a half?"

"Is *that* all? I thought you grew up together or something."

"Nah. We met when he had me take a picture of him with his Boxer. Yoda."

"Excuse me?"

"Yoda is his dog, a white Boxer. He brushed him with green food coloring last year for Halloween." Mark chuckled. "It was frickin' hysterical, although Butch's sofa will never be the same."

I laughed. This was exactly the kind of weird humor that attracted me to humans, but what had Yoda the dog thought of the experiment? Since elves could communicate with animals, I might get the chance to ask him. "Do you have a pet?" I wanted to know more about him—everything, in fact.

Mark shook his head. "Not with the traveling I

do. If the money's there, I try to take a trip every year—some place picturesque, so I can sell a calendar of the pictures. Last year I went to Italy. The exchange rate was terrible, but I stayed with relatives."

"You have relatives in *Italy?*"

"Sure. What part of 'big Italian family' did you not understand?" We had reached Canyon Boulevard, and he pushed the button on the pole at the crosswalk, to activate the flashing lights. "Let me guess. Your relatives are all WASPy types who came over on the *Mayflower.*"

I didn't say anything.

"C'mon, Adlia. We always seem to wind up talking about me. What's your story?"

I'd rather tell Mark than anyone else, but I wasn't supposed to, and he wouldn't believe me, anyway. "Well, I told you my parents are dead, and I don't have any brothers or sisters."

"I can't even imagine what that would be like."

"What's it like, having a big family?"

He gave me a look. "We're talking about you, remember?"

"Right." I sighed. "I was brought up by a sort of cousin to the family. Aunt Kootie, I call her, even though she isn't really my aunt." We walked through the Canyon Gallery parking lot. Now was when I should go into work. Instead I led the way across the bridge that spanned Boulder Creek. "Anyway, Aunt Kootie isn't one of these warm, cookie-baking women. She's kind of stern and negative. Plus, she has a hairy mole on her face, so we didn't go out and socialize much."

"You said you were homeschooled. Did you go to college?" Mark asked.

"No. What about you?"

"I've got a BA in photography from the School of Visual Arts in New York. Do you have a job?"

"Aunt Kootie manages the investments for our family, and I help her. It's boring, so I took up photography. And that's how I met you. There's really nothing more to tell."

"Sure there is. What do you do for fun?"

"Fun . . . I take pictures and draw a little. I write in my journal, although I'm not sure that qualifies as fun." Describing my life was starting to depress me. I steered us toward a brick quadplex. "This is my place."

"Do you still live with your aunt?"

"No, thank God. I live alone." I stepped onto the sidewalk that led to the apartment building.

He didn't seem inclined to leave. "Do you at least have a pet—something to talk to? Maybe a goldfish?"

No. I'm boring, and you have no reason to like me. "Absolutely. A cute little goldfish named Squint."

"Squint." He stepped a little closer. "And Aunt Kootie, who has a hairy mole. You made all of that up, didn't you?"

"Of course not. I couldn't make *all* of it up."

"So Squint is really a hamster." He reached out and took my hand, as if it were a vase he just happened to pick up to admire.

"What are you doing?" I asked, watching him stroke my fingers.

"Even though you're bizarre and untrustworthy, I still find myself wanting to kiss you." He cocked his head and looked at me. "Can you explain that?"

"Not really." I felt so breathless, it came out as a whisper.

Mark closed the gap between us, pulling me into an embrace. I saw all of this as though I were standing a little distance away, and then his lips met mine and I was catapulted back into my body, which pressed up against his.

So this *is what all the fuss is about.* Lenny had introduced me to sex in a detached, light-hearted way, but I had never kissed a human before, and it was the difference between a breeze and a storm.

We merge with the land, but it's as though they are *the land—all the pull and gravity of it.* I hadn't realized how tired I was until I felt energy suffuse me in a rosy, fizzing tide. I pushed closer to Mark, widened my mouth against his, and moaned. He responded by burying one hand in my hair and practically lifting me off my feet.

I wasn't sure how long we'd been kissing when I heard several sets of heels on the sidewalk, followed by giggling.

Mark pulled away and glanced at the approaching group of college girls. Taking my hand, he pulled me toward the entrance to the apartment building, which had a little roof over it and was somewhat sheltered between two spruce bushes.

As soon as we stopped moving, I wound my arms around his neck. He rested his forehead against mine and grinned, his teeth white in the dusk. "So you do have *some* social skills."

"Be quiet and do that thing with your mouth again."

He bent his head obligingly, and I stood against him, feeling his heat along the length of my body and running my hands over his back, feeling his muscles flex under the thin cotton of his T-shirt. He turned me toward the door and pressed me against it.

A light came on just over our heads, illuminating us as though we were on a very small stage.

I pulled away. "What the hell?"

"It's just your security light." He chuckled, holding my hands. "Did you forget about it?"

"I guess so." I looked around nervously.

He bent his head and kissed me lightly. "We could always go inside. I promise to behave myself, at least as much as you want me to."

I was still breathing heavily. "Inside. No, I don't think so." I stepped away from the door, pulling him after me. "Look. There's a little bench around the side. Let's sit there."

The bench sat under a window, but the window was dark, and trees sheltered it on either side. He sat and pulled me onto his lap. I was enjoying this new position when I heard a scrabbling noise from the other side of the window, followed by crazed barking from inside.

"Oh, honestly!" I sent a mental message to the dog on the other side of the door. *I don't mean any harm. I'm just an elf trying to get some, okay?*

My house! Mine! Get off my property! Go! Now! Go!

Just because you can communicate with a dog doesn't mean it'll listen to you.

A light came on inside. Mark grabbed my hand and pulled me back to the sidewalk. "I feel like a teenager," he said, laughing. "Any minute now, some old grouch is going to come out and say, 'You kids should be at home!'" He still had my hand, and he pulled me back into the circle of his arms. "Or is that *your* dog, and your boyfriend is going to come out and catch me kissing you?"

He didn't seem worried, because he moved his hands to the back of my head and kissed me deeply enough to make me forget everything else.

"What do you want to do, Adlia?" he asked, when we came up for air. "Shall we go inside?"

If I were human, I would have a home to take him to. We would make love, and then we would talk for hours, holding nothing back. For the first time, I would know that someone cared about me. But I wasn't human.

"Adlia?"

I glamoured him, and watched all the affection and expectation drain from his face. "Go home, Mark Speranzi," I whispered, kissing his unresponsive lips. "You deserve more than lies. So do I, for that matter."

After making him think I'd taken a taxi home and he had gone for a walk, I turned him around and sent him on his way. He strolled down the block, hands in his pockets, with no idea that I was behind him.

Chapter Seven

"You're late," were Kutara's first words to me when I showed up at work.

"I didn't know we had official hours now."

Fia wandered across the room. I stepped in front of her aimless trajectory and caught her eye. "Hi, Fia. Remember me?"

"Addum," she said, without much conviction.

Galan and Dag were beavering away. Dag was even in my chair, though he immediately got up and went to get a guest chair.

Kutara studied me across our desks. "What have you been doing?"

"I went to Bonaire to see the flamingos. When did my private life become interesting?" I clicked through the menus on my computer screen to check Dag's work.

"I've always taken an interest in your life."

Glancing up, I saw that Galan was grinning at me. "What?"

His grin got even wider. "You've been with a human."

"How can you tell?!"

"Glossy hair, glowing skin . . . There's a certain kind of energy glow you get from being with a human who has feelings for you." Galan tilted his head and studied me some more. "Although I'd expect you to look happier."

Dag cleared his throat. "Perhaps we should respect Adlia's privacy."

Kutara looked at him like that was the most ridiculous thing she'd ever heard. "Who was this human?"

"Nobody. A guy from my photography class. He wanted to kiss me, and I'd never been kissed by a human, so I let him."

Kutara nodded approvingly. "Getting energy from humans is a valuable skill."

I had suffered agonies over Mark, and she made him sound like a car I should learn to drive. "Is that the only reason you hang out with Guy?" I snapped.

She looked a little surprised at my angry tone.

I swallowed hard and tried to sound calmer. "I mean, you're practically living with him, right?"

"In addition to sexual energy, he is a valuable source of information. As an architect, he knows about possible building projects in Boulder that could affect elves."

Dag nodded. "Choosing to have sex with a human who can benefit you in other ways is always a good idea."

What was *wrong* with them? Or was it me who was broken? I turned to Galan. "I know *you* didn't choose Erin for those reasons. After all, you and she performed—"

Galan cut me off with a warning shake of his head. "Erin and I have common interests that help both of us."

"Right." Galan and Erin had performed the elven marriage ritual, but we weren't supposed to talk about it. If other elves knew the extent of our involvement with humans, we might lose all influence with them. "You guys have that whole jewelry-making thing in common." I glanced at Dag, hoping he wouldn't ask any questions. "They basically share a talent."

Dag raised his eyebrows at Galan. "And she knows what you are?"

Galan and Kutara exchanged a look, and Kutara shrugged slightly. *He'll find out sooner or later,* it seemed to say.

"Erin and I accidentally bonded," Galan said. "As a result, she can't be glamoured by elves."

Dag looked startled. "Is there a way to break the bond?"

"I have no desire to break my bond with Erin," Galan said.

The coldness in his voice made me feel a twinge of longing. Would anyone ever feel that protective of his relationship with me?

Kutara was doing her best this-is-no-big-deal impression. "Erin turned out to have talents that benefit all of us, and she's sympathetic to our situation."

"I see." Dag gave me a secret look, as if to say, *It takes all kinds.*

I didn't acknowledge his covert communication, but studied my computer screen instead. Dag had entered a huge amount of account information into Quicken—information Kutara had given to me to enter. "You've got a real knack for this."

He smiled modestly. "Thank you. If we're not battling dark elves, I can at least practice strategy with money."

"Keep up the good work." I stood behind him, so he didn't notice when I caught Kutara's eye and jerked my head toward the door.

She raised her eyebrows at me, but got up and followed me into the hall. "What is it?"

I walked sideways toward the lobby. "C'mon. All the way outside."

When were out of the building, I turned and whispered, "I like Dag, but do you think it's wise to trust him with all the account numbers for Fellseth's money?"

"I haven't given him all the account numbers."

"Yeah, but we're still talking about a lot of cash."

She shook her head. "Why would he want money, Adlia?"

"Why do we want money? Why did Fellseth?" I countered.

"We want money so we can help elves. Dagovar is doing that through us. Fellseth wanted money because he was a dark elf, determined to do as much harm as possible. Dagovar is not a dark elf."

"I know, but—"

"Do you know of some reason we should distrust him?"

"No, it's just that we don't really know him."

She sighed. "We're elves, Adlia. I can't ask for his last job reference or check to see if he has a criminal record. We need people. Dagovar shows a facility for accounting and he wants to help."

I heard an unspoken criticism in that last statement. Dag was eager to help, whereas I wasn't.

"Dagovar will continue with the finances," Kutara went on. "I think you would be more entertained by helping Galan look for properties."

Now I just wanted entertainment. "Fine. You don't mind if I check up on him from time to time, do you?"

"By all means." She turned and went inside.

I would have expected Kutara to be more cautious. Maybe she was insulted because I was suspicious of her first big fan. I went down to the creek and sat for a little, in an effort to cool down.

When I went back inside, Dagovar looked over his shoulder at me and said, "I'm sure I'll have questions for you."

Not wanting to look like a sore loser, I said, "I'm sure you'll do great. Trade chairs with me. You should have the one with wheels."

"This one is no trouble."

"Take it, Dag. Anyway, it goes with the desk."

I dragged the guest chair around to Galan's workspace.

"A noble sacrifice," Galan murmured, not looking at me.

"Yeah, yeah. Fill me in."

* * *

Later that night, Fia and I sat by the creek, watching the moon through the trees.

Galan joined us. He stretched, and I automatically admired his biceps as his T-shirt sleeves fell away from them. He sat next to me and said, "Dagovar's not very talkative, is he?"

"He talks to me." I was starting to feel bad about suspecting him earlier.

"It's weird, Kutara being famous enough for elves to travel here."

"You're a little famous, too," I pointed out. "Sorry I mentioned Erin to Dagovar."

"That's all right. He'd find out sooner or later."

I looked at Fia, who was piling fallen leaves together. "What's it like, being bonded to a human?"

"Wonderful." He smiled. "And challenging. I was married before, you know, to one of us. Being with a human is very different."

"How is it different?"

He leaned back on his elbows and studied the sky. "I was used to thinking of humans as kind of insubstantial. They're not connected to *Ma'Nah* the same way we are and they don't live very long. Then there was Erin, giving me all the energy I needed."

"I guess it's hard to think of her as insubstantial when she's what keeps you going."

He chuckled. "I still did, at first, and it was terrifying. Then I discovered that she's like a miniature *Ma'Nah*—only with all these emotions and demands." He shook his head. "That sounds like I'm complaining, but I'm not. Erin asks for more than *Ma'Nah*, but it feels like I've *become* more so I can give her what she needs."

I fumbled in my bag and took out my notebook so I could write down what he'd said. "I wish I had someone like that." I cleared my throat.

"I think you'd do well with a human, Adlia," Galan said. "We both have more emotion than most elves I know."

I sighed heavily. "That's not necessarily a good thing."

"Oh, I don't know. Maybe elves are too much like *Ma'Nah*. Animals disappear, serious changes are accepted, and life still seems to go on, right up until it doesn't. If we were more attached to the result, it might be a better one—certainly for us." He stood and offered me his hand. "Back to work?"

"Yeah." I let his warm grip pull me to my feet. "I used to have a crush on you, you know."

"And you don't anymore? Aw. I feel like less of an elf."

I laughed and shook my head. "Trust me, it's better this way. C'mon, Fia." We waited until she joined us, then strolled back toward the annex.

"Does your lack of crush have anything to do with the human you kissed?" Galan asked.

"No, I got over you ages ago. As far as the human goes, I want more than kissing, but it seems so futile and *sad,* somehow. We're not supposed to tell humans about us, but if I lie to him and glamour him, it's not real affection. That's not fair to him, and it's not what I want, anyway."

"You'll figure something out."

I shook my head. "You were lucky to be bonded to Erin, with no choice in the matter."

He grunted. "If you call it lucky to have my land taken from me and almost die. I'm lucky it all worked out."

"Well, there you are, then." I ushered Fia into the office ahead of me.

Kutara looked up from her computer screen. "Galan, come here."

I hesitated in the doorway for a moment, then followed him. If it was something to do with property, I'd need to hear it, too.

"What's up?" Galan asked.

Kutara's slender finger tapped her screen. "Isn't this one of the potential elf-habitat properties on our list?"

Galan leaned over to look at it. "Fifteen acres in Longmont. Yes."

"It appears to have sold. Did you make an offer on it?"

Galan's brow furrowed. "Sold? Already?"

"So you *didn't* make an offer?"

"Um, could you give me a moment? I'd like to check my notes."

"Certainly," Kutara said, all chilly graciousness.

I felt my stomach clench sympathetically as Galan went to his desk. Instead of following him, I went to see what Dag was doing. Looking at his

computer screen, I asked, "Is that a new account?
With thirty-five thousand dollars?"

He shook his head. "It's the same T-bill account
I was working on earlier."

"That one ended in 3674." I pointed to the top
of the screen. "This is 5311."

"Huh." He pulled up a new window. "Let me
bring up the overview. It'd be great if I entered the
password wrong and accidentally found new
money."

"That *would* be great, but I don't think it's very
likely."

He brought up a succession of screens, finally
pointing to the top of one. "Here's the issue. It's
the same money, but a different screen view. We
were looking at the customer number instead of
the account number."

It was nice of him to say *we* when it was really me
who had been confused. "Thanks. Now you're
teaching me things." Maybe one of them was that
Kutara was right and I was jealous.

There was a clatter from the other side of the
room. I looked up to see Fia rubbing her head, a
phone cord draped around her neck. On the shelf
above her, a cardboard box lay on its side, electrical
equipment spilling out of it.

"Ow," Fia said.

I went over and took the cord off her neck. "What
were you trying to do?"

"Don't know."

"Dag, can you get that box down so I can repack
it?" I pointed to the shelf. "It's too tall for me."

"Sure."

I would have had to stand on a chair, but Dag didn't even stretch to get the box. I looked at the spread of his shoulders as he put the box on the floor. Mark had the broad-shouldered, elegant build of a diver, but Dag was just huge.

Fia, looking up at him, rubbed her head and murmured, "Not my blond man."

I stared at her. "What did you just say?"

Everyone else must have heard her, because they converged on us. Fia backed away a step.

"Back up a little," I said, raising a hand. "I think we're making her nervous."

We all shuffled away from her. She looked at us curiously, as if wondering what trick we might do next.

Kutara nudged me and whispered, "She's used to you. Ask her about the blond man."

"Dag *is* blond, isn't he?" I said brightly. "Is he blonder than your man?"

She nodded slowly.

"Who's your man?"

She looked at me blankly.

"If you have a mate, he might be looking for you," I suggested.

"I'm hungry."

"Fia, we were just talking about your blond man. Remember him?"

"No." She rubbed her head, then squatted to poke around in the box Dag had taken from the shelf.

"Well," Kutara said. "That was briefly exciting. Why is she rubbing her head like that?"

"She pulled that box over," I said. "I think the phone hit her on the head." I picked up the phone from the floor and put it in the box. Fia shoved it aside as though it had never interested her.

Galan watched her thoughtfully. "You know, I seem to remember a movie where someone lost their memory from a head-related injury, and then another knock on the head restored it. Do you think that's the case here?"

Fia opened a box of binder clips and dumped them on the floor.

I squatted next to her. "Maybe if we hit her with something larger, she'd remember more. Fia, quit making a mess." I scooped up the clips and dumped them in the larger box, then handed it to Dag. "Would you put this back?"

"It's something hopeful, anyway," Kutara said, as Dag replaced the box. "Which we could use right now."

Had I displeased her in some new way? "What now?"

It was Galan who answered me, his handsome face lined with worry. "I was supposed to make an offer on that property in Longmont last week. The folder was on my desk, but I just . . . forgot to check."

"And now the property has sold to someone else," Kutara finished crisply. "I know this work is unfamiliar, but other elves are depending on us."

She sighed. "Perhaps we should limit casual conversation while we're at work."

"You've got to be kidding!" I said. "We'd lose our minds."

Kutara folded her arms. "Then I suggest we all learn to use the reminder program that came with our e-mail."

I groaned, and Galan's shoulders slumped. Having never used computer technology until a few months ago, each new thing seemed like a huge ordeal.

"You may as well start now," Kutara said.

Fia had gone back to Galan's desk and covered her thighs with colored sticky notes.

I pulled her upright. "Fia, how would you like to stick those on the wall? Come sit on the floor over here."

"I'm hungry."

"We'll take you out soon." I got her situated.

Galan sighed as I resumed my seat next to him. "Not only did I miss that property, but I've made extra work for everyone."

I patted his shoulder. "Like Kutara said, we're not used to this kind of work. Maybe our brains aren't equipped to deal with it."

"Maybe. I know humans forget things, but we usually don't have that problem."

"Well, except for Fia." In the silence that followed, Galan and I looked at each other. I spoke first. "Um, you don't suppose whatever she has is contagious?"

"*B'nah flok!*" Galan said, which translates to, *I have*

accidentally traveled through soil contaminated with sewage. "Kutara!"

"I heard you." She rapidly typed something. "I'm sending an e-mail to the elf who contacted us before about memory loss. He only mentioned the one case. Surely there would have been others."

I turned and looked at Fia nervously. "Unless the affected elf wandered off so quickly that he didn't come in contact with anyone else."

Kutara smacked a final key and looked at me. "He came in contact with *someone*, or they wouldn't have known he was forgetful."

"Oh, right. Maybe you have to be exposed for a certain amount of time."

Galan blew out a breath. "You're just full of cheerful hypotheses, aren't you?"

"It's a possibility," Kutara said.

Dag was the only one of us who looked calm. "I honestly don't think it's contagious. We come into contact with human germs, but they disappear when we become incorporeal. How would this be different?"

"That's true." Kutara thought for a moment. "However, something of us remains to become corporeal again. Perhaps that *something* can carry disease."

He still looked skeptical. "Look at the stack of folders on Galan's desk. Which is more likely—that Galan missed *one* detail in work that's very new to us, or that Fia is contagious? I believe Fia is suffering from some injury, or even a birth defect."

Kutara looked at me.

I sighed. "That's not unheard of, says the elf born without a talent."

"Let's hope Dagovar is right," Kutara said. "Regardless, there's not much we can do except remain watchful, since all of us have been exposed to Fia." She gave Galan a look. "And pay more attention to our work."

Chapter Eight

We all left at about six AM. Galan decided to see if Fia could be merged with his old land for a while, so none of us would have to baby-sit her during the day. Erin picked up the two of them in her car.

I hoped he'd be able to pull it off, and that it would do Fia some good, but what I *really* hoped was that she wasn't carrying some horrible elven disease that would make us all mental deficients.

After Erin's car left, Kutara walked behind a tree and disappeared, leaving me with Dag. This was a good opportunity for me to find out more about him. "So where do you go during the day?"

"I sit by the creek and take energy, or go in the library to listen and learn about this place. Sometimes I find a human woman who is willing to take me home, so I can get energy."

"A different woman each time?"

He shrugged. "I enjoy women."

We walked to the creek together, crossing to the other side and stopping at some boulders at the edge of the water. Dag chose one of a pair, and I sat on the rock next to him.

"Do you ever think it would be better just to make ourselves known to humans?" I asked, swishing my hand in the water. "Tell them, *We're here, make room for us*?"

He shook his head. "They would never trust us unless we gave up glamour—our one defense."

"Could we not tell them about it? I mean, humans have their own types of glamour—money, fame."

"But other humans can see those things and choose whether to be affected by them."

"I suppose." This was the kind of philosophical discussion I would have enjoyed with Mark, but that wasn't going to happen.

At least Dag was willing to talk about it. Once Kutara made up her mind about something, she didn't see any point in discussion, and Galan liked to stick with happy subjects. Given some of the things he had been through, I guess I could understand. "What do you think about Galan letting his human know about elves?"

"I think he's a fool," he said. "Humans don't understand our need for secrecy. Erin will tell her friends, and word will spread until someone shows up to capture Galan and take him away."

I shook my head. "He could just glamour them."

"What if they shot him from a distance?"

"They wouldn't want to *kill* him."

He smiled, but it wasn't a nice smile. "All right. They use a tranquilizer gun, then turn him over to a staff of humans who have elf ancestry, so his glamour won't work on them. And then the experiments begin." He looked thoughtful. "Maybe that's what happened to Fia."

I was starting to understand why Galan preferred to think cheerful thoughts. "Humans in this town talk about all kinds of strange things, like fairies, and no one shows up with a tranquilizer gun."

Dag's brow wrinkled. "Aren't we the same thing as fairies in human mythology?"

"I think fairies have wings."

"Oh." He shrugged slightly. "The point is, humans and elves are natural enemies. It's like men who train tigers, thinking they understand them and are safe. Then one day, *Rrrrr!*" He half lunged at me, his hands like claws, and I jumped.

"So you think humans are like tigers?" I asked.

"In that scenario, yes."

I went back to my land, but felt restless after only a few hours and rematerialized. When I did, my phone beeped to tell me I had messages.

Erin's was first, and she sounded panicky. "Adlia, something terrible has happened. We were on the way to take Fia to Galan's land, and I stopped to get gas at Folsom and Arapahoe. I sent Galan in to buy a candy bar, then I went in because pretzels sounded good, too. I didn't even *think* that Fia might leave the car, but there was a long line at the register and when we came back she was gone! We've been calling and looking, but there's no sign of her. I was hoping you might have an idea of where she would go, but you're not answering, which means I have to call Kutara. Oh, God."

Kutara was next, sounding angry and disgusted. "Apparently Erin has already told you that she lost Fia. I checked at the library and all through the park, but there is no sign of her. If you see her, obviously you should bring her back."

I braced myself, then called Kutara. "Still no sign of Fia?"

"None. This was so careless of Erin, not to mention Galan."

"I can see how it could happen, though. None of us is used to looking after someone like Fia. I'll go through the park again, just in case."

She gave a gusty sigh. "Thank you."

"Maybe her mate spotted her and took her. He wouldn't know to tell us anything." When Kutara remained silent, I said, "Anyway, it's not like she was your responsibility."

"*All* elves are my responsibility," Kutara snapped, and hung up.

I searched for several hours with no luck. Late morning saw me sitting by the creek sketching ducks, wondering if they were the same ones Fia had watched. Someone tapped me on the shoulder, startling me.

Mark grinned at me, camera in hand. "Surprise."

The urge to embrace him was so strong, I was halfway up before I remembered that I'd glamoured our kisses from his memory. I stretched, as though that had been my plan all along. "Hi."

"I see you got home all right the other night."

Remembering I'd made him think I had taken a cab, I said, "Yeah. No problem." It hurt to see him again. Why couldn't I have feelings for an elf? The irony was that I'd have more elves to choose from if humans weren't edging us out of existence. "You know, I might not be able to come to class anymore. Aunt Kootie has a lot of work for me right now." There was no reason to keep torturing myself by seeing him.

"Oh." He cleared his throat. "I understand if you're too busy to come to class, but if I've made you uncomfortable by being too friendly, I'll cross the street the next time I see you coming." He tilted his head. "I don't want to make you give up something you enjoy."

Oh, this was hard. For a moment I considered making him think I was married, or had been in jail for throwing bricks at babies—anything that would make him take his beautiful, kind, ethical self far, far away from me. But apparently I wasn't that strong, because instead I said, "You're not too friendly. I'll see how it goes."

His face relaxed a little. "Great. Oh, I hope you don't mind." He looked at the rear of the digital camera he held and clicked a button. "I took a picture of you—*Woman Sketching Ducks.*" He started to hand the camera to me, then drew it back and stared at the screen. "That's funny."

"What?" I leaned over to see.

"Your ear . . ." He reached toward the side of my head.

I jerked away, glamouring him into stillness. A

woman walking toward the water stared at Mark's strange, statuelike posture, and I panicked and glamoured her, too. If the university marching band had come toward me, I would have glamoured the whole bunch of them.

I took the camera from Mark's hand and had him move into a more natural position, keeping his mind blank. Then I made the woman worry that she had lost her keys. She headed for the nearby parking lot, rooting through her purse as she walked.

I zoomed in on the photo Mark had taken. It showed me with one hand raised to rub the nape of my neck. The motion had pushed a section of my hair aside, revealing my ear's pointed tip.

"Delete," I muttered, pushing a button. Another photo appeared, almost identical to the first but with less of my ear showing. I deleted it and found one more. In that one, my hand held my notebook and my ear didn't show at all. I hesitated, my finger over the button, then left it.

There were a *lot* of pictures on the memory card. It took me five minutes to scan all of them. There were no more of me, but I did find one with Dag in a crowd of people by the library. His ears were covered by his thick blond hair, but I deleted it anyway. It wasn't that great a shot.

Maybe humans would catch us with tranquilizer guns or maybe it would be with a camera. Why had we never thought of this before? Of course we covered our ears with our hair, or hats, or braids, but my unconscious gesture, captured by Mark's camera, proved how reliable that was.

Did Mark have more potentially dangerous pictures? Of course, I could find out just by making him take me to his house. Once there, I could root through his file cabinets and closets, find every photo in the place, and have a little bonfire on his couch, if I wanted. But I wouldn't do that to Mark. A more subtle plan was in order.

Putting the camera back in his hand, I made him think he had just asked me to dinner. Then I took a step back and released him from the glamour. His face went from blank to expectant as he waited for my reply.

I smiled for all I was worth. "I'd love to have dinner with you tonight!"

"Great! What time should I pick you up?"

"I have a meeting downtown that's going to last until six. What if I just meet you somewhere?"

"How about The Kitchen—that little place near Pearl and Tenth?"

"Perfect. See you then." I gave him what I hoped was a charming smile.

He waved and walked away, tall and broad-shouldered.

Unbelievable. I could have made him give me his house key and gone there when he wasn't home, but no . . . Instead I had arranged to spend the evening with Mark Speranzi—the human I couldn't have in the way I wanted. Apparently I was not only gloomy, I was a masochist.

* * *

I went home and soaked in my land like a woman soaking in a hot bath.

A date meant dressing up. Elves hadn't even worn clothing until they started encountering humans on a regular basis, and our fashion sense hadn't changed much since the Renaissance.

As young elves, we saw what our parents wore and thought up something similar. The more practice we got with one outfit, the easier it was to form out of the raw materials around us as we emerged from the earth, so I transformed the surrounding mulch into the some kind of T-shirt and jeans every time I became corporeal.

Tonight was not a jeans-and-T-shirt night. Merged with *Ma'Nah*, my physical body didn't currently exist, but I planned to put it in a dress—something red that came to just above the knees—and high heels, which I'd never worn. Jewelry? Unfortunately, while making clothing was a basic elf ability, metal-working was yet another artistic talent I *didn't* have. I'd have to stick with the basics.

When the time came, I emerged in the park dressed in a blood-red dress that set off my gold hair. Everything above the waist clung, including the V-neck and small cap sleeves. The skirt flared over my hips, rippling like falling water.

I took a step and staggered in the red high heels I had conjured. How did human women walk in these? Hanging on to a tree, I let my feet sink into the ground up to the ankles, then pulled them out one at a time in curvy sandals with a low wedge heel.

Looking down at myself, I caught sight of my

messenger bag, its brown canvas looking more like mulch than ever. I pushed it into the ground with both hands and pulled it back out as a stylish black shoulder bag. *Much* better. I took a few steps to test the new shoes, then walked across the grass toward Canyon Boulevard.

"Hey, pretty lady! Spare a dollar for a man who can't afford to have a girlfriend like you?"

I sighed. The homeless could be complimentary, but it always came down to money. "Sorry, guys," I said to the trio of dirty, bearded men seated under a tree. "No cash."

"You could get some, looking like that," another said. "Don't do anything we wouldn't do!"

They all laughed.

I put my hands on my hips. "Would you go on a date with a man so you could destroy incriminating photographs, then wipe his memory afterwards?"

Giving me nervous looks, they got up and shambled quickly away, dragging blankets and knapsacks behind them.

Chapter Nine

The Kitchen was a cozy little restaurant with a long, narrow dining room, bright with white paint and funky glass chandeliers.

Mark was waiting for me at the tiny bar just inside the front door, and he smiled in delight when he spotted me. "Can I just say, as a photographer, that you are a picture?"

"Same to you." His well-tailored black slacks and crisp white shirt boosted his Italian good looks to an alarming degree.

The hostess smiled warmly at Mark and showed us to a front table with the eager deference of someone who knows the establishment's style points have just gone up.

The place was packed, and I glanced around nervously. Should I try to glamour everyone, or just make Mark think I was eating and not worry about the rest? When I turned back, my date was studying me over his menu.

"Looking for someone? We're not going to run into a jealous ex-boyfriend, are we?"

I gave a bark of laughter. "Not hardly." Hundreds of years old and I had never had a steady guy. "Just checking for exits in case of fire."

"You could start one, in that dress." He grinned sheepishly. "Sorry. Had a construction-worker moment, there. What I meant to say is that you look wonderful."

Beneath my hair, I felt the tips of my ears grow warm. "You already said."

"It bears repeating."

The waiter came and poured water into our glasses from a bottle. "Have you both been here before?"

Mark shook his head.

"This is Eldorado Natural Spring Water, compliments of the house, and I'll keep it coming."

"Does it have lemon?" I asked. Elves could drink water without becoming mortal, but lemon might count as food.

The waiter shook his head. "Would you like some?"

"No, I'm allergic."

Mark picked up the wine list. "Should I order a bottle of something?" he asked me.

"I'm just going to have water, but you go ahead."

He consulted the list a moment, then turned to the waiter. "A glass of the Mazzi Valpolicella."

"One of my favorites," the waiter said.

When he was gone, Mark whispered, "I bet he says that about all of them."

"Maybe he's had all of them."

When the waiter returned, I ordered salad, figuring it was the easiest way to keep people from thinking I was odd. I hoped Mark wouldn't notice if I merely rearranged it.

Mark entertained me with stories about his last trip to Italy, where his elderly female relatives kissed him and called him their little *principe*, or prince, and cried when he left.

He told me about how he and his brothers always fought over the heel ends of ciabatta at Thanksgiving dinner, and why fresh flowers on wedding cakes were such a headache, and about crazy Nonno Nino, who smoked so much he lost his front teeth.

"Nonno Nino?" I asked.

"*Nonno* is Italian for *grandfather*," he explained. "He said he wasn't going to be cheated out of a name or a nickname, so we have to call him both."

"He sounds funny. It must be nice, having all those relatives."

He nodded. "We have a good time, when we're not driving each other crazy."

"What drives you crazy?"

"Different opinions on what makes for happiness, I guess. My sister can't understand how I can be happy when I'm separated from the rest of them, and I can't understand how she can be happy when, between our parents, her husband, and her kid, she never has a minute alone."

I laughed. "To hear you talk, you'd think you weren't social."

"I am social." His dimples deepened. "Especially compared to you."

My smile faded. "If you don't like how I am, why'd you ask me out?" It would have been a snappier comeback if I hadn't glamoured him to ask me out.

Mark reached across the table and caught my hand. "I'm teasing, Adlia. I guess you're not used to it, being an only child."

"I'm not." I watched his thumb stroke the back of my knuckles. "When Aunt Kootie criticizes me, she means it."

He tugged on my hand a little. "Hey."

I looked up.

"I'm sorry. I like the way you are. I like *you*."

This time, it was more than my ears that turned pink. "Thank you." *I like you, too, even though I shouldn't.*

He let go of my hand to put a credit card in the bill folder the waiter had left. "What's your favorite kind of day?"

Had he purposefully asked a question I could answer? "A snowy day."

He looked up. "Really? Why?"

"Because it makes everything so quiet. The animals and birds stop racketing around and there's all this silence, this *peace*. You can think things you never had room to think of, or you can not think at all."

He rested his chin on his fist. "I grew up taking pictures of wedding cakes, and I get *paid* to take pictures of people, but I have taken more pictures of snow than anything else."

"I would *love* to see your pictures of snow," I said, leaning forward.

The waiter returned with the bill. Mark signed the receipt with a flourish. "How about right now?"

"Let's go." I'd be late to work, but since it was all for a good cause, Kutara could just deal. Whether the good cause was looking through Mark's photos or having him to myself, I couldn't admit, even to myself.

Photos covered the walls of Mark's condo. I slowly walked the perimeter of his living room, stopping in front of a picture of an old man and a boy with their heads together, both of them showing gap-toothed smiles. "Is that your grandfather?"

"That's him. A bunch of us went to the zoo and Nonno Nino taught my nephew Tommy to spit at the tapirs. The only reason we didn't get thrown out was because Mom once dated the security guy."

I laughed, even though the thought of animals in captivity made me shudder inside. "Who's this?" I pointed to a dark-haired bride sitting on the floor, her wedding dress pooled around her. Her eyes were crossed, and she had stuck out her tongue at the photographer.

"My sister Amy. She was so nervous about being the star of her own wedding that she threw up for two hours the night before. We thought she'd have to go to the hospital." He laughed, then looked serious. "Of course, it wasn't funny at the time."

He stood so close to me, I could feel the air move with his breath. Now was when I should leave him sitting blankly on the gray-tweed sofa while I searched through his stuff. Instead, I asked, "Where are the pictures of snow?"

"In the bedroom."

I turned to face him, and saw the fingers of his right hand straighten, as if he were consciously relaxing them.

"Maybe you want to see them later," he said.

"No." I smiled. "Let's see them now."

Mark's bed wasn't made, and he quickly picked up a few articles of clothing from the floor and threw them into a closet, shutting the door after them.

The bedding was white, the headboard a black grid, and a double line of photos with thin black frames circled the room, as though the walls were bisected by a 360-degree window. I sat on the end of the low bed and sighed with contentment.

Touches of color in the pictures gently caught my attention: one red leaf, sugared with frost; the blurred cobalt of a Steller's Jay as it flew through a white-draped pine forest; withered green apples with caps of snow, hanging from a leafless tree. The rest were studies in gray, brown, black, and pure, serene white. "The only thing more perfect would be if you had some on the ceiling."

"Look up."

I did, then lay back on the bed, laughing. "*Very* good." The ceiling was almost covered with unframed photos.

He lowered himself beside me. "I sell a line of framed Colorado collages. This is how I decide how to group them."

I pointed. "Those two are excellent together.

The three rocks, and the three chickadees on the branch." I turned my head to look at him. "I thought you didn't do wildlife photography."

"I saw the rocks on my way to class, and the birds were in the aspen outside my kitchen window."

Turning toward him, I could practically count every one of his long lashes. "I'd call you an opportunist, but you seem deaf to all this knocking."

He turned onto his side, facing me. "You mean the fact that we're in my bedroom, on my bed, and you look like a naked flame in the middle of winter?"

I swallowed. "Yeah. That."

He leaned over me and whispered, "Just wanted to be sure," before lowering his mouth to mine.

Kissing Mark on the street had been absorbing enough. In the quiet of his bedroom, surrounded by beauty he had created, I felt consumed by my desire for him. It was a close thing as to who would wind up on top, but he won and I was glad.

How could anyone think humans were insubstantial? His weight, his heat . . . It felt as though energy were crackling across the entire surface of my skin, fighting to get in. He kissed past my jaw and I arched my neck under his lips, groaning, *"Li'don-ahshuk . . ." You make me wet.*

He came back up, nipped my earlobe, and whispered, "What did you say?"

"Nothing, just nonsense words." I buried my hands in his hair and dragged his mouth back to mine.

His lips curved as we kissed. "Speaking in tongues. I like it."

"I'll show you speaking in tongues." I opened my mouth under his and he moaned into it, pressing his hips against me.

We took off our clothes in between kisses and gasps. When we were both naked, he sat back on his heels and smoothed his hands down my breasts and ribs to grasp my waist—his olive skin dark against my paleness. "I've never seen anyone so beautiful, Adlia," he breathed. "You're perfect."

No one had ever told me I was perfect—or even above average, for that matter. As he bent to kiss my breasts, I raised my hands and ran my fingers into his thick, wavy hair, finding the rounded top of one ear and marveling at its strangeness.

The muscles in his shoulders shifted as he moved lower. He paused to gently close his teeth on the flesh of my thigh, and my legs opened as if that animal gesture were the key to my lock. His hand came up, sliding over my belly, and I gripped his strong fingers with my own as my eyes closed.

By the time Mark came back up, my eyes had rolled back behind their closed lids and I could barely think.

"Adlia," he whispered.

"Mark," I whispered back. I hadn't glamored him when he heard me speak Elven, but I did make him forget to wear a condom. I wouldn't have a child unless I wanted to, and nothing was going to come between his flesh and mine.

I felt the light touch of his lips on my eyelids, my cheek. He pressed his mouth to mine, and our tongues touched slowly, languidly. Then he slid inside me and I arched backward, hands gripping his arms as he pushed deeper.

I whimpered and moaned as energy filled me from my core outward. I felt my hair lift slightly away from my head, as if stirred by a breeze, and I was glad Mark's eyes were closed.

We panted and grunted, hands slipping as they sought purchase on each other's sweaty skin. And when I could hold no more, when it felt as if sparks would crackle from my fingertips and earth themselves in his bones, I came.

He pushed into my arching body with a shout, and we shuddered helplessly together.

After a minute or so, he rolled sideways, taking me with him. "That was amazing. You're amazing." He planted gentle kisses across my face. "I can barely think."

"I like not thinking," I murmured, trailing my fingers up his ribs and then letting my hand fall, exhausted.

"Adlia?" His warm breath stirred my hair.

I buried my face in his neck, breathing his scent. "Hmmm?"

"I think I have a spare toothbrush, if you want to spend the night."

I could call Kutara and tell her I needed to look for photographs of elves. I squirmed closer, not wanting to think about Kutara or photographs. "I can stay."

"Good. I'll make omelets for breakfast." He pulled back so he could look at me, then sucked in his breath.

"What?"

"You look *incredible!* I mean, you're always beautiful, don't get me wrong, but this . . . I . . ."

Uh-oh. Elves were more attractive than humans in our regular state, but a big hit of energy made us even more so. I assayed a grin. "Haven't you heard of a sexual glow?"

He blinked as if to clear his vision. "I think you actually *are* glowing. Is that possible?"

"No." I sighed. After having just had the best sex of my life, I had to make my lover think I was less attractive. It was *so* not fair.

Chapter Ten

I lay watching Mark sleep—the way the bow of his upper lip deepened as his mouth relaxed, the slow settling of his hair after he turned over, and, finally, the twitch of dreams behind his closed eyelids. Then I eased out of bed and went looking.

It wasn't hard. Besides a rather spartan guest bedroom, the only other room was clearly Mark's home office. I closed the door quietly and switched on the light.

To my right, three tall file cabinets stood next to a closet with louvered doors. On the exterior wall, a laptop sat on a computer desk below the window. A worktable held a slide viewer and some other, more arcane equipment, making it clear this was a photographer's room. Plastic boxes filled the space between the table's legs.

I crossed my arms over my bare chest as I wondered where to begin. Mark hadn't grown up in Boulder. It might make the most sense to start with his computer. The most recent digital photos had to be on that.

I sat on the cheap rolling chair and brought the laptop out of hibernation. Mark was organized, I was happy to see, so I could skip folders with names like *Italy06*, *Portraits02to04*, and *HikesWithMike*. Instead I opened *Boulder08-09* and went straight to *CreekPath*.

I scanned thumbnail images to save time, pulling up a full-size picture only if someone in it looked familiar. I knew less than a dozen local elves, after all, and Dag had only just arrived.

It felt as though about an hour had passed when I clicked the last folder closed. All that searching, and I had found one picture of Lenny wearing his knit cap, two of Galan (one with Erin), both with his hair over his ears, and one picture that might have shown the back of Kutara's head. Since we were in the park a lot and Mark made a habit of taking pictures there, that was surprisingly few. Maybe we needed to get out more.

Mark was more likely to notice something fishy if I deleted the photos, and none of them showed ears, so I left them.

After closing the laptop's lid, I knelt on the floor to pull the lid off one of the plastic boxes stored there. Portrait proof sheets—hundreds of them. As far as I knew, no elf had ever purposely gotten his picture taken, so I replaced the lid and went over to the closet, where I pushed open one of the doors with only the smallest of squeaks. More boxes, containing negatives. No *way* was I going through those tonight.

The two filing cabinets remained. The left one contained only business documents, and I closed each subsequent drawer with relief.

The right cabinet held prints in both black and white and color, and the haphazard way they were filed made me think that they were old. The first two drawers had mostly wedding photos, and the third, pictures of snow. I looked through a few of the latter, smiling. Mark's composition had improved a lot since these rather ordinary shots of humpy bushes and the shadows cast by aspen groves.

I sat cross-legged on the rug and read the label on the bottom drawer—*Family*. The folders inside were neatly labeled. *Mom, Dad, Amy, Maria, Gianni.* There were others, including *Nino, Tommy,* and *Faith.* I removed Faith's folder and pulled out the first print.

Mark had obviously taken this by holding the camera at arm's length. He was grinning from ear to ear while Faith pressed her lips to the side of his face, her arms wrapped around his shoulders.

He looked younger here, a little thinner in the face, and his hair was very short. The bones beneath his temples and cheeks seemed sharper and more vulnerable without his wavy hair covering them. I put that photo back and pulled out the next.

In this one, Faith reclined nude on a sheet-covered couch, shadows artfully accenting the hollow of her neck and the long line of her thighs. A classic study of the female form, it wasn't designed to be titillating, but I wondered exactly how close she and Mark were on the family tree.

Why am I doing this? Still holding the print, I rested my hands on my knees and shook my head in disbelief at my own behavior.

Was the occasional photo of someone with pointed ears really a threat to us? In these days of photo manipulation and online costume supplies, would anyone's *first* thought be that someone with pointy ears was actually an elf? Of course not.

Was I so afraid of Kutara's disapproval that I had to violate Mark's privacy in the dead of night in order to justify sleeping with him? How pitiful was *that?*

The door swung open, and Mark stood there. "Adlia?"

I glamoured him without stopping to think and put the photo back where I had found it.

Mark slumped in the doorway, naked and beautiful, a crease mark from his pillow on his cheek. I took his arm to lead him back to the bedroom and decided to make the best use of the glamour while he was under it. "Have you ever seen an elf?"

"Uh-huh."

I stopped and stared up at him. *"Where?"*

"*Lord of the Rings.* Anime."

I steered him toward the bedroom again. "Have you ever seen a person with pointed ears in real life?"

"Uh-huh."

I made him get in the bed and turn on his side, toward the center. "Where did you see real people with pointed ears?"

"Actor at Shakespeare festival. Donkey guy. Also cat woman at Halloween party."

I got in the bed and pulled the sheet over us before backing up against him and pulling his limp arm over my waist. "Do you believe there are elves in real life?"

"No."

I released him from the glamour and felt him pull me closer. He pressed a kiss to the nape of my neck and I turned in his arms, hooking my chin over his shoulder so I wouldn't see his tender, trusting expression. Moonlight shone through the window and lit the picture of the jay flying through his winter wonderland. Maybe that was the reason I loved snow. It hid everything that was ugly.

Early evening of the next day saw me back at the office, one very energized elf.

Kutara wasted no time. "Did you find any photographs?"

"There wasn't a pointy ear in sight." I sat down at Calan's desk and turned on his computer, since he wasn't there yet. In my peripheral vision I saw that Kutara's gaze was still on me like a laser.

"Were you able to look through everything?" she asked.

"No." I picked up a real-estate magazine that had fallen to the floor and indulged myself in a smile. "I guess I'll just have to go back."

"Go during the daytime," Kutara said. "I would prefer that it not interfere with your work."

I pointedly turned away from her.

Lenny came in to talk to Kutara about cell phones, and I busied myself with property descriptions of *close-in location, ready-to-build,* and *septic already installed.*

Looking at potential real estate was actually pretty interesting, and an hour went by before I even thought to take a break. I was about to go outside when my cell phone rang. Lenny and Kutara both waited for me to answer, patently expecting that it was elf business.

The display showed Mark's number. I stood to go outside. "It's a personal call." In response to Kutara's incredulous look, I said, "What? Guy calls you on yours."

I walked briskly into the hall and flipped open the phone. "Hi, there."

"Hello, angel."

I gave a little shiver of pleasure as I left the building. Outside, a breeze whispered through the tall cottonwoods lining the creek, blowing away the heat of the day. "What are you doing?"

"What am I doing? Um . . . I'm training elephants for the circus."

"You are not." I walked to the creek and looked down at the water, opaque in the fading light.

"Okay. I'm dyeing white doves green for a leprechaun magician."

I laughed. "What are you really doing?"

"Right this moment? I'm walking to meet a beautiful stranger."

I heard a footfall behind me and turned.

Mark pulled me to him in a fierce embrace. My phone fell to the grass as I wound my arms around his neck and kissed him, the rush of sensation and energy making my head swim and my knees weak. He was heat and passion, and I couldn't seem to get enough.

I was almost ready to shuck my clothes when he cupped the back of my head and moved his mouth to my neck. "I know we don't have plans this evening." He kissed the skin below my ear. "But you seem to hang out here a lot and I couldn't stop thinking about you, so I took a chance."

I pressed myself against him. "I'm glad you did."

He pulled back enough to see me, and I saw his eyes widen. I glamoured him just enough to not notice my enhanced appearance.

He pushed a curl away from my face. It hovered in my peripheral vision, waving slightly. "Have you had dinner? Should we go somewhere?"

I heaved a sigh. "I can't. I'm working."

He glanced at his watch. "At seven o'clock?"

I waved a vague hand at the annex building. "We're setting up a new exhibit. It's all . . . hammering, and stuff."

His face brightened with interest. "You work at the Canyon Gallery?"

"No. I mean, I have a friend who does, and they needed some extra people. That's all." Any second now, he was going to ask more questions, and I didn't have the answers. I pulled at the collar of his shirt. "I have to go back in soon. Kiss me again. Please."

Mark's mouth moved slowly over mine, warm and soft. His hands on my back felt as though they were all that held me up, and I wanted to arch backward and feel him bend over me.

Quite suddenly, he let go.

I staggered backward, almost falling. Mark stood limp and dazed, while behind him, Kutara and Lenny approached.

Lenny gave Kutara a disapproving look. "Was that really necessary?"

Kutara pushed my messenger bag at me. "Come with us."

"What? No!" I took Mark's unresponsive hand. "You have no right to—"

"Erin called," Lenny said gently. "Galan is losing his memory."

Chapter Eleven

We materialized behind the spruce tree at the side of Erin's house. Kitty Girl, Erin's cat, ran up to us as we approached the front door. Kutara avoided her with a look of distaste.

I reached down and stroked the animal just to annoy Kutara, but found myself comforted by the vitality in the small, warm body. *Life goes on, no matter what,* I thought, then gave myself a mental shake. Galan wasn't dead.

Lenny knocked on the door and we heard Erin call, "Come in!"

Galan lay on the oversized couch in the middle of the living room, his head in Erin's lap. She didn't look up as we came in, but continued to stroke his silver-blond hair, a wrinkle of worry between her brows.

Galan opened his eyes and gave us all a weak smile. "Sorry to cause alarm." He sat up and rubbed his temple absently.

Kutara moved behind the couch and put her hands on either side of his head. "Do you hurt?"

"No. It's more of a foggy feeling, as though I have to consciously make myself think."

Erin spoke to Kutara. "I thought he'd gone to work, and then I found him in the backyard, just . . . sitting. He seems almost normal as long as I keep him talking, although he had trouble coming up with the right word a couple of times."

Kutara took her hands away from Galan's head. "I don't feel anything obviously wrong. There might be something slightly off, but it could also be that I'm expecting to feel that."

Erin nodded. "It was the same for me."

"Are you sure you're not just tired?" I asked Galan. "You have been working a *lot*."

He shook his head regretfully.

I sat on the couch next to him, and Lenny took a seat on the big hassock.

Kutara paced the room, tapping her upper lip with the fingers of one hand. "Adlia has spent the most time with Fia, but she hasn't had any problems." She gave me a sharp look. "You haven't, have you?"

"Not as far as I know." The thought of having problems and not realizing it was terrifying.

"So why Galan?" Kutara mused.

I chewed my lip and thought. "He was the first to contact her. Could she have been more contagious then?"

Lenny chimed in. "Or maybe it's some kind of parasite, and it transferred from Fia to Galan."

Erin spoke to Galan. "Honey, you haven't noticed any kind of itchy spot or wound, have you?"

"No."

"If only he could merge with *Ma'Nah,* that might get rid of it," Kutara said. "It's possible that we've all been exposed, but since Galan is bonded to Erin, he can't bond with his land to cleanse himself."

"Does that mean Fia is bonded to a human?" Lenny wondered. "I wish you could have tried merging her with Galan's land. That would have told us something."

A thought at the edge of my consciousness finally clarified. "What if she *is* merged with his land?" The rest of them stared at me. "No, listen . . . Fia disappears. We can't find her anywhere. The only land close to where she disappeared that's available for an elf is Galan's old land. What if she merged with it and that's somehow affecting him?"

"But Galan isn't bonded to that land anymore," Lenny said. "Is he?"

Kutara spoke to Galan. "Are you?"

Galan continued to gaze into space, and I felt the first pang of true fear for him. While we were discussing his sanity, possibly his life, he had drifted away.

"Galan!" Kutara barked.

"What?" He looked at her, his forehead creased.

"You don't have any bond to your old land, do you?"

"No. I get my energy from Erin or the creek."

Lenny looked disappointed. "Do you visit it, though?"

Galan stared at him, as if willing himself to pay attention. "Occasionally."

"Your land isn't very far, is it?" Lenny asked.

Erin answered. "Only about three blocks."

"Could it be trying to establish a connection, but also contaminating you because Fia is there?" Lenny pressed.

Kutara frowned at him. "I've never heard of land reaching out for an elf. Even if such a thing were possible, why would it bother when it has an elf in residence?"

"She's not much of an elf," Lenny said.

I gave him a look.

"Well, it's true."

Erin appeared to be holding on to her temper with some difficulty. "Would someone *please* check to see if Fia is there?"

"I'll go." I pushed myself off the couch.

"I'll go with you," Lenny said, beating me to the front door.

When he opened it, Kitty Girl bolted inside and ran to the couch, where she jumped onto Galan's lap. He looked surprised for a moment, then picked her up and lay his cheek against her fur. I turned away, my throat tight.

Outside, the day had finally darkened. As Lenny followed me behind the tree, he said, "If Fia is there, you don't suppose traveling through that land could contaminate *us*, do you?"

I chewed on my lip a moment. "Maybe we should walk."

* * *

We walked.

It was strange to limit ourselves this way. As we passed the occasional dog walker, my thoughts went from the inconvenience humans experience to the fear they feel.

Elves didn't die of old age. We died because humans developed our land or, on rare occasions, because of attack by a dark elf. But with the discovery that we could survive off water energy or hook up with a human on a more-than-temporary basis, Boulder elves had started to feel safe again.

I didn't feel safe anymore.

If my mind began to drift, who would take care of me? Would Mark, if I told him what I was? Maybe if we had been together longer, and if Kutara didn't glamour away his memories of me.

I turned off the paved road onto the trailhead. "It's not far now." We crossed an irrigation ditch, where a dog walker resignedly watched his Labrador wallow in the muddy water, and continued up a rocky path beneath the pines.

Fewer people passed us as the stars came out. I led Lenny to the base of a rocky outcrop that looked like the giant spine of a prehistoric animal. "This is it." I cupped my hands around my mouth. "Fia! Hey, Fia! *Vol'kellet!*"

Lenny did the same. "Fia!"

We fell silent as a woman with a Dalmatian approached.

"Lost your dog?" she asked, disapproval in her tone.

I didn't bother answering, just glamoured her to move on and leave us alone. "Fia!"

We called and called, but there was no response. Finally Lenny knelt and put his hands on the ground.

I watched as his palms sank slightly into the dry, stony earth. He was brave, to risk contamination like that. "Anything?"

He cocked his head, as if listening. "I don't feel anything, but her energy was so nebulous the last time I felt it. She could be there and I might not know it."

"If I merged, do you think I could tell anything more?"

He lifted his hands and sat back on his heels. "Don't do it, Adlia. Tracking is my specialty. I can tell more from that small contact than you could by merging, and it's not worth the risk to you."

He didn't need help rising, but I held out my hand to him anyway.

He looked at my outstretched hand. "Are you sure you want to touch me?"

"I could ask you the same thing. I spent more time with Fia than anyone."

He grasped my hand and stood. "I guess we're all in this together."

Erin was not pleased to hear that we didn't have an answer. "So we still have no idea what causes it."

Kutara picked up my messenger bag.

"Hey! That's mine, you know!"

She pulled out my camera and brought it to me. "This has a video feature, doesn't it? I'm going to ask Galan questions. I want you to document it."

Document his deterioration, she meant.

Erin covered her face with both hands, and Galan wrapped his arms around her. "Sweetheart, don't," he said. "If we approach this systematically, we might find a clue as to how to cure me."

She nodded and wiped her face with her hands. "All right."

I think we were all a little heartened at his logical statement. He was able to answer all of Kutara's questions, too, although it was clear he had to work to focus. The only moment of real tension came when Kutara asked the names of his parents.

Galan shook his head slightly. "I should know this."

Erin took his hand. "It's not like you're close to them. *I* don't remember their names."

"Anatelia and Trion," Galan said, looking relieved.

"Good." Kutara signaled for me to stop recording.

As I put the camera away, Kutara said, "Determining what causes this and locating a cure is now our top priority. It occurs to me that this might not be a contagious disease. There could be an environmental trigger and Fia was simply the first to succumb. Erin, see if you can think of anything odd Galan might have been exposed to."

Erin nodded thoughtfully. "That's a good idea. He sometimes drinks water."

"That should stop," Kutara said. "We don't need it, after all. If we're lucky, it'll be something that simple."

I put my hand on Galan's shoulder. "Try not to worry."

He covered my hand with his and smiled up at me. "I don't think that'll be a problem. I'd have to concentrate pretty hard to worry."

Kutara, Lenny, and I went outside and gathered behind the spruce, although we probably didn't need to bother. In the dark, anyone who saw us disappear would assume their eyes were playing tricks on them.

"Let's meet back at Elf Ops," Kutara said. "No going off to play with your human boyfriend, Adlia."

"I wasn't *going* to." Although being with Mark was the most comforting thing I could think of right now. "Speaking of him, did you bother to include any explanation when you glamoured him, for when it wore off?"

"Of course I did. Your friend called with a baby-sitting emergency, and you had to go."

"Oh." That was really good, actually.

"Now can we leave?" she asked.

"Wait," Lenny said. "Maybe we shouldn't travel incorporeally."

When Kutara looked blank, he clarified. "If it is something environmental, we might want to avoid merging."

Kutara shook her head. "We are part of *Ma'Nah*. You might as well say we shouldn't be elves. Now let's get back so Dagovar can hear about this." She melted into the ground, and we followed suit.

For the first time, traveling through *Ma'Nah* gave me no sense of comfort. Did merging safeguard me from this disease, or was I being poisoned even as I flowed through the ground?

Ma'Nah was a living creature, but I couldn't communicate with her directly. Her language was in the thickness of roots, the color of leaves, and how many foxes were in a litter that year.

I felt a longing for Mark. If I told him what the Boulder elves were going through and told him my fears, would he listen, or would he just think poor Adlia was crazy?

We reached the park and emerged, making sure we weren't watched.

Inside, Dag was clearly shocked to hear of Galan's condition. "Apparently I was overconfident that we would all be safe."

Kutara ran a finger over her laptop's touchpad to bring the screen to life, but her gaze rested somewhere above the computer. "I want to make it clear that you are all free to go home." She focused on our astonished faces and smiled thinly. "It might be safest to remain incorporeal."

"I can't help but notice your use of the word *you*, as opposed to *we*," I pointed out. "Does that mean you're not going anywhere?"

"I will continue to try to find a cure." Kutara

shrugged. "But it's a risk. I won't be disappointed in anyone who chooses not to take it."

Silence descended on the room for a minute. Dag opened his mouth to speak, but before he could say anything, I found my own voice. "I'll stay."

He gave me a look, as though I had stolen his thunder. "I also will stay."

"Then that makes it unanimous," Lenny said.

Kutara smiled at him. "Lenny, I want you to go home."

"What?" He was clearly offended. "It's my decision!"

"Of course. But you, Galan, and I have been working on Fellseth's estate from the beginning. If I manifest the disease, I want someone who has all the knowledge to replace me."

"Then why don't *you* just go home?"

Kutara raised her eyebrows at his tone.

Lenny pushed his hair back in a nervous gesture, and I saw that the tip of his ear was pink. "I didn't mean that the way it sounded. I'll go. But I think I'm just as likely as you to get it."

"It can only be a precaution, of course. But if necessary, I have faith that you can replace me as *ka'chil*, Lenny."

Lenny looked mollified at this, but I saw the corners of Dag's mouth turn down. Of course, if anyone had *ka'chil* written all over them, it was Dag, but he hadn't been with us very long.

I was quite sure that my name had never been up for consideration. I gave Dag a commiserating smile, and his frown deepened. "So what's next?" I asked Kutara.

"You're very good at Internet searches, aren't you?"

"I guess so." Actually, I was excellent at them, due to my appetite for time-wasting content, but I didn't realize Kutara had noticed.

"See if you can find any online elven groups we're not aware of," she went on. "I'll recontact all the known groups and put pressure on them to ask as many people as they can about this. Up until now, I don't think any of us realized just how serious this could be."

Dag folded his hands on his desk. "I admit to not being very good at searches. If you like, I can continue to work on the accounts and property search, so we don't miss too many opportunities."

She nodded. "Perhaps that would be best, although I hate the thought of putting you at risk for anything so trivial."

Trivial was not a word I had ever expected to hear Kutara use when speaking of business matters.

Dag shrugged. "We may find a cure quickly, and then wish we hadn't dropped everything else."

"True. Then we all have our tasks." Kutara smiled in a way that suggested pride and camaraderie, then said, "Lenny, go home."

I searched the Internet all night long, without stopping to read sarcastic blogs or surf eBay, but I couldn't keep my thoughts from wandering to Mark. If I told him what was happening, would he believe me? By now he would be in bed, and the thought of his warm, sleepy body gave me a lump in my throat.

When morning neared, I still hadn't found a hint of elf groups outside the two we already knew. What if another one existed and knew of the cure, but we never found them among the millions of online communities? Even worse, what if no other groups actually existed? The thought gave me a creepy, end-of-the-world feeling.

My left hand felt numb from resting against the edge of my laptop. I stretched my wrists and yawned.

Kutara looked up from her own work. "Perhaps we should all rest. I would hate to work toward finding a cure for this, only to succumb prematurely because we're overtired."

Since I had seen Kutara work for thirty hours straight on more than one occasion, I knew she was taking Galan's situation—and all of our situations—very seriously. "You're going home, too, right?" I asked.

She closed the lid of her computer. "Yes. Dagovar, you should leave as well. We all need rest."

He did look a little frazzled. "Let me just finish this e-mail." He finally closed his machine and raised his clasped hands above his head in a stretch before standing.

Kutara locked the office door behind us. "Let's hope for better luck tomorrow."

When we got outside, she melted into the ground immediately. The early-morning light had already warmed the grass, and I found that I wanted to sit in the sun for a little.

Dag followed me to one of the concrete planters, and we sat down with almost identical sighs. I closed my eyes and enjoyed the light's warmth on my lids.

Dag spoke, his voice a rumble next to me. "What will happen to the Boulder elves if Kutara becomes incapacitated? Will Lenny really be able to take her place?"

I squinted my eyes a little tighter. "He'd do fine."

"But would he be the leader Kutara is?"

"No." I opened my eyes. "There are times when I dislike Kutara, but I guess that's part of being an effective leader. You can't spend your time pleasing everyone, and sometimes you have to make decisions that seem harsh."

He grunted and fell silent for a while. "Do you think we will find a cure?"

"If there's one to find, we'll find it. Kutara never gives up."

He nodded slowly. "I suppose that's how she finally defeated Fellseth—by never giving up."

Kutara hadn't been the one to kill Fellseth, but we kept that a secret. Most elves wouldn't appreciate hearing that a human had killed an elf—even a dark elf. Humans were responsible for too many of our problems already. "Fellseth made it easier by coming back," I said, "but if he hadn't, I think Kutara would have eventually tracked him down."

He stood. "Her determination gives us some hope, at least."

"You bet." I shaded my eyes with my hand and looked up at him, haloed with sun like a Viking god. "I don't trust Kutara with my feelings, but I do trust her with my life."

Chapter Twelve

I did eventually go back to my land, but merging didn't give me the ease it usually did. Elves had been aware of pollutants for some time, both man-made and not. Was some contaminant in the Boulder area making us sick?

Galan hadn't merged with land for over a year, but who knew how long the sickness took to manifest? As creatures that morphed from a physical to an energetic state, we might be affected just by walking on top of the land. It could be magnetic fields, air pollutants, or even sunspots. If only we knew more about Fia's history.

I diffused farther into the soil around me. It was a gesture of defiance, but also an acknowledgement that I couldn't avoid the unknown. I wouldn't even see it coming.

I woke about midday, feeling jittery. During August, the plants in this part of the country stored energy for all they were worth. Staying immersed too long gave me a buzz that must feel like three shots of espresso to a human.

Still craving sun, I emerged onto the surface naked and spent a little time basking. The hum of a nearby highway sounded from over a ridge, but it wasn't visible, just as other elf communities might be out there but invisible.

I wasn't supposed to go to the office during the day, but I could still go to the public Internet terminals at the library. I remerged and gathered the atoms of my messenger bag, determined to find other elves if they were out there.

There were no chairs at the library's Internet terminals. My feet hurt from standing so long, and the college student waiting for my terminal was well inside my personal space.

He set down his backpack so it nudged my shoe. "You've been here a long time."

I gave him a cold stare and a shot of glamour.

"Although there's no official limit on terminal use," he continued loudly, "so, really, I'm being a complete asshole. I'll leave now."

I made him curtsey, pinching the sides of his baggy jeans.

Searching the Internet had always come easily to me, but after hours and hours of it, I couldn't bring myself to follow another lead. And why were people still cluttering up the Net with *Lord of the Rings* stuff, anyway? Those movies had come out *years* ago. Apparently there had also been some kind of book.

I left the library. Outside, people were scattered across the grass by the creek, reading, sunbathing, and playing with their dogs and kids. They all looked so normal, although any one of them might be dealing with some terrible disease or tragedy. The difference was, they had people who loved them.

I took out my recovered cell phone and called Mark. "Hi. It's Adlia."

"Hi! How did the babysitting go?"

I didn't know what real babysitting entailed. In movies, the kid always managed to wreck a car or something. "It was fine," I said, figuring that was safe.

"You sound kind of down. Is everything okay?"

It was on the tip of my tongue to say I was just tired, but then I wondered . . . Why couldn't I confide in Mark, at least a little? I took a deep breath. "Actually, I am kind of down. I have a friend who's really sick, and no one seems to know what to do."

"I'm so sorry. Do you want to get together? I could take you to lunch on the Pearl Street Mall."

What I wanted was to go to his bedroom and leave the world behind, but this was a start. "Sure. How about I meet you outside the Boulder Book Store?"

"I'll be there in twenty minutes."

The pedestrian mall was busy, but I found a place to sit on the raised landscaped area across from the bookstore. Trees shaded me, and water bubbled from the mouth of a fountain shaped like a man's face with wild hair, set flush with the brick surround.

I had heard Erin refer to the fountain as a green man, although it was made of bronze.

Mark arrived about five minutes later, with wet hair and a sprinkling of damp spots on the neck of his red shirt.

When I stood to meet him, he engulfed me in a hug. I closed my eyes and savored the feeling. The scents of his shampoo and soap didn't do much for me, but underneath was the warm smell of animal vitality. We stayed that way for a few moments.

Finally he pulled back, kissed me softly, and took my hand. "Sorry if I'm late. I did a shoot in a warehouse this morning, and had to shower."

"You're fine."

"Did you want to eat at the bookstore café?" He gestured to it with his free hand.

I shook my head. "You know, I'm not that hungry. Maybe we could just walk? Unless you want to eat."

"No, I'm fine." He gave my hand a squeeze and we walked east, past a guitar player and the patrons seated outside a sushi restaurant.

"So what's wrong with your friend?" he asked.

"He's losing his memory." I sighed.

"Like Alzheimer's? How old is he?"

I was pretty sure Galan was about 250 years old, but that didn't mean anything to an elf. "It's not Alzheimer's, and he's not old. No one knows what's causing it. I feel so helpless."

He pulled me closer, letting go of my hand and putting his arm around my shoulder. "I know what that's like. My Nonna was sick with cancer for a long time."

"Nonna?" I asked.

He smiled. "Italian for *grandmother*. I kept thinking, maybe there's some information out there that could fix it, if I spend enough time looking."

"That's exactly it!"

He gave my shoulder a squeeze. "And it's uncomfortable to spend time with sick people, because it makes you wonder if you'll have the same thing someday."

I stopped walking and stared up at him. "How can you possibly know that?"

"Because I know you."

But he didn't know me.

He gave a half smile. "And because I looked through my mother's book on grief while I was in the hospital lobby one day. Some things are universal, aren't they?"

"Apparently." I started walking again. The idea that Mark could understand and care without knowing all about me was strange. "What was the name of that book?"

"I don't remember. She had four or five self-help books on the subject and said they were all the same. I'm sure they have some at the Boulder Book Store. Do you want to walk back?"

I didn't have any money. "I'll look for one at the library."

"You're a big fan of the library, aren't you? Which reminds me, what show are you working on at the Canyon Gallery?"

"Art glass." I had seen a poster for the next event, but that was all I knew about it. Not wanting to lie, I decided to change the subject. "Have you seen your cousin Faith? She works at the gallery, right?"

"She's their bookkeeper. She specializes in non-profits." He gestured to the cross street we'd come to. "C'mon, let's make this light." We trotted across the street. "Anyway, I showed up at her office yesterday afternoon, so she couldn't avoid me. It didn't do any good."

"She still wouldn't talk to you?"

He shook his head. "I asked her to lunch. She said she had too much work to do. I asked if we could talk for five minutes. She said she didn't have five minutes. Her coworkers were staring at me like I was a stalker. I can't *make* her talk, but something is definitely wrong."

I could make her talk. It was on the tip of my tongue to offer, but I was supposed to be working on elven problems, not human ones. I curved my arm around Mark's waist again. "I hope you find out what's wrong."

"Thanks. I will." He pointed up ahead, to where a crowd had gathered. "Someone's got a bunch of kids around him. Must be a magician."

"Let's go see." Human children fascinated me. Elves usually had one child at a time, and they didn't often get together. Because of my long hibernation in *Ma'Nah,* I hadn't even known *myself* as a child. The fact that these tiny creatures grew into complex people seemed like the essence of magic.

When we got closer, we saw that mothers and toddlers had gathered around the children's fountain, which spouted random jets of water from a concrete foundation. A tiny girl in a sopping pink T-shirt ran flat-footed through the puddles, gurgling with laughter as she chased something silver along the ground.

Mark laughed, a delighted sound. "That's a good trick!"

"What is it?" Someone tall had stepped in front of me.

"Looks like a metal fish." More children had joined in the chase. "There's at least three kids between him and that gizmo, so he can't be using a line. Must be remote control." He pointed. "See him?"

Now I did. Galan squatted at the edge of the crowd, silver-blond hair dripping down his high cheekbones, a huge grin on his face. For just a moment I felt a spurt of pure joy. He must be recovered! But why was he shirtless and barefoot? And why was he doing magic in the middle of a crowd of humans? Unless . . . "No." It came out as a moan.

Mark looked at me, his face concerned. "What's wrong?"

"The magician—he's my sick friend. It's a mental thing."

I looked around for Erin or Kutara, but Galan appeared to be alone. "I need to get him back to his wife."

"I'll help. Is he likely to struggle or anything?"

"I don't think so." But of course I didn't *know* that, and for a moment I imagined a confused and angry Galan, shooting bolts of energy amid screaming children. "The thing is, I don't know if he'll recognize me." I could glamour the mothers, but I couldn't glamour Galan.

"Stay here. I have an idea."

It didn't occur to me to protest, I felt so lost. Mark walked casually around the back of the crowd, to the edge of the lawn that fronted the courthouse. Then he straightened, taking on a purposeful air. "If I can have your attention? We're glad you enjoyed this portion of the show. If you'll walk to the end of the block, Marissa the fairy princess is doing face painting."

Most of the mothers called to their children and began to move away, but a few stayed. Some obviously enjoyed Galan's shirtless state, and watched him more than they watched the fish.

As the tiny girl in pink ran by, her mother reached out and grabbed her with a laugh. "C'mon, sweetie. Face painting!"

I came closer and glamoured the rest of them to leave. "Galan?"

His gaze skimmed me with no sign of recognition, his expression showing only disappointment that his audience was going.

And then I felt him counteract my glamour. The little girl in pink ran back, and Galan smiled as the fish, made from silver foil, darted between her feet.

He still squatted, so I put my hand on his bare shoulder. "Galan. It's time to go. Don't you want to see Erin?"

He looked around, as if Erin would appear. "Where?"

"Let's go see her now." I slid my hand under his arm and raised him to his feet. The fish fell on its side in the water, and the little girl grabbed it with a squeal.

"Is he all right?" her mother asked, picking up her daughter with no regard for her dripping state.

"He's fine."

The mother's face relaxed as my glamour took hold, and she turned and walked away. Her daughter wailed as they left, reaching over her mother's shoulder toward Galan, the foil fish crushed in one small hand. Glamour never worked very well on small children. When they wanted something, they wanted it absolutely.

"We'll have to take your car," I told Mark.

"Of course." He scanned the area around us. "Where's your shirt, man?" he asked Galan.

"I don't think he brought one," I answered. Was Galan's focus so poor that he couldn't remain fully clothed? If so, I was amazed Erin's name had meant anything to him.

Erin must have been looking out the window, because she opened the door and ran down the walk before Galan was fully out of the car. She wrapped her arms around him and he clung to her, eyes closed tightly.

Mark put his hands in his pockets and turned slightly away, looking at the ground.

Kutara appeared in the doorway to Erin's house. "Come inside."

Mark's expression became vacant and he turned toward his car, but I grabbed his arm and did a little counteracting of my own. Kutara glared at this sign of disobedience on my part, but I held firm. "I couldn't have brought Galan home without Mark."

Erin turned back, her arm around Galan's waist. "Thank you so much."

"I'm glad I could help," Mark said. "I hope he feels better."

"Yes, thank you." Kutara made a peremptory gesture toward me. "Adlia."

"Stay here," I told Mark, and walked to where she stood in the doorway. Once there, I said, "Is the house on fire?"

"I think you can see that it isn't."

"Then could you give me a minute to say good-bye to Mark?"

She sighed. "Please be quick. The less we involve humans in our business, the better."

I turned away, muttering, "Except for your human, of course."

Behind me, the door shut a little harder than necessary.

Mark leaned against his car. "Who was that?" he asked, when I reached him.

"Galan's nurse."

"Kind of bossy, isn't she?"

I rolled my eyes. "You have *no* idea."

He pulled me against him. "Are you going to stay here?"

I nodded against his chest. "There might be something I can do."

He kissed the top of my head. "You're a good person, Adlia."

I tilted my face up and looked into his dark eyes. "You might not think so, once you get to know me."

He laughed. "I think I can tell."

Chapter Thirteen

Kutara and I took turns searching the Internet on Erin's computer, trying to find a record of Fia, or other elf groups, or even Alzheimer's information that could apply to elves, although that seemed very unlikely.

When we got tired, Erin meditated to raise energy for us. When she got tired, we watched Galan for her.

It was after Erin had relieved me of this duty that I found Kutara in the kitchen, sitting at the small table and staring into space. I pulled out a chair and sat. "Have you heard from Lenny or Dag?"

"Lenny is using someone's computer in Broomfield. Dagovar is at the Boulder Public Library. He e-mailed to ask when he should come in. I told him the usual time." She glanced at the clock on the wall above us. "I suppose we should leave soon."

I wondered if Mark wanted me to spend the night. If so, we were both going to be disappointed.

Thinking of Mark, I realized I had never found the source of the elven glamour I had sensed on him.

"The guy I was with tonight, Mark . . . Had you ever glamoured him before that one time when we were kissing?"

Kutara lifted one shoulder. "It's possible. I probably glamour fifty humans on an average day."

"Are you serious? Why so many?"

"They always seem to be in the way. Shall we go?"

We stopped outside Erin and Galan's closed bedroom. Kutara tapped on the door and said, "We're going now," in the gentlest voice I had ever heard her use.

"Okay," came Erin's muffled reply. "Thank you."

We waited a moment, then went outside, closing the front door quietly behind us.

I heaved a sigh. Traveling through the earth took energy when you weren't on your own land, and I was already tired.

Kutara must have divined my thoughts. "Why don't you ride with me?"

"You have Guy's car today?" Sure enough, a beige Geo Metro was parked by the curb.

"I'll have it every day. He gave it to me."

I watched her root through the small purse she carried. "He *gave* you his car. Of his own free will?"

"Yes." She pulled the keys out of her purse and jingled them at me. "This morning."

"What's he going to drive?"

She unlocked the car and we got in. "He bought a new car."

I couldn't resist a little dig. "That's quite a present.

I didn't know you were that kind of couple." I expected her to come back with something like, *He's a kind person who saw that I had a need.*

Instead she said, "There's a lot you don't know about me."

Dag was working away when we reached the office. "I thought I'd found a group of elves in Texas." he said when we came in, "but it turned out to be some people acting in a game."

"Tell me about it." It felt weird to sit in my usual chair, in our same old office, without Galan. Just two days ago, real estate was our biggest worry. Now we were in danger of losing everything, as we had already lost Fia.

I brought up my browser, only to stare at the search field. Kutara also seemed to be stumped.

"Maybe we should talk about the ways we've been searching," I suggested, "so we don't waste time doing the same things."

She nodded. "An excellent idea."

It turned out that Kutara had searched within Yahoo Groups, while I had ranged freely through the labyrinth of Google.

"What about you, Dag?" I asked.

"I have searched for elven names."

"Huh." Considering that elven culture didn't have standard names such as *John* or *Mary,* that meant Dag had been searching for the names of elves he had met or knew of. That would take me about five minutes. Maybe there was something here I wasn't getting. I glanced at Kutara.

Her face was carefully neutral. "How many elven names are you aware of, Dagovar?"

"Twelve, specifically, but what I meant is that I have used elven words that *might* be chosen as names."

"Oh," I said, relieved. "Like *bright water,* or *moon on the hills.*"

"Yes."

I turned back to Kutara. "You know, searching on Elven language isn't a bad idea."

She raised her eyebrows. "Except that I don't see any Elven characters on these keyboards."

"Well, no, but if you were an elf online, you'd use a phonetic version of *Vol'kellet* or whatever. We could try a bunch of spelling variations on common expressions."

"I'll do that, if you like," Dag offered. "It's something specific, and I don't think my search skills are as advanced as either of yours. Perhaps you could each come up with a list of words that almost any elf would know, regardless of area or dialect."

I started typing. *Hello, good-bye* . . . What would an elf say online? At Elf Ops, we talked about land and money, with tactics against dark elves thrown in for good measure. But if I were a solitary elf discovering the invisible web of connections that was the Internet, what words would I send out, like an electronic message in a bottle?

Vol nas. I am elven. *Hol lin'tu fal?* Is anyone there?

I typed these in, plus two dozen more, and e-mailed them to Dag, copying Kutara on the message. "I just sent a list of words to start on, if you want to take a look." I glanced at Kutara, waiting to see if she would approve.

She stared at her screen, brow furrowed and mouth pursed in concentration.

"Did you not get it yet?" Patience was not *my* elven name. Kutara had named me Adlia. It meant *Unknown.*

Her fingers jittered absently on the keys, making a soft clicking. "What's the word for *new?*"

"*Sheng.*" But why would she ask me that? Elves' facility with languages was an evolutionary trait, allowing us to blend in during the centuries we'd lived among humans. Once we learned a word, we never forgot it.

Fear dawned on her face, even as my own heart sank.

Our tension must have communicated itself to Dag, because he looked up. "What's happening?"

"Apparently merging with *Ma'Nah* is not a cure for Fia and Galan's condition. I am losing my memory," Kutara said, her voice quite calm.

I was desperate for this not to happen. "Maybe you were looking for a synonym, like *novel* or *revolutionary.*"

"And did you have any trouble remembering those words?" Kutara shook her head. "It's time to close up the office and do what we can to salvage the situation."

"What? Why?" I wailed. Elf Ops had been my only community. The thought of being isolated again momentarily terrified me, until I thought of Mark.

"But isn't that why you designated Lenny as your successor?" Dag asked.

Kutara shook her head. "I sent Lenny away hoping to limit the exposure of at least one of us, but he may still succumb. I believe it is a contagion, and that this office and everything in it may be contaminated."

"He could buy a new computer and start a new office," I insisted.

"And if he loses his mind and wanders away from his new office and computer?" Kutara asked. "Then Fellseth's fortune would be lost to us. No, we will close down operations while we can still do it in an organized fashion. Fellseth's financial information will be uploaded to online storage, where it can be accessed without fear of contagion, and we will turn everything over to the Kansas elves. As for the rest of it—"

"What rest?" Dag asked.

"We're not working with Fellseth's entire estate. Galan, Lenny, and I collected laptops and papers from five houses and eight safe-deposit boxes owned by Fellseth. We stored some of the computers in Guy's garage, and none of us have touched those since before Fia arrived."

Dag gave her an incredulous look. "Are you saying those machines have account information you haven't even *looked* at? You might have been able to buy a whole island for elves by now!"

"The items at Guy's house all relate to *foreign* accounts and investments," Kutara said. "Unfortunately, humans can't be controlled over the phone, and there are language difficulties as well. I flew to Switzerland and glamoured most of a bank to obtain one password. It could take years to track down everything. Some of it may never be accessed."

"I see. Will you send those laptops to the Kansas elves, too?" Dag asked.

"Guy will drive them there."

Dag frowned. "You may not have touched those computers since before Fia came, but you have certainly touched your human. What if he contaminates them?"

"It's a possibility, I admit," Kutara said. "Guy will take hygienic precautions. But I think it will be best for him to put them in a rental storage unit when he arrives in Kansas. The Kansas elves can wait to approach them, if they wish. We certainly had enough money to manage without having overseas funds as well."

Dag still didn't look convinced. "And can your human be trusted with information that could be worth a fortune?"

"Guy is completely trustworthy." Kutara's voice would have sounded neutral to a stranger, but I heard the anger in it. "Even if he wasn't," she went on, "all of those laptops have been password protected."

"Are you sure you're having problems?" I asked. "Because it sounds like you've thought of everything."

"I typed it in a file some time ago." She smiled at me, and it was the first time I had seen her look wistful. "And now I must apologize for an action I felt I had to take."

This couldn't be good. I had never heard Kutara use the word *apologize.* She went on. "I took pictures of all of us and sent them to every elf we know. If we do become like Fia, I've instructed them not to approach us. Rather, they should do whatever they feel necessary to keep us from contaminating anyone else."

Dag and I stared at her in silence. Finally I said the only thing that came to mind. "I didn't know you had a camera."

Kutara tapped her cell phone where it lay on her desk. "So handy, for so many things."

"Truly, you are *ka'chil,*" Dag said, his voice husky. "And this means I cannot go home."

Kutara nodded slowly. "We can't risk the chance of this disease spreading."

I could barely take it in. Fia gone, Galan and Kutara losing their minds, Elf Ops disbanded, and now I could be killed on sight if I came across another elf.

"There is one more thing to discuss." She pinched the bridge of her nose, then rubbed her forehead.

When she remained silent, I began to worry that there was something worse, though I couldn't imagine what it was. "Kutara?"

She looked up, her gaze slightly unfocused. "I'm sorry. What was I saying?"

"One more thing to discuss," Dag prompted.

"Yes. The possibility of becoming mortal."

"Mortal?" Where was she headed with this? "Do you think that's what happened to Fia?"

"No, I mean that we could choose to become mortal. It might stop the course of this disease, or even reverse it. It's a slight possibility, I admit, but I have already mentioned it to Erin."

"Are you considering this?" Dag asked.

She nodded. "It might give me another sixty years in which to help other elves with my knowledge. Depending on how fast I feel I am degrading, I might make the decision tomorrow. Pizza has always fascinated me." She tried to grin, but the result wasn't entirely successful.

I tried to imagine Kutara eating, aging, dying . . . All of this would happen if she ate food and triggered the change from elf to human. "Shouldn't you wait until . . . Or maybe . . ." I trailed off.

Kutara shook her head. "There is still time for us to craft human identities. Glamour someone at a hospital for a birth certificate, then a passport clerk. You know what to do."

Dag pushed back his chair. "If you'll excuse me for a moment. I'm going outside to think."

We watched him go in silence, but as soon as Kutara heard the front door close, she leaned forward and spoke rapidly to me.

"There is money in an account for you. The information is on your laptop, in your poetry folder. The file name is 'accountability,' the user name is your name, and the password is my name."

"You put money aside for me?"

She straightened from her urgent posture and

gazed slightly to one side. "You have been a valuable part of this team. It was the right thing to do."

"Thank you." Of course she had thought of my future, and probably Lenny's, Galan's and Dag's futures as well. Taking care of elves was what Kutara did. "Do you really think we're all going to get this?"

Now she met my eye. "I do. Tomorrow I will make the change to human."

When Dag came back, he seemed calmer, or more resigned. We worked through the night, finding an online service that would store files, making electronic notes about accounts and investments when they needed explanation, and then saving everything to the service. It took hours and hours.

During the times when my laptop's drive light flashed and I waited to push the next button, I thought about the things Kutara had said.

Could I make the decision to become human? Admittedly, there was a dramatic, tragic allure in the idea. It would remove all obstacles to a serious relationship with Mark, for one thing. I would age like him, eat like him, and eventually die like him.

Would Mark still want to be with me if I were merely human? I would be just another woman, short and mouthy, with normal attractiveness and no special tricks in bed.

It was a little after six in the morning when Kutara rubbed her eyes and pushed back her chair. "I have finished. At least I *think* I have." Seeing my expression, she said, "That was a joke."

"Stick with your day job." I stretched to loosen my shoulders. "I still have a few things left to transfer. How about you, Dag?"

"I'm finished." He closed the lid of his laptop and sighed. "What will happen to these machines?"

"I'll store them at Guy's house, after he's left town. Adlia, you can keep yours." Kutara picked up her cell phone. "I'll call Guy now and tell him what to do."

Dag loaded some more papers in boxes while I uploaded more files to the service, but I know I listened as Kutara told Guy he needed to shower at the neighbor's house, make an excuse to borrow clothes there, enter the garage from the side and load certain items into his car.

His *brand-new* car, I remembered, and wondered when Kutara had first planned this and how much Guy knew.

She finished by saying, "I won't get home before you leave. When you return, I will have a surprise for you." She listened for a moment, then said, "That means more to me than you know."

As soon as she hung up, Dag said, "I'm sorry to ask this, but under the circumstances—

"What?" Kutara asked.

"Now that everything is saved to online storage, did you remember to send the Kansas elves a list of the account passwords?"

"I sent them in an encrypted file." She frowned. "However, they can't access the laptops currently stored at Guy's house—the ones with the international accounts. I password-protected those machines before we gave up on them. I don't have that list with me, but I can send it later. They're going straight into storage anyway."

I had a sudden thought. "You know, we might be premature with all of this!"

"What do you mean?" Kutara asked.

"The last time you merged, you weren't showing symptoms, right? Maybe you just need to spend some time in *Ma'Nah*."

"I will definitely try that. But if I catch it again every time I become corporeal, my abilities as a leader are severely limited. No, it's better to turn everything over to elves who are not handicapped in any way, while we still have time. The money isn't ours, after all. It's for all elves."

"That's true." But apparently I had enjoyed working with it more than I knew.

"If merging with *Ma'Nah* doesn't clear up this disease, as I suspect, then it's probably not safe for another elf to take over my land." Kutara let out a small sigh and returned to her keyboard. "One more detail to tell the Kansas elves."

I felt a tug at my core thinking of my own land, and the possibility that I could no longer care for it. "At least there's no chance that *your* land is contaminated, Dag. Someone will use it."

"That's true." He combed his hands through his hair in a distracted gesture. "Dark elves I was prepared to face. Not this."

"It must be extra hard for you," I agreed. "You barely know us, and now you've been sucked into this horrible situation."

"It could have happened anywhere, I suppose." He got up and pushed a chair aside on his way toward the door. "I'm going outside to take some creek energy. I *think* I'm just tired, but every sign of fatigue makes me think my mind is going."

"I'm sure it's just because we've been working so long." I tried to sound confident, but my voice was tight with fear as I watched him leave. Would the three of us, working so closely together, show symptoms within hours of each other? Had Lenny left in time? Was he safe in his land, or was he wandering the city mindlessly?

Dag hadn't shut the door behind him. I got up and closed it, then returned to my files, determined to finish everything so I could leave. The very air felt contaminated.

We hadn't been working much longer when Kutara made a call. "Guy? There's something I need to retrieve before you go. I'll be there shortly." She closed her phone and got up.

"You're leaving?" I asked.

"He didn't answer his phone, and it occurs to me that the list of passwords that protect the stored laptops might be in one of the boxes I told him to pack. It's not exactly secure to send the passwords *with* the machines they protect."

"I guess not." I stood. "Kutara . . ."

She turned. "Yes?"

"If I don't see you before you . . . I mean, if you do decide to become mortal . . ." We had never hugged, but now I moved toward her.

She held up a hand. "You should not touch me—

just in case. But yes, I'll be back as soon as I take care of this password business."

"All right."

I finished in half an hour, comforted by the fact that my brain still appeared to be functioning perfectly.

Dag wasn't back from the creek yet, but the Gallery's human staff would be here soon. Of course, in these circumstances, we might work through their arrival. I went outside to see what his plans were.

Down by the creek, our usual rocks were deserted. I looked back toward the office. Dag could have crossed the bridge and walked back on the other side. Or maybe he didn't remember where our office was.

"Surely he can't have gotten sick *that* quickly," I muttered to myself as I walked back to Elf Ops. But of course there was no guarantee of that, and Dag might be wandering down Canyon Boulevard at this moment.

Still, I expected to find him in the office. When I didn't, I got out my cell phone and called his number. Lenny had outfitted him with a phone days ago.

It rang, then went straight to voice mail. I listened to Lenny explain that this was Dagovar's phone and I should leave a message.

"Dag, where *are* you? Call me!"

Maybe he had gone with Kutara for some reason. I called her next, but she didn't answer, either. This was really freaking me out. Locking the office behind me, I went outside and shouted, "Dagovar!" There was no reply, but seeing a passing jogger got rid of the creepy feeling that I was alone on an abandoned planet.

I dialed Kutara's number again with no luck, then went back into the office and looked up Guy's phone numbers, which I had never had occasion to call.

His home number rang a long time before switching over to the message. "Nobody's home, nobody's home," Guy's voice sang to some familiar classical melody.

"This is Adlia. Dagovar is missing, and I need to speak with Kutara." I added, "It's urgent."

I called Guy's cell, but he didn't answer that, either. This time, I didn't bother to leave a message—just went outside and melted into the ground.

Chapter Fourteen

Guy's house, in a Boulder subdivision called Martin Acres, clearly belonged to an architect. Kutara had told me that Guy was inspired by Frank Lloyd Wright. I didn't know who that was, but the house certainly had an aesthetic edge over its neighbors.

I didn't stop to admire it, because Kutara's car sat in the driveway and its door, the front door of the house, and the door to the attached garage all stood open.

"Kutara!" I yelled, ducking beneath a branch of the huge spruce under which I had materialized. What looked like receipts littered the lawn, tumbling slowly in the light wind.

Just inside the house, an open staircase led upstairs or down. I headed up but slowed before I reached the top level.

Guy's dining room table was shoved out of place, two of the chairs knocked to the floor. In the kitchen beyond, a bowl and a glass lay smashed on the floor.

The open floor plan allowed me to look into the living room next, where an entire bookcase lay on the floor, a delta of paperbacks spilling from underneath.

"Kutara? Guy?" I called, more quietly.

I went back outside and noticed the rut from a car tire in the grass beside the driveway and a flattened bush at the edge of the yard.

Inside the garage, more papers littered the cement floor, along with a computer mouse, a broken pair of eyeglasses, and some manila file folders. A jumble of rakes and shovels lay beneath a pegboard. I walked through the side door, also open, and into the backyard. "Kutara? Guy? Anyone?"

Juniper bushes grew at the very back of the lot along the wooden privacy fence. One of these shook, as though an animal stirred underneath. I walked slowly toward it, prepared to melt into the ground at the slightest sign of danger.

The shaking stopped as I neared. I bent down and pulled aside a branch. Guy looked up at me, his face pale and bruised-looking. A cut bisected one eyebrow, and his lower lip oozed blood.

"Where's Kutara?" I asked.

"I don't know," he whispered, grimacing as he spoke. "Call an ambulance, please."

I called 911 and gave them Guy's address, then hung up. "Is there anything I can do for you?"

He shook his head.

"What happened? Can you tell me?"

"I heard noises, in the house. Thought it was Kutara. Then this guy comes in garage and starts going through stuff. As soon as I spoke, he went crazy. I know he would have killed me, but Kutara got here."

He made a garbled noise, and I gripped his wrist. "Guy, stay with me."

"*Fzzz . . . Pchoooo . . .*"

I realized he was making little explosion noises. "Kutara fought him with *energy?*" My next thought was unthinkable, but I thought it anyway. "What did he look like?"

"Long blond hair. Big, like a Viking."

"*Dag?*" My mind could barely process the thought. Surely it was someone else.

Guy nodded. "*Dagovar*. That's what Kutara screamed at him." He rested for a moment, struggling for air. "She fought like a tiger."

"How did you get out here?"

"Dragged myself. Not fun." He stopped and panted shallowly for a moment. "I think I might have a collapsed lung. Maybe punctured."

"I'm assuming you don't want me to pull you out of there, but could you breathe easier if I rolled you onto your back?"

"Don't." He tilted his head toward his lower body. "Leg's broken."

I got up from my crouched position and parted the bushes farther back. Guy lay on his side, and when I saw his topmost leg below the hem of his shorts, I drew in a sharp breath. The white end of a bone poked through the fleshy part of his thigh. Blood streaked both legs and had darkened the ground below.

"Did you see what happened to Kutara?"

"I was halfway across the yard when they both came out, fighting. Kutara had a paper, in her hand. He wanted it."

The passwords to the laptops? "Did he get it?"

"Don't know. Kutara ran away. He chased her."

"She *ran* away?" Why hadn't she dematerialized into the ground to escape? Unless she *couldn't*.

I studied Guy's face. His eyes were closed. "Guy, do you know that Kutara is an elf?"

"I knew there was something . . . special. I thought, she'll tell me when she's ready."

"Yes, but . . ." How could I ask him this? "Have you noticed anything different between the two of you? It could have been really recent."

"I fell in love when I first saw her. She . . . could have had any man." His voice was so faint, I could barely hear him. "She told me she might need me to take trip, for her. Bought new car, more reliable." His eyelids opened, drooped, then closed again. "When I gave her my old car, something different in the way she looked at me. For the first time, I thought . . . she might love me."

I heard the wail of an approaching siren. Had Guy's gift of a Geo Metro caused Kutara to bond to him? That was the only explanation I could think of for why she had *run* from Dagovar—she had bonded to Guy and could no longer become incorporeal. It would also explain why Dagovar couldn't glamour Guy and had instead beat him. "Where's your car? Did Dagovar take it?"

He nodded slightly. "I think so. He came back,

but didn't see me. I heard noises from house, then a car leaving." He sucked in a breath and grimaced.

"Hold on, Guy." I put my hand on the top of his head, the only uninjured part of him I could see. "Is the pain worse?"

He panted slightly. "Dizzy."

The siren reached the front of the house and cut off. I heard car doors slam. "Back here!" I yelled.

Two white-uniformed men carrying a stretcher ran to join us. I glamoured myself out of their awareness as they extricated Guy from the bush.

I approached the stretcher once the paramedics had stabilized Guy's leg. "Guy, can you hear me?"

His eyes were tightly closed against the pain, but he nodded.

"When Dagovar came back, could you see if he had a paper in his hand? The paper Kutara had?"

He rolled his head slightly. "Don't know."

The paramedics lifted him, and I got out of the way as they carried him alongside the garage and out to the street.

Dagovar might or might not have caught or killed Kutara. Where would he go next?

I melted into the ground and headed for Elf Ops.

Upon emerging, I had to immediately glamour five people. A crowd filled the area outside the Canyon Gallery and Theater, the crackle of police radios cutting through the hubbub of voices.

I pushed my way toward the building, since it was impractical to glamour that many people to let me

Esri Rose

through. Yellow tape roped off the area in front of the Canyon Gallery, and shards of glass and pottery littered the pavement just outside.

One of the current pieces of art on display, a huge terra-cotta vase, had obviously gone right through the plate-glass window and lay in pieces on the concrete outside.

I ducked under the yellow tape and glamoured the cops not to see me.

"Hey!" a voice from the crowd said. "How come she gets to go through?"

I went inside, stepping carefully. Some of the artwork lay on the floor. There were more police here, and I glamoured strategically, trying to conserve energy.

Inside Elf Ops, my chair was overturned. All of the laptops were gone, which meant that my access to the money was gone. Cords hung over the desks where the laptops had been yanked free. I wasn't sure what resources I had to catch Dagovar, but money wasn't one of them.

I waited until the police photographer turned away from the desks before unplugging my phone charger from the wall. The edge of one of the file cabinets had a big dent in it. That concerned me more than anything, since there was nothing nearby that could have hit it.

Was there anything here that could be useful? I opened Kutara's desk drawer. Paper clips, a spare phone battery, some pencils—nothing to help.

Back outside, the police were questioning a bicyclist. His legs were scraped and bleeding below his spandex racing suit. "I mean, the guy was *huge,* but this woman kept fighting him with what must have been some kind of Taser. You should have seen the sparks. I picked up my bike and hit the guy with it. He sort of batted it aside, and then he threw me. That's the last thing I remember."

The officer looked up from his notebook. "You didn't see what happened to the woman?"

"Or him. By the time I came around, I guess someone else had called you guys."

Most of the crowd now surrounded the bicyclist. I walked away, toward the creek, but stopped when I spotted something green and shiny in the grass— Kutara's phone. I picked it up.

"Hey!" A policewoman marched toward me. "What's that you've got?" A quick shot of glamour and she said, "Oh, that's okay then," and made an about-face.

Elves dissipated when they died. If Dagovar *had* killed Kutara, there would be no corpse, not even clothes. But finding Kutara's cell phone didn't necessarily mean she was dead. It could mean she had lost it in the battle. I held on to that thought as I walked down to the rocks by the creek.

I opened myself to the creek energy. Dagovar and I had sat here together. I had liked him, even *admired* him, and all the while he had been a traitor in our midst.

A tear rolled down my cheek and I blinked, trying to clear my vision. The creek washed the tangled roots of the tree I had photographed for Mark's class, feeding it now, but killing it over time. Was that what our association with humans amounted to?

My gaze traveled up the trunk, where I spotted the corner of something white protruding from between two branches. I got up and waded through the shallow water, icy from glacial runoff.

A piece of paper had been folded small and stuffed into a crevice in the bark. I unfolded it and glanced at five nonsense words and their permutations—passwords that unlocked the computers from Guy's house.

A careful, S-shaped tear went from the top edge down. Another small tear went to the left, from the center of the *S*. Long before paper and pens, elven scouts left marks on leaves and bark to help those who followed—elf sign.

Unimportant. That was the message Kutara had left. And at the bottom, another careful tear. *Don't seek.*

A sob escaped me, and I ran my hand under my eyes to wipe away the tears. An elf left that last symbol when he knew he was dying and didn't want anyone to waste time looking for him. It had a second, implied meaning—*remember*—because those who read it took a moment to honor the lost elf.

Kutara had put this where she knew I was likely to see it, and presumably before she fought Dagovar at Elf Ops.

Why had she gone into the building? Why had Kutara not escaped when she had the chance?

The answer came as I stared at the curving, rippling surface of the water. *Because she thought I was inside.*

I could imagine Kutara darting through Guy's neighborhood, then out to the street to glamour an unsuspecting driver and take his car—Kutara arriving at the library and hiding the password list.

Had she taken a moment to recharge from creek energy, or had she gone immediately to Elf Ops? Maybe she tried to call Lenny, only to drop the phone and run when she realized Dagovar was already inside.

Kutara had not been a warm surrogate mother. She had badgered and manipulated and made me want to get far away from her, but I wasn't sure I could bear it if she were dead.

I took out my own cell phone and left Lenny a message explaining what had happened. Next I called Erin. "Have you seen Kutara?"

"Not yet," she said. "Yesterday she said she might come over in the afternoon to use the computer."

"I don't think she'll be there."

After I explained to Erin, she was silent for a bit. Then she said, "There's nothing to show for sure that she's dead."

"*Don't seek*," I reminded her.

"It also means *remember*, right? I think she's telling you that what's important is finding a cure for the forgetting disease. *Remember.* See?"

"There may not be a cure. I'm pretty sure Kutara and Guy bonded just recently. It looks like bonding to humans is what causes the disease."

"And Galan and I have an unbreakable bond."

Erin sounded near tears. "But why did it take a year for Galan to show signs?"

"I don't know. Maybe it takes longer for male elves to show symptoms."

"Or maybe it's just a coincidence," Erin said. "If only we knew what Fia's situation was. I can't *believe* I lost her."

"There might be another way to help Galan. Kutara felt the beginnings of memory loss last night. She was planning to become mortal, hoping it would cure the disease." I was reluctant to ask my next question. "How is Galan today?"

"Not good." Her voice caught on the last word. "I have to watch him constantly. Lily is taking care of the store."

"You could give him some food, in case Kutara's theory is right."

"I can't make that decision for him. Not yet." She paused, and I heard her blow her nose. "Do you think Dagovar will keep trying to get the passwords?"

I blew out a breath. "I don't know. Instead of copying files to online storage, he probably spent that time changing accounts so only he could access them. I hope that's enough money for him, and he's on his way out of town."

"It's possible Kutara killed him, you know. She killed him and now she's resting somewhere."

"Maybe. I suppose it's also possible that Dagovar has her, and will offer to trade her for the passwords."

"And you would, right?" Erin said.

"Of course I would." Although ideally I would get rid of Dagovar once and for all.

"What are you going to do now?"

"Go back to my land and recharge. Dagovar has never been there, and I never mentioned where I live. I should be safe. *Whatever* happens next, I want to be ready."

My little patch of *Ma'Nah* lay just off the highway between Boulder and Golden, next to Kutara's larger area. I went to her land first and called her name for some time. There was no answer.

Fia, Kutara, Galan . . . Their names went round and round in my head. We had lost so much, but even if Dagovar never reappeared, I would lose something more—Mark. My feelings for him meant that I could no longer spend time with him. The risk of bonding was too great.

Looking on the bright side wasn't easy, but at least Lenny and I were probably safe from the forgetting disease. We could start a new Elf Ops, maybe ask for some of Fellseth's fortune to manage, and spread the word that bonding to humans wasn't a compromise between freedom and extinction. It was something much worse.

Chapter Fifteen

I emerged in late afternoon and checked my cell phone. I had missed one call, from Lenny. I called him back.

"Erin told me. I can hardly believe it," were the first words he said.

"I know."

We were both quiet, struck by the enormity of what had happened.

After a moment, Lenny said, "Poor Galan and Erin. They only had one year together."

"It was a year he wouldn't have had without her," I pointed out.

"I guess so. What's weird to me is that Dagovar isn't even a dark elf! I would have sensed that on him, and there was nothing. He's just . . . *bad*."

"You know what I wonder? Did he come here wanting to help and then was tempted by the money, or did he plan this all along?"

Lenny was silent for a moment. "I don't see how he *could* have planned it. I mean, I was with Kutara when she spoke to elves. Yes, she said we were setting up an organization to help elvenkind, but I don't remember her *ever* saying, 'And we have an enormous sum of money to do it with!'"

I laughed, surprised I still could. "You're a good elf, Lenny."

"You, too. I guess I should contact the Kansas elves. Dagovar probably won't show up there, but you never know."

"And warn them about bonding to humans," I reminded him.

"That too, although I don't think that's very likely. I've always gotten the impression they dislike humans even more than most elves do."

"All right. I'll talk to you later, okay?"

He sighed. "Who else are we going to talk to?"

After we hung up, I took a deep breath and called Mark.

"Adlia!" His voice was warm. "I was just thinking about you."

Soon he would have to forget me. I closed my eyes, wishing I didn't have to do this. "Are you at home? Can I come over?"

"Absolutely. I'll make you dinner."

"You don't need to do that, but I'll be right there."

I would break up with Mark in person. I owed him one last lie.

Mark answered the door with a dishtowel in his hands and a dark spot on the front of his black

T-shirt. When I was inside, he took one look at my face and pulled me into his arms. "Tough day at work?"

For a moment I considered dodging his kiss, then couldn't bring myself to do it. But when he opened his mouth over mine, I pulled back, frightened that I would bond with him then and there.

He looked at me questioningly.

"Your shirt is wet," I said, as if that were an excuse.

"Spaghetti sauce." He led the way into the kitchen. "I always think it'll wipe off with less water than it takes."

I trailed after him. "I said you didn't need to make dinner for me."

He went to the stove and lifted the lid on a pot. "You don't need to eat any, but I'm hungry."

"Right. Sorry."

I sat at his kitchen table and stared at a stack of mail. What if Erin was right, and it *wasn't* bonding that caused the disease? Was there a way to break up with Mark but leave the option of getting back together?

He stirred the pot's contents with a wooden spoon. "So what'd you do today?"

My mouth opened and closed before I said, "I have to leave the country."

"What?" He paused in midstir and looked over his shoulder at me. "Leaving the country as in you're taking a holiday in Greece, or you're going for good?"

"It's for my Aunt Kutara's business."

Mark put down the spoon and came to sit across from me, his face perfectly neutral. "For how long?"

"That's the problem. We don't know."

"Well, what kind of business is it?"

"It's confidential." I chewed on my lip.

His brow furrowed. "So don't tell me the details. Is she going to open an office somewhere? Is it a new client?" He shook his head. "You know what? It doesn't really matter unless you're going to be gone for more than a year. I mean, I won't ask you to be exclusive, but that doesn't mean we can't keep in touch with e-mails, some Skype phone calls . . ." He stopped and frowned. "Unless you'd rather not and this is just an excuse."

"It's not like that, I swear!" I cleared my throat to loosen the tightness there. "It's just that I might be moving around a lot, sometimes in areas that don't have electricity, and I wouldn't want you to worry if you didn't hear from me for . . . months, maybe."

"Months."

"Maybe a year."

He ran a hand over his head. "Does your Aunt Kootie work for the government or something?"

What the hell. "Yes."

Mark looked at me closely. "You're serious?"

Liar, liar, pants on fire. "Yes."

"Adlia!" He reached across the table and took my hands in his. "Will you be safe?"

Only if I stayed away from him. "Probably."

"Can you spend the night?" he asked, rubbing his thumbs across my fingers. "How long before you have to leave?"

I made a show of looking at the time on his microwave clock. "Now, actually. I'm sorry."

He let go of my hands. "You're kidding me, right?"

I had pushed it too far, but I couldn't risk making love to him. It was time to take the easy way out.

I glamoured Mark to undress and fall asleep on his bed, believing we had made love. He lay there, naked and beautiful, the only person to care for me with no sense of obligation—just for *me*. Or at least what he believed I was.

I took one last look, tears streaming down my face. Then I left, making sure to turn off the stove first.

Back home, loneliness and guilt overwhelmed me, despite my incorporeal state. Kutara was probably dead, Galan might soon be. I shouldn't be thinking about humans, but though I suffered plenty over my elven friends, I couldn't get Mark out of my head.

Whenever I went into Boulder, I might see him. Not only would it hurt, but each time, I would have to see the happiness of our meeting on his face, then glamour him to forget me. Eventually he'd grow old and die, of course, and then it wouldn't be a problem.

I should stay away from humans and stick to elves, but there weren't that many of us left. Traveling far wasn't easy when you drew energy from one small part of *Ma'Nah*. It was possible for me to live for hundreds of years, thousands, and never see another elf besides Lenny.

He and I should mate and install our child on Kutara's vacant land. If it was a girl, I would name her Kutaran—*in memory of Kutara and Galan*.

Lenny would be a good father. For a minute, it seemed as if I could hear his voice calling to our child, and then I realized I *did* hear Lenny, somewhere above me.

I emerged to find him standing with his back to me, hands cupped to his mouth.

"Adlia!" he yelled.

"What?"

He spun around. "There you are."

"What is it?"

"It's Dagovar. He wants to meet."

Dagovar had sent the same text messages to both of us:

Seven PM, in front of the Boulder Book Store. Bring laptop passwords.

Lenny and I sat on the ground where I had emerged, discussing the possibilities.

I read the message once more before closing my phone. "Do you think he has Kutara?"

Lenny blew out a breath. "Wouldn't he say if he did?"

"You'd think." I tapped the phone against my

palm. "Seven o'clock on the pedestrian mall, on a summer evening."

Lenny nodded. "It's going to be mobbed with humans, and that's one of the busiest spots."

"There's a big landscaped area there, but I don't suppose we should materialize among the pansies. We'd have to glamour fifty people at least, and we might not catch them all."

"On the other hand, he's not likely to attack us with so many humans looking on," Lenny said.

"I don't know. He fought with Kutara at Guy's, and then again at the Gallery."

"That's true. It was early in the morning, but still."

I looked at my phone's readout. "It's six twenty now. I guess we should get going." I reached into the ground, gathered my messenger bag and pulled it out, then stood and brushed dirt off my jeans.

Lenny stood as well. "You have the passwords?"

I patted my bag. "In here."

He sighed. "I guess we have to bring them, in case Dagovar does have Kutara, but I hate to think of that bastard taking any more from us."

We materialized not far from the creek path and walked toward the mall, splitting up one block from our destination. Lenny would approach the meeting spot from the east end of the block and call me when he saw Dagovar.

I planned to cut through the bookstore itself, but in the meantime, I waited behind it, under a small tree planted in the median. A constant stream of people strolled down the sidewalk beside me, and the sound of a nearby band came through the warm air.

My phone vibrated in my hand, and I flipped it open. "Is he there?"

"Yeah." Lenny's voice was a little hard to hear over the general noise.

"Does he have Kutara?"

"I can't tell. He's sitting with someone at a table outside Old Chicago. I'm pretty sure it's a woman, but she's wearing a hoodie and I can't see her face."

It was hard to imagine Kutara sitting peacefully next to Dagovar, but if she had degraded as far as Fia had or if she had become mortal, that's exactly what she would do. "Where are you?"

"Inside Old Chicago. I ran down the alley and came through the patio entrance. He's looking toward the landscaped area between here and the bookstore, and I'm looking at the back of his head."

"You're not wasting a lot of energy glamouring people, are you?" I asked sharply.

"No. I'm at the bar. I told them I'm waiting for someone."

"Okay. I'm going to walk through the bookstore and add Dagovar to this call when I can see him."

I went in the children's wing of the Boulder Book Store and continued through the store to the front window. It was difficult to be sure with people streaming past, but I thought I spotted Dagovar's blond head at one of the tables across the way.

"Is he still there?" I asked Lenny. "Does he look like he's seen me?"

"Not that I can tell."

Between us lay two lanes of human traffic: residents out for an evening stroll, tourists, students, and vagrants, sitting on the edge of the walled enclosure that held pine trees, shrubs, and flowers. Measuring about twenty-five feet square, the enclosure became a series of steps on which people sat and chatted, or watched the world go by. Kids dabbled in the water that burbled from the bronze fountain's lips.

"That dirt has to go all the way down, right?" I murmured into the phone.

"I think it would have to, with those trees in it," Lenny said. "They're not small."

"Okay. I'm going to add Dagovar to the call. Don't say anything unless you need to warn me." I dialed Dagovar's number.

"Adlia?"

How dare he say my name like that, as if we were friends? I stepped outside, but instead of going straight across, I walked to the right, following the low wall that buttressed this small outpost of *Ma'Nah.* "What do you want, Dagovar?"

"I want the passwords that unlock the laptops—the ones with the international accounts."

I turned the corner that bordered the street, staying close to the soil. "Why should I give them to you? Do you have something for me?"

"Where are you?" he asked.

I turned the second corner and stepped onto

the wall. "I'm coming right towards you." I could see his blond head now, momentarily looking away from me as he scanned the constantly moving crowd.

He turned and spotted me, and I saw his lips move as he asked, "Where's Lenny?"

Forty feet and as many humans separated us. Standing on the wall, I looked over the top of most of them. The woman next to Dagovar sat with her head bowed, the hood of her shirt shielding her face. "Who's that you're with?" I asked.

Dagovar stared across the intervening space at me. "Give me the passwords and you'll find out."

"Let me see her face."

"Passwords first."

My messenger bag hung across my chest. Still staring at the woman, I reached to open the flap.

A breeze sprung up, making the pine branches whisper and ruffling the edge of the woman's hood. A lock of her hair fell forward—blond hair. Kutara's was black.

"You *bastard*," I hissed into the phone.

Dagovar stood up.

My right arm rose of its own accord, fingers tingling. A couple walking past looked toward Dagovar, as if wondering what I was pointing at. I lowered it with an effort.

Dagovar's voice came over the phone, low and scathing. "So ready to fight, Adlia? You wouldn't have a chance and you know it. Now give me those passwords or I'll kill everyone you know, starting with Galan and his mate."

"Did you kill Kutara?" Cigarette smoke drifted past my face, burning and acrid.

Dagovar started to walk, making his way between tables and out of the fenced eating area—toward me. "No."

My right hand tingled, and I clenched it. "Stay back, Dagovar."

"You wouldn't dare, with all these humans around. You brought the list here, didn't you? It's in your bag."

I stepped backward, onto the soil.

Dagovar stopped. "I know where Erin lives. I know she's home, taking care of poor Galan. Give me what I want and I'll go away. If you don't, I'll pay them a visit, right now."

We stared at each other across fifteen feet of space. A handful of people sat on the brick wall between us, some of them watching, their interest captured by two angry-looking people who chose to talk over cell phones when they were so close.

I was higher than everyone around, and Dagovar had ceased to play by the rules. *He has a clear shot at me. No amount of watching humans will keep me safe.* I realized this as his arm came up with the speed of a snake striking, a stream of silver energy arcing toward me.

I threw myself backward, but not before pain seared my right arm and the edge of my chest.

Lenny. Lenny would warn Erin. It was my last thought as I sank into the ground.

Chapter Sixteen

I regained consciousness but not form sometime later. The particles of my bag were in the process of dispersing near me, and I gathered them together with some difficulty.

Ma'Nah held me, but since I had no link to where I was, she offered no help. I drifted, hearing the excited babble of people above me and wondering if the effort of movement was worthwhile, or even possible.

I would not reach my land in this state, but Mark's condo wasn't as far. Making love with him might bond us, but it would also raise the energy that could save my life.

Blackness. I drifted into consciousness again and willed myself to focus and move. It might be the wrong direction, but if I waited to be certain, I might not move at all.

Eventually I raised my face from the ground, like a swimmer breaking the surface of a pond. Some time had passed, because streetlights shone above and headlights raked the curb directly in front of me. I rotated slowly in the other direction, gasping in pain. Pieces of dry grass fell into my open mouth.

A granite sign with etched writing jutted from the ground. My eyes blurred, and I blinked to focus. GUNBARREL ESTATES. Mark's condo complex. I was close.

I emerged in Mark's backyard. It was too much effort to form clothes, but I managed to drag my messenger bag from the earth. I left it lying as I crawled across the grass toward the patio door. Lights and the sound of television came from inside.

I knocked at the base of the sliding glass door. It took two tries to make much of a noise. As Mark's feet appeared around the end of the sofa, I rolled slowly onto my uninjured side, unable to support my weight anymore.

A light flicked on overhead, and I heard the door slide open.

"Adlia! My God!"

I didn't think I'd be able to glamour Mark, but I felt stronger as soon as his hands touched me. *Help me up.*

He put his hands under my arms and lifted, while I did my best not to scream. *Carry me to the bedroom.* My head fell forward, and I saw that there was no sign of injury. My right arm and breast were unmarked, even as they burned with agony.

He carried me into the bedroom and lay me on the bed. I panted with pain and exhaustion as I

directed him to undress. The outdoor light he had
switched on streamed through the window, bathing
his body and casting shadows across his face.

I wouldn't be able to keep up the glamour during
lovemaking. My thoughts fluttered darkly, wanting
to fade into unconsciousness. I closed my eyes, the
better to concentrate while I planted memories in
Mark's mind.

*You answered the front door. I told you I had changed
my mind and decided not to leave the country. We came
in here to make love.*

I couldn't compel his affection when the glamour lifted. Would Mark still *want* to love me, or had
my erratic behavior and ridiculous stories de-
stroyed his trust? Now was the moment of truth. I
let him go and opened my eyes.

For a moment he remained motionless, and then
he put one knee on the bed and slid next to me.
"Adlia."

I hadn't consciously held my breath—rather,
it was an effort to breathe, and I had forgotten to
make myself do it. "Mark." My voice was the merest
sigh.

He brushed against my right arm. My gasp of
agony sounded like passion, and his tongue swept
inside my open mouth. But even as I wondered if
his cure would kill me, I felt the pain lessen slightly.
His lips traveled over my face and down my neck,
feeling as though they trailed cool light. Still, I
didn't think I could bear his weight.

I glamoured him for just a moment, long enough
to have him roll me onto my left side. His body fit

behind mine, cradling me in warmth and strength. My breathing eased.

"Thank you," I whispered.

"For what?" He kissed the side of my neck, one hand skimming my side from ribs to hip.

"For letting me come back. For putting up with my strangeness."

"I kind of like your strangeness." He pushed my top leg forward with his knee.

"You do?"

"Yeah." He rocked me backward and snaked one arm beneath my neck, then crossed the other over my chest, covering my breast with his warm hand.

I found the strength to lift my leg and sighed with pleasure as the warm length of him nudged between my thighs and entered me. My thoughts drifted as I abandoned myself to the slow push-pull of his movements. I had never seen the ocean, but this must be how it felt to swim on a calm night—embraced in the slow movement of something powerful yet comforting.

Something fell away inside me, and for a moment the falling felt like death. My eyes opened wide as energy pinpricked across my skin, starting at my chest and spreading outward like a net that bound us together.

Behind me, Mark gasped and moved more urgently. I arched backward, all pain vanishing in a rush of pleasure, my mouth open in a silent scream. We shook and pulsed together, Mark's teeth grazing my shoulder.

When our shudders had subsided, he put his lips to my ear. "I'm glad you came back."

My hand found his, and I felt the tingle of our new bond as our fingers twined. "Don't worry," I whispered, a tear sliding down my cheek. "I won't be leaving again."

I woke with the sense that important events had happened, although I couldn't immediately remember what they were. Then my eyes opened on a sudden intake of breath. "Dagovar."

Beside me, Mark stirred. "Bag o' what?"

"Nothing. I was just dreaming."

He stretched. "I've had those dreams. You have this profound insight, and then it turns out to be something like, *egg whites on the blackboard allow you to skip wearing shoes.*"

"What?"

"Exactly."

He snuggled behind me, pulling me tight against him. I braced myself but didn't feel any pain. I gripped his hand and heard his sigh of pleasure.

Mark had saved my life, but at what cost? Now that we were bonded, my memory would soon desert me.

In the meantime, I could no longer travel through *Ma'Nah* or draw energy from her. I remembered Kutara's words to Lenny. *We are part of Ma'Nah. You might as well say we shouldn't be elves.* My bond with *Ma'Nah* was broken. My life force now came from Mark. What kind of elf was I?

Mark's stomach growled. "Man, I'm *starving* this morning!" he said. "You'd think I didn't eat anything yesterday." He rolled me over and gave me a smacking kiss. "I'm going to make us an enormous breakfast."

I smoothed my hair over my ears as he climbed out of bed. Our bond meant that elven glamour no longer affected Mark. I wouldn't be able to hide my ears, or the fact that I didn't eat. I wouldn't be able to hide anything, but that wouldn't matter for long. I didn't have much time before the forgetting disease claimed me. Before it did, I had one goal—to kill Dagovar.

Mark stretched, crossing his wrists behind his head and stretching backward with a grunt, magnificent in his nakedness. He straightened and grinned at me. "I'm not posing, I swear. I do that every morning." His grin faded. "Is everything all right? You're really quiet this morning."

I smiled. "I'm quiet every morning, I swear."

"No regrets?" He bent down.

I lifted my face for his kiss. "No regrets."

As soon as Mark went in the bathroom and closed the door, I bolted from the bed. I had left my messenger bag in his backyard last night, too weak to carry it. I had arrived naked, too, but the yard was completely enclosed by a wooden privacy fence.

I peered out the glass doors for just a moment before darting outside to get my bag. A quick check relieved my mind. The passwords were still there.

I pressed one hand to *Ma'Nah* and felt a shock as

she resisted me, even though I had expected it. I would have to borrow clothes. I ran back to the bedroom.

An almost musical buzzing noise came from behind the closed bathroom door. Who knew what humans did in there? I threw my bag on the bed and rummaged through Mark's dresser until I found a pair of tan drawstring shorts patterned with little blue surfboards. They had net underwear built in, but whatever.

I had seen several movies where women borrowed men's button-down shirts. I found a blue one in Mark's closet and fumbled it closed, tying the ends at my waist just as he came out of the bathroom.

He stopped and stared. "Are you going swimming today?"

"I can't stand to put on dirty clothes." I gestured to my bag, as if it contained my previous outfit. The sleeve of Mark's shirt flopped over my hand. "You don't mind, do you?"

He came near, still naked. "I couldn't object if I wanted to, because you look so adorable." He took hold of my sleeve and gently rolled first it, then the other, to elbow-length. "Do you want eggs and bacon, or waffles? I could eat both, frankly."

"I can't eat this early. It makes me queasy." When he raised a hand as if to brush back my hair, I grabbed it and kissed his palm, then pulled both his arms around my waist and looked up at him. "There are some things I need to do this morning. You know, since I'm not leaving town after all."

"Gotcha." He bent and kissed me.

I stood on tiptoe as our mouths met, and felt strength flow into me from his touch. When my hair began to stir, I reluctantly pulled away. "I have to go. Enjoy your breakfast."

Mark put a hand to his stomach. "Maybe hash browns, too."

I left the house and stood for a moment, the sidewalk cool and rough under my bare feet. I wasn't sure where I needed to go and I needed to make some calls, but standing here in the open didn't seem very safe.

A black SUV came down the street. I glamoured the driver to stop, then climbed in the back and sat on the floor, out of sight. The first thing to do was to check on Erin. I instructed the driver not to notice me while he drove wherever he was going, then I called Erin.

"Adlia! Are you okay?"

"Yeah." I couldn't bring myself to tell her about my new bond. "And you? Did Lenny warn you about Dagovar?"

"He called us, and I dragged Galan to the car and got us the hell out. We're staying at the Outlook Hotel on 28th Street."

"What about Lenny?"

"I called to let him know we were safe. I think he went home after that."

"How's Galan?"

She was quiet.

"Erin?"

"I'm here. Galan can't seem to stay still, and he's stopped talking. I have to really work to get his attention, and I don't think he recognizes me anymore."

"I'm so sorry." Sorrier than she knew.

"Lenny said he would keep searching the Internet, either for a cure, a confirmation that bonding to humans is the cause, or even to see if anyone is looking for Fia, so we can find out what her situation is."

"Good for him. I should call him now. He doesn't know if I'm alive or dead."

"He said you were tough, but I could tell he was really worried. Do you think you'll come by today, to talk about what we should do next?"

I was touched by her use of the word *we.* "We'll probably be by sometime today."

"Thanks. I should let you call Lenny now."

Lenny answered his phone by saying, "Adlia! You're alive!"

"You don't have to sound so surprised."

"You have no idea how bad it looked. Dagovar's shot sent you flying."

"No, it didn't. I saw it coming and threw myself backward."

"Really? I couldn't tell. Anyway, I called Erin immediately, but there were all these humans in an uproar around where you had fallen. I went over and put my hands on the ground, but I couldn't feel you."

"I was kind of weak. Where are you now?"

"At some guy's apartment in Golden. I glamoured

him to show me his computer before he left for work. Figured that was safer than being in a public place like a library. What about you?"

"I just left Mark's house."

"Who is Mark?"

I realized I'd never told anyone Mark's name. "Mark is the human I've been sort of dating, only now it's a little more than that." I took a deep breath. "Dagovar's shot really hurt me, Lenny. I couldn't make it home. Mark's place was closer."

"Oh, Adlia . . . Tell me you're not bonded to him."

"You'd rather I were dead?" I snapped.

"No, of course not."

In the silence that followed, the car I was in slowed and stopped, and the driver got out. I poked my head up and looked out at a vast parking lot bordered with fields. A huge building loomed nearby—IBM.

"So what are you going to do?" Lenny asked.

"Kill Dagovar before I get too stupid."

"Don't say that."

"It's easier for me if you don't show too much sympathy."

"All right," he said quietly.

"We still have the passwords. Maybe we can lure him somewhere with those."

"That's something to talk about. Let's meet at Erin's hotel."

"Okay, but there's something I need to do first."

"What?"

"Tell Guy about Kutara. He doesn't know what's happened."

Guy answered his cell phone himself. That was a good sign.

"Guy, it's Adlia."

"Adlia! Where's Kutara? I've tried her phone, but she doesn't answer."

I had turned off Kutara's phone. I took a deep breath. "We don't know. It's possible Kutara is dead. I'll know more soon." I would know more as soon as I could see Guy, because if Kutara were dead, their bond would be broken and he would be vulnerable to elf glamour again.

"I see." Guy spoke heavily. "Before you come, would it be possible for you to bring me some things from my house?"

"Sure. Where are you now?"

"At Boulder Community Hospital."

Guy's house was still a mess inside, although someone had shut his doors. Maybe the paramedics had done that. The house was unlocked, however, and I went inside.

Seeing the wreckage left by Dagovar and Kutara's fight, I was struck by how shocking and immediate the violence felt. Two people had tried their best to kill each other in these rooms. Guy was lucky to be alive.

I pushed up the rolling top of his oak desk, in

the living room, and found his spare glasses and checkbook. Guy remembered last working on his laptop in the bedroom. It sat on top of the sage-green coverlet, the screensaver image drifting. I closed the cover and unplugged the power supply to take with me.

Matching nightstands flanked the queen-sized bed. The one with a bottle of Tylenol P.M. must be Guy's, which meant . . .

I went over and picked up the framed photo on the other nightstand. It showed Kutara sitting at a small table in a restaurant. Guy stood grinning behind her, his chin resting on her shoulder and his arms around her. Kutara's expression was a little prim, but her head tilted toward his and the tips of her fingers curled around his left arm.

I put back the picture and squeezed my eyes shut for a moment. More to distract myself than anything else, I opened the drawer below. It held several silky, brief nightgowns and a small carved piece of wood. What on earth?

When I turned over the carving, the past rushed up and hit me between the eyes. Woodworking was the most common of elven talents, and Kutara had asked me to try it soon after finding me. Friction had yet to develop between us, and I had shaped this representation of her face, hoping to please her. I remembered her disappointment when I presented it.

This isn't your talent, but I'm sure you'll discover it someday.

I put it back and shut the drawer. Then I reopened

the drawer and put the carving in my bag. There was no sense in cluttering up Guy's house with something that would have no meaning to him.

I returned to the kitchen. The business card for his cleaning service was supposed to be on the refrigerator, but I found it on the floor under the table, along with a bunch of coupons and some broken glass.

I went ahead and called them, leaving instructions to come and tidy things up as much as possible, and telling them Guy was in the hospital and would mail a check.

Guy's cell phone was next on the list, and he'd said it was probably in the garage. I went in through the side door, from the house, and froze.

The scattered papers were gone. Someone had been in here, and I didn't think it was Kutara. I quickly searched the floor and shelves, wondering if Dagovar would appear at any moment.

Guy's phone was nowhere to be found. Dagovar had probably taken it in case there were useful phone numbers, or maybe just to hinder us.

Kutara's cell phone was still in my bag. I went back inside, found her charger plugged into a bedroom wall outlet, and put it in my bag. As I left, I grabbed the photo of Kutara and Guy from the nightstand and took that, too.

Guy was clearly better than the last time I had seen him, although the bruises that darkened his face made him look worse.

He carefully positioned the photo on the cabinet next to his bed and stared at it for a moment before turning to me. "Do you know anything more about Kutara?"

"I'm still waiting for information." Now was as good a time as any to see if glamour still worked on Guy. I gave him the thought that there were no such things as elves. Kutara was just a woman—missing after someone had broken into Guy's house and attacked them both.

Guy pushed his replacement glasses up from where they had slid down his nose. "So, do elves have a special way to look for people? What are you doing to find her?"

"You still remember elves?" I asked, hope blossoming inside me.

"I sure as hell remember that big sonofabitch who attacked me. Now what are you going to do about Kutara?"

"We're a little disorganized at the moment, but we will try to find her." Because the only reason I could think of for glamour not to work on Guy was that somewhere, Kutara was alive.

Chapter Seventeen

The Boulder Outlook Hotel, where Erin was staying, looked more like a trendy mall than a hotel. A rack of rental bikes lined the front, and twenty-somethings sat at the outside café tables, chatting and working on laptops. No one gave me a second glance as I walked by, barefoot, in Mark's swim trunks and shirt.

Lenny accosted me as soon as I stepped through the doors. "What took you so long?"

"Getting rides, what do you think?"

"Oh. Right. Sorry."

"Let's not talk about it." I followed him through an immense common area with a restaurant, bar, and swimming pool with faux rocks and fountains. "Why is there no pool smell?"

"I don't know. It's some kind of environmental thing. They also have a zero-waste policy, whatever that is. Erin seemed to think I should be impressed."

"What'd she do—take a minute to call around before she ran from Dagovar?"

"No. She picked this because it's right on the

highway, in case she needed a quick getaway." He led me up some stairs and down a hallway and knocked on a door.

Erin opened the door. Normally a hip, stylish woman, her hair was a mess and she wore mismatched flip-flops. "I was starting to get worried."

Galan wandered up behind her, stared at us with no sign of recognition, and wandered off, bumping into the corner of the large bed as he did so.

"Oh, that's not depressing," I muttered to myself as I followed them inside. A joke felt like the only thing that would keep me from bursting into tears.

Lenny walked to a small table and sat down in one of the two chairs. "Erin, do you know of any way to break the bond between an elf and a human? I'm not talking about *penansel*—just a regular bond."

Apparently Lenny was taking his inherited leadership role seriously, and we weren't bothering with small talk.

"Why?" Erin looked from Lenny to me. "Don't tell me one of you has bonded to someone. Please."

I dodged Galan and sat on the bed. "I took a hit from Dagovar and couldn't make it home. I needed energy to heal."

"Oh, God." Erin sank into the other chair and put her face in her hands.

I looked at Galan, automatically expecting him to comfort her, but of course he didn't. I turned away from his blank face.

Erin composed herself. "When Galan and I first bonded, we asked everyone if there was a way to break it. The only person with a suggestion was Fellseth. This was before our *penansel* ritual, and he told me that if I wanted to break our bond more than anything else, it would dissolve. I tried, at one point, but couldn't make it work."

That sounded too easy. I closed my eyes and concentrated. "Would I feel something? I guess you wouldn't know." I squeezed my eyes tighter.

"I think you would," Erin said.

I let out my breath. "I'm going to go outside and see if I can merge."

A few minutes later I was back. "It didn't work."

Erin nodded sadly. "Playing with me like that was the sort of thing Fellseth would do. Who are you bonded to?"

A small armchair sat in the corner of the room. I dragged it over and joined them at the table. "His name is Mark. We've had one date, so it's not like he's a stranger."

Erin sniffed. "That is so sad."

"Don't. I'm barely keeping it together as it is." I took a breath and pasted a smile on my face. "On the other hand, I have some good news. It looks like Kutara is still alive." In answer to their excited questions, I explained about Guy and my failure to glamour him.

Erin's excitement faded. "There could be another reason you couldn't glamour Guy. He could be part elf. All it takes is a relative with pointy ears and he'd be immune."

I looked at Lenny. "Kutara would have mentioned that, wouldn't she?"

He thought for a moment. "I don't know. I always got the impression that Guy pretty much worshipped Kutara and never pressed her for any kind of information. Glamour may never have come into it."

I groaned. "He said as much to me, come to think of it."

Lenny folded his hands on the table. "I'm not sure finding Kutara is a priority, and her last message to us reinforces that. We've already found out that the forgetting disease is caused by bonding to humans, and it may not have a cure. Which leaves Dagovar as our most immediate problem—"

"And there's definitely a cure for him," I finished.

In answer to Erin's questioning look, Lenny said, "Adlia is determined to kill him. Not on her own, of course."

"Why not on my own?" I demanded. "What have I got to lose?"

"It's not that, Adlia," he said. "It's just that you've never fought before. You might need help."

"I suppose. Wait a minute . . . Dagovar probably thinks he's killed me, right? Lenny, what if you arrange a meeting, and I hide somewhere and blast him?"

He looked thoughtful. "That's a possibility."

Someone knocked on the door, and Lenny and I shot to our feet.

"That's probably my friend Lily." Erin got up and looked through the peephole. "Yup. And don't bother trying to glamour her. She's the reason I know about elf ancestry." She opened the door.

Lily was a pretty, slightly plump woman in her

forties, with a wealth of curly black hair. Printed cherries decorated her white sundress. In addition to a purse over her shoulder, she carried a paper grocery bag and a plastic cage of some sort. She set down the cage, saying, "Oof," as she did so.

"Kitty Girl!" Erin cooed, and opened the cage.

A black-and-white cat emerged cautiously.

Erin picked her up and looked at Lenny. "Is she angry?" she whispered.

Lenny looked amused. "She doesn't understand English, except for the occasional word. And why would she be angry?"

"Because when I heard Dagovar was coming, I took Galan but not her. I didn't know if she was inside or out, and there wasn't time to look."

"Don't worry about it," Lenny said. "Animals figure on taking care of themselves once they're adults." He stared intently at Kitty Girl, and I felt the buzz of their mental conversation. "She says Dagovar came to your house."

Lily sat down in one of the chairs. "He wasn't there today, was he?"

Lenny communicated with Kitty Girl a bit longer. "No. He came right after Erin left, and didn't stay long. Kitty Girl was outside, so he didn't see her."

Lily nodded. "I could have used some of that elf know-how when I was trying to get her into the carrier, but half a bag of treats finally did the trick."

I wondered if Erin had told her friend about the threats Dagovar had made toward humans we knew. "Weren't you afraid to go there?" I asked Lily.

"A little, but he can't glamour me, and it helps

that I bought a Taser." She lifted the paper bag she had brought onto the table and took out a box. "This one's yours, Erin."

"You bought me a Taser?" Erin opened the box and took out a pink-and-gray device wrapped in a plastic bag.

"What exactly *is* a Taser?" Lenny asked.

"It delivers a big ol' shock to your assailant," Lily said. "It incapacitates most people, and I figure it might do even more to an elf. You guys seem to run on electricity." She rummaged in the bag and took out a smaller box. "Here's an extra cartridge."

Erin looked up from examining the device. "How many shots do you get per cartridge?"

"One, but it shoots out on wires, up to fifteen feet. Then you have to reload." When Erin looked disappointed, Lily said, "I know, but it's better than nothing and it does less damage than a knife or a gun if someone takes it away from you."

Erin hugged her. "I really appreciate it, and you're right, it's definitely better than nothing."

Lily pushed the bag toward her. "I also brought toiletries, clothes, the mates to your shoes, and some jewelry supplies in case you get bored."

"You didn't stay at my house long enough to pick all of that up, did you?" Erin asked.

"No. The jewelry stuff is from the store, and I bought the toiletries. And I wore a disguise to your place—carried a bucket and cleaning supplies."

Erin pointed to her feet. "Did you wear those shoes?"

Lily looked down at her red patent-leather heeled sandals. "Um, maybe."

"Most elves probably wouldn't think of that," I comforted her. "Of course, most elves wouldn't know what a cleaning woman was, either." I held out my hand. "Hi. I'm Adlia."

She shook it. "Lily Savchuk. Are you Kutara's replacement?"

I laughed. "Hardly."

Lenny stepped forward. "Kutara designated me as her successor."

Lily nodded. "Hi, Lenny. I'd say congratulations, but it doesn't seem in order. And now I have to get back to the store. Could you tell the cat she's going to be my guest for a while?"

Lenny looked at Kitty Girl.

After a moment, she walked back into the box.

Lily closed the front, then kissed Erin's cheek. "I promise to take good care of her. Do you need anything else right now?"

"No." Erin caught her hand and held it for a moment. "I can't thank you enough, but you probably know that."

When she was gone, Erin began taking things from the bag Lily had brought. "Okay. What's the plan for getting rid of Dagovar?"

Lenny got up and began to pace. "The question is whether contacting him will make him suspect it's a trap. But if we wait for him, there's no telling what he might do in the meantime, and it would be so much better if we could pick the time and place." He glanced at me. "We'll both want to be as strong as possible."

"Speaking of which," Erin said, putting down a pair of small pliers she had just taken out of the bag. "When are you going to be with Mark again, Adlia?"

I avoided her gaze. It was hard to think of Mark. "I don't know."

"But he *knows,* doesn't he?" she pressed.

"Knows what?"

"Adlia! You told him you're an elf, right?"

I looked at Lenny for support. "Last time I checked, we were supposed to be keeping our existence a secret. Has that changed?"

Lenny looked uncertain.

Erin put her hands on her hips. "At the very least, you have to tell him that he's in danger from Dagovar."

"Dagovar doesn't know about Mark," I protested.

"That you *know* of."

"If it's a matter of keeping Mark safe, I just won't see him again. I'll stay here and protect you and Galan while we decide what to do, and you can meditate for me." The thought was painful, but not as painful as thinking of what Dagovar could do to Mark.

Lenny shook his head. "Erin could keep you alive, but I don't think you'd be in great shape to fight. You should really have sex with Mark right before you try to kill Dagovar."

I made a face at him. "Maybe I'll ask if he can

drive me to the meeting. We can do it in the car while you and Dagovar chat."

"I know!" Erin said. "Why don't you tell Mark something that makes it clear you're in a dangerous situation, but gives him the choice of whether he wants to help you or not?"

"Keeping in mind that I can't glamour him anymore, what would that be?" I asked. "What could possibly explain my bizarre behavior, pointed ears, and the fact that someone crazy is after me?"

"Tell him you used to be in a cult."

I called Mark to make sure he was at home before going to his house. Erin gave me one of her outfits, so I would look more believable when I told my story.

Mark opened the front door. "Hey!" He bent and gave me a quick kiss, and I immediately felt better. "I'm working on the Tenenbaum's wedding photos, but I can talk while I do it. Come in and keep me company."

Would he still want my company after I told him it could get him killed?

"Did you take care of everything you needed to?" he asked. We went by the kitchen, where I had lied to him repeatedly, past his bedroom, where I had gotten him to make love to me under false pretences, and into his home office, where I had violated his privacy. "Aunt Kootie found someone to take your place in the drug-infested jungles of Columbia, or whatever?"

"Something like that."

Once in his office, he sat down at his laptop, then looked around the room. "There doesn't seem to be a chair for you, does there?" He pulled me into his lap and wrapped his arms around me. "Wonder if I can reach the mouse around you?"

"You'd come to resent the way I got between you and your work." I kissed his nose and got up.

"Maybe so. I'll be right back."

I looked at the thumbnail photos on the screen while he went to get me a chair. Human weddings were such public affairs—apparently it wasn't just the bride and groom who cared that they were married, but also their family, friends, neighbors, and coworkers. What would it be like to have more than a handful of people interested in your life?

Mark came back with one of the kitchen chairs and set it next to his rolling one. "I have about half an hour more before I'm done with this."

I wanted his full attention when I told my latest whopper, so I mostly listened while he chatted about posing kids in the wedding party, and how one bride had specified that he never photograph the left side of her face because she swore it was crooked.

Finally he finished. "I had a huge breakfast, but now I'm hungry again," he said, pushing his chair back. "I wonder if I have a tapeworm?"

"I read that food isn't as filling anymore. Something about the lack of nutrients."

He smiled. "You made that up."

Depending on how good he was at spotting my lies, I could be in trouble.

"C'mon." He patted my thigh. "Food."

We went to the kitchen, and I watched as he opened the fridge and took out dark bread, plastic-wrapped meats and cheeses, mustard, mayonnaise, and pickles.

When he had put the finishing touches on his sandwich, I said, "Mark, there are some things I want you to know about me."

He looked up and gave me a quick smile. "Now that's something I never thought I'd hear you say." He cut the thick sandwich in half. "Half of this is yours."

I shook my head. "I had a late breakfast."

"Good, because I think I want all of it." He pulled out a chair and sat.

I watched him take the first bite. "The reason I haven't talked about my past is that I'm ashamed of it. I made some stupid choices, and some of them affect me today. But if you and I are going to see each other, then there are things I can't keep secret."

He didn't look worried, just swallowed his bite and said, "Do you have a kid? Because I've dated women who have children. I like kids."

"I don't have a kid. Remember I told you I was an orphan?"

"That's right."

"Well, before Aunt Kutara straightened me out, I hung out with a group of really bad people—a cult. We called ourselves the Elven Eleven, and we stole money to give to environmental groups. I never did any of the thefts myself, but I would scope out convenience stores, or call when a car or house was unlocked." I paused before going on. Erin had come up with a pretty detailed story.

Mark was listening with grim interest. "Go on," he said, ignoring the sandwich on the plate in front of him.

"Eventually I found out that they were using a lot of the money for drugs. And then they shot someone they were robbing, and he died. With my help, the police caught all but one of them. Aunt Kutara really is with the government, and she helped me change my name. But there was one thing I couldn't change." I put my hands to the sides of my head and slowly pushed back my hair. "We all had our ears surgically altered, to show our dedication to the cause."

"Oh, my God." Mark got up and came over to look closer. "Where did you have something like this done?"

"Our oldest member was a plastic surgeon who had lost his license. The whole thing was his suggestion. He was pretty crazy."

"I guess." He traced the tip of my ear with a finger, making me shiver. Then he looked at me suspiciously. "I never heard about any of this."

"It happened in Canada." Our handy neighbors to the north. They so seldom made a blip on our news.

Mark squatted next to me and took my hand.

"You said they caught all but one. I assume you're not talking about yourself."

"No. Dagovar was the most violent and the smartest. The reason I was going to leave the country for a while is because he's still looking for me, and they think he's closing in."

"Adlia!" Mark stood and pulled me to my feet so he could wrap his arms around me.

I pressed my face against his chest, feeling his heat. Now came the hard part. "It would be safer for you if we didn't see each other until the police catch him." A rational man, a cautious man, *a man who didn't love me,* would agree. This was when I found out what kind of man Mark Speranzi was.

"Angel. Sweetheart," he murmured, nuzzling the top of my head. "It would be safer for both of us if you moved in with me. I don't know what I'd do if you got hurt."

I reached up and brought his mouth to mine in a kiss that said everything I couldn't—that he was the kindest, bravest person I had ever met, elf or human, and I would give him my body and mind for as long as possible. I only wished it could be longer.

He kissed me, one hand on the small of my back, the other behind my head, and then he bent and lifted me in his arms. "I've wanted to do that since the day I met you," he said, as he maneuvered me through the doorway. "You're so small and perfect, it was all I could do not to run off with you."

"You should have," I murmured, thinking of how many more times I could have made love to him, without feeling how short our time together would be.

In the bedroom, he put me on the bed and quickly shed his clothes, but I was faster.

"Lie down," I said.

He obliged, and I climbed on top of him, sighing with pleasure as our skin made contact. His height meant I had to straddle his waist to kiss him.

He cradled my face, touching the corner of my mouth with one thumb. "How could anyone want to harm you? When you came into my class, all blue eyes and gold hair and with that prickly attitude, I thought, *I wish I could have protected this girl from whatever's hurt her.*"

"I've never known anyone who wanted to take care of me," I whispered.

His brown eyes were so serious, so beautiful. "If there's anything I can do to help catch this guy, let me know, and I'll do it."

I scooted down, then guided him inside me. I gasped as energy flowed from our joined flesh, the pulse of his life filling me. "Just having you with me does more than you know."

Mark fell asleep after we made love. When he had turned over and let go of me, I slid out of bed and called Lenny.

"Did he believe you?" he asked.

"Yeah, but I don't feel good, dragging him into this."

"The stronger you are, the more chance we

have of getting rid of Dagovar, and the safer Mark will be."

"That doesn't make sense, because Dagovar wouldn't know about Mark if I stayed away from him."

"For all you know, Dagovar *already* knows about Mark and is planning something horrible," he said.

"You're really filling Kutara's shoes, you know that?"

"I'm trying. Listen, I'm going to go home and think about what we should do. I'll call you later."

"Okay." After hanging up, I looked in my bag for the charger I had taken from Guy's house. My model was the same as Kutara's. Was Kutara still alive—maybe even in Dagovar's control? Did she wonder why we didn't come for her, or was she past wondering?

I went back into the bedroom and plugged in my phone. Mark woke as I climbed back into bed.

"Come here," he murmured sleepily.

I snuggled under the arm he lifted and rubbed my cheek against his chest hair. "Want to go again?"

"Yes, but I should get some work done. Do you have a car? Do you need help bringing your stuff over?"

"I don't have a car, and it's better if I don't go back to my place. I'll pick up a few things at some point."

"We can do that later this evening, after dinner."

How would I fake eating, now that I couldn't glamour him? And while he would probably pay for anything I needed, wouldn't it look less odd if I had money of my own?

It occurred to me that my last big lie was just the beginning of many, many more. Could we kill Dagovar before I started to forget what lies I had told?

Chapter Eighteen

I was helping Mark by filing his business correspondence when his cell phone rang. He picked it up from his desk, glanced at the display, and flipped it open. "Faith! It's good to hear from you."

He turned slightly away from me, but I still heard the high, panicked voice coming from the tiny speaker.

"No, I'm not going to say *I told you so*. Just tell me what I can do to help. Do you want me to come over?" A pause. "Okay, I'll be right there."

"Is something wrong?" I asked, when he had hung up.

He stuck the phone in his pocket. "You remember Faith, my cousin, who I couldn't seem to get hold of?"

The one whose picture he carried. "Uh-huh."

"Well, I would much rather have been wrong, but her new boyfriend has turned out to be an asshole. She wants me to come over while she tells him to move out."

"Isn't this a job for the police?" Even I knew the dangers of getting involved in domestic disputes.

"It's not that serious. I don't know why she picks these jealous, insecure guys, but this isn't the first time I've done this for her."

"I'll go with you." When I got through glamouring the guy, he wouldn't remember Faith's name or address, and Mark wouldn't have to face off with some idiot.

"Shouldn't you stay here? What if Dagovar sees you riding around? Although I suppose we need to go out so you can pick up some clothes. What are the odds of meeting him at Target?"

"Very low."

He brightened. "I know—Faith can loan you some things. You're about the same size."

That would also solve the problem of me not having money. "That sounds great. I'll hide in the back of the car, so no one knows I'm there."

Faith's apartment building wasn't much to look at. Dark-brown siding covered it, and exterior stairs and landings crisscrossed the front. But overhanging cottonwood trees and a prettified irrigation ditch gave it a secluded charm.

Faith sat on the wooden steps leading up to her apartment, smoking a cigarette. This was not the glamorous creature in Mark's photograph, or even the somewhat tired woman I had seen at the Canyon Gallery.

After a moment, I realized she wasn't wearing

any makeup. Presumably to make herself even more unattractive, she wore mud-brown sweatpants and a baggy green T-shirt. Her hair hung in a lank, messy ponytail.

Mark stopped on the landing below her. "You're smoking again?"

"Shut up. It's the stress." She ground out the cigarette on the wooden tread and let it fall to the gravel landscaping below.

"Where's Daniel?"

"He's using my car to put some stuff in storage, and that's the last thing I'm doing for him. I've put the rest of his shit in boxes." She grabbed the banister and pulled herself to her feet, then gave me a hostile look. "Who are you?"

"This is Adlia," Mark said. "We're seeing each other."

"Does she have to see me as well?"

"Be nice," Mark said.

I glamoured her calm.

"Come on." She turned and started up the stairs. "We might as well start putting his stuff outside."

We followed her to an apartment on the third floor. Inside, dirty dishes filled the sink and cluttered the countertop and kitchen table. Clothes, junk mail, and empty grocery bags littered the floor.

Mark looked around. "Are you trying to drive him away with filth?"

"It's the passive-aggressive way." Faith grinned suddenly, and I saw a flash of what she must usually be like.

She waved a hand toward six liquor boxes that sat near the door, haphazardly loaded with papers, computer cables, and men's clothes. "This all goes downstairs. The main reason I asked you to come is that I want to make sure he gives me my key back." She glanced at me. "It's probably good that you're here. The more people, the less likely he is to make a fuss."

"He could have made a copy of your key," Mark pointed out. "You should stay at my house while you get the locks changed."

"If you think so." She closed her eyes for a moment, sighing. "I'll put some stuff in a suitcase."

Mark bent and picked up a box. "I'll take these downstairs. And can you do *me* a favor and loan Adlia some clothes?" He rested the box on his hip while he opened the door. "I'll let her tell you as much as she wants to."

Faith looked at me curiously. "Did you lose everything in a fire, or what?"

I might not be able to glamour Mark, but I could still glamour other humans, and for a moment I was tempted. But probably Faith should be made aware of Dagovar, too. "I have my own creepy guy problem, so I can't go back to my place. If you ever meet a big blond guy named Dagovar, stay away from him."

She sighed. "Sounds like just my type. I'm a sucker for foreigners. Come on."

I followed her into the bedroom. This more personal space was notably tidier—apparently mess didn't come naturally to her. A lavender bedspread in some silky fabric covered the bed, and a large print of a tulip hung over a white wicker desk.

Faith opened her closet door and waved at the contents. "Pick anything you want. Do you need underwear, too?"

"That's okay."

She knelt and pulled a red suitcase from under the bed. "While you do that, I'll get my toiletries together. I have a bunch of nice samples you can have."

"Thanks." Generosity was apparently a family trait.

Faith's closet was an almost solid mass of clothes. I pushed aside hangers until I found a pair of jeans. They were lower in the waist than the ones I used to conjure, with a delicate spray of pink flowers embroidered above the back pockets. Would Mark think they were pretty?

By the time Faith came out from the bathroom, I had a small stack of things on the bed.

"Are you sure that's all you want?" she asked.

"Yeah." Clothes probably wouldn't be an issue for more than a couple of days. After that, I wouldn't be aware of what I wore, and I hoped Dagovar would be dead. "Do you need any help?"

"No. Tell Mark I'll try to be fast. I just don't want to leave anything valuable, in case he did make a copy of the key."

I went back into the small living room.

Footsteps sounded on the staircase, and then Mark came in, looking sweaty. "Everything's out there. I was going to say we should just leave it for him to find, but there are some valuables. I know he's a jerk, but I don't want to be blamed for someone taking his things." He looked toward the bedroom. "Is she almost ready?"

"Not quite. She doesn't want to leave anything he might steal."

He sighed. "We're going to be here forever. Faith!"

Another fifteen minutes, and he had helped and chivied her into being ready. In addition to her rolling suitcase, she'd also packed a large box. Mark carried that downstairs, while Faith bumped along behind him with the case.

When he reached the curb, he put down the box with a thump and flexed his hands. "What the heck did you put in there?"

"Computer stuff. There are some books, too. And shoes."

He sighed. "I had to park all the way around back. Stay here and I'll bring the car around."

Faith shook her head vehemently. "What if he comes back while you're gone? He'll start yelling."

"It's only going to take a minute." He started walking.

She followed, suitcase bouncing over the rough asphalt.

He turned. "Faith . . ."

"I'll stay here so no one messes with the stuff," I offered. "He doesn't know I have anything to do with Faith." Plus, I could take care of the jerkiest of human males.

Mark looked around. "I guess you're not visible

from the street. There's no reason Dagovar would come here, right?"

"Nope." I waved a hand at him. "Go on. I'll be fine."

They walked past the staircase and out of my sight, although I could still hear the bumping of Faith's suitcase wheels.

A thin layer of clouds had covered the sun for most of the day, but now the sky cleared, and heat bathed the two rows of cars in front of me. I sat on the curb and listened to bugs sing in the trees overhead.

A hot wind blew from the west, ruffling the papers in one of the liquor boxes and signaling even warmer weather to come. A sheet of paper blew out of one of the boxes. I got to my feet and snagged what appeared to be a financial spreadsheet. A name toward the top leapt out at me—*Village Developments.*

"No way," I whispered. Three steps took me to the box. I pulled a paper out at random and stared at a note written in Kutara's tiny, precise handwriting.

> *Adlia, make sure this money is transferred to a CD or bond—something with a better rate of interest.*

I squatted and rummaged through the box, finding account names I knew, bank books belonging to Fellseth . . . A sheet of neon pink caught my eye, and I pulled it free.

Fia's face smiled up at me.

*Have you seen this woman? Missing: Fia Avis,
aged 25, last seen in the Martin Acres neighborhood.
No birthmarks or tattoos, but her ears have been
altered to have points. PLEASE contact Josh Temple
or the Boulder County Sheriff's Office.*

Three phone numbers and an e-mail address followed this plea.

I stuffed the flyer in my messenger bag and stood. Had Dagovar known of the connection between my lover and his, or had he simply picked Faith because she worked at Canyon Gallery? Whichever it was, I had to get both Mark and Faith out of here.

I jogged toward the corner of the building where they had gone. If I glamoured Faith to say that her ex-boyfriend had mentioned a gun, would Mark agree to leave immediately? If he argued, would it be quicker to grab her box and go?

The sound of a car came from behind me. I spun in time to see Dagovar's face behind the wheel as he gunned the engine and drove straight for me.

He wasn't close enough, and I dodged right, hearing the engine roar and brakes squeal as I ducked between the two rows of parked cars.

A car door opened as I ran quietly back the way I'd come, keeping low. Any minute, Mark would drive around the corner and wonder where I was.

Dagovar didn't know I was bonded to a human and couldn't merge. He would expect me to head for the grassy area to my left, where *Ma'Nah* beckoned. Instead, I went to the far right of the cars and stood behind the wide tire of a pickup truck. A quick glance showed me that Faith's car, still running where Dagovar had left it, wouldn't block Mark's way.

Several moments of tense silence followed, and then Dagovar's head appeared between the roofs of two cars.

I fired for the first time in my life. As green fire blazed from my fingertips, I realized I was too far away for a good shot. He ducked in time, and a moment later I heard him coming toward me.

I didn't try to run, but got between two cars and lay quietly on the ground. From somewhere behind me I heard the sound of a car approaching—Mark. I lifted my arm and sighted along it, waiting.

And then Dagovar's feet came into view. I aimed at the space under the next car. *Not yet . . . Wait . . . Now.*

Dagovar gave a hoarse yell and his feet disappeared, upward.

I heard a scrabble and a *thunk* as he hauled himself on top of a car hood. Now was the time to finish him off. I got to my feet, still keeping low.

"Adlia?" Mark called. "Where are you?"

"Get down!" I screamed, and saw silver fire arc over my head. Had he been hit? I ran toward where I had heard Mark, keeping my head low.

He crouched beside his car. The trunk stood open. "Is it Dagovar? What the hell was that?"

We both turned at the sound of the passenger door opening. Faith came around the back, wearing the dazed expression of someone under a glamour.

"Faith! What are you doing?" Mark shouted, lunging for her leg and missing. "Get in the car!"

There was too much going on, and I couldn't see

Dagovar. "You drive, I'll get her in the car. And for God's sake, stay down."

It was hard to overcome Dagovar's glamour on Faith. I was closer, but he was *good*. I pulled her around the car by her arm.

Mark slouched in the front seat. A blast hit the door frame above him and he cursed.

I got in the back, dragging Faith behind me. "Not yet," I told Mark. As soon as he raised his head, he would be vulnerable. With my window finally down, I rested my left arm on the door and put Faith in a headlock with my right. "Okay, go!"

I saw Dagovar as Mark accelerated. He lay on the back of a car, even closer than I had thought. I fired shot after shot in his direction as Mark roared out of the parking lot, our open trunk bobbing up and down.

Mark didn't slow down until he reached Canyon Boulevard, with its four lanes of traffic. "Is he behind us?"

I thought of Dagovar's awkward position on the back of the car, and my shot hitting his feet. "No. He's not going to be driving for a little while." That wouldn't keep him from traveling through *Ma'Nah,* but if his land really were in Texas, he'd need to raise energy with a human to recover from his injury—as he no doubt had done with Faith.

Mark turned to look back at Faith, who sat blankly, still under my glamour. "Is she okay?"

"She'll be fine."

"Then I have just one more question. What in the

fucking hell *was* that? Were you shooting stuff out of your *hands?*"

Should I just tell him? Would I have to tell Faith?

"Adlia? Talk to me."

I opened my bag and took out the flyer with Fia's face on it. "Have you seen this woman? I have to talk to someone before I can answer that question."

It was time to find out if Fia had been bound to the man who made this flyer.

Josh Temple lived in an older home in North Boulder. An empty hummingbird feeder hung from an elm tree in the front yard, and the birdbath standing on the lawn below needed to be cleaned.

"Who is this person?" Mark asked, then turned to study Faith anxiously as she stood beside us on the doorstep. "And why isn't Faith saying anything?"

I rang the doorbell.

"Faith will be fine. She's under a light hypnosis."

He started to say something else, but put a hand to his midsection instead. "Ow!"

"What's wrong?" I grabbed his arm. "Are you hurt?"

"Cramp." He rubbed his stomach. "Can you get an instant ulcer? It must be the stress of not knowing what the hell is going on."

"You'll know soon enough, and you probably just need to eat." I had used so much energy fighting Dagovar, it was a miracle Mark was upright.

Footsteps sounded behind the door, and it swung open.

The man who stood there was in his early twenties.

He wore loose jeans, but his tight T-shirt revealed that he got some kind of regular exercise. With his fine-boned features and blond hair pulled back in a ponytail, he could almost pass for an elf, had it not been for the stubble on his face.

"Josh Temple? I'm Adlia. I'm here about Fia."

"Did you find her?" Hope showed in his eyes, only to fade a moment later. "Is she dead?"

That was one of the things I hoped to find out. "Can we come in?"

"Yeah. Sorry."

Josh led the way into a spacious living room that probably mirrored his state of mind. The large windows were covered with curtains. A plasma-screen TV showed a paused video game. Josh gestured for me to sit on a worn leather couch and picked up a remote that sat on the floor, next to a pile of dirty dishes. "Sorry—the place is kind of a mess." He switched off the set.

"That's okay," I said.

He sat and turned toward me. "Are you with the police department?"

Mark looked at me, obviously eager to hear the answer. Instead I glamoured Josh. He went under with no problem. I looked at his blank face and sighed. If he had been bonded to Fia, they weren't bonded anymore.

Mark made a noise of impatience, and I gave him a pleading glance. Glamoured or not, I couldn't just ask, Were you bonded to an elf? Instead, I confirmed his idea that I was from the police and released him. "How long were you and Fia together?"

"About a year." Josh fiddled with a braided leather bracelet on his left wrist.

"Were you close? Had anything changed between you? Anything at all, no matter how personal, would be helpful."

His face crumpled. "We had a fight."

That wasn't exactly what I was looking for. "What started it?"

"We were showering, and I noticed her ears were different."

Here it came. "Different how?"

"They were pointed." He shook his head, confusion tightening his features. "I couldn't understand why I hadn't noticed them before. They weren't fake, and I think I would have noticed if she'd had surgery. Finally she started saying she was an elf." He looked up, his expression inviting me to share his disbelief.

I shook my head, speechless.

"She said if I loved her, I would believe her." His eyes welled with tears. "God knows I loved her, but how could I believe something like that? I asked her to see a psychiatrist or even a regular doctor, to see if she had some condition that made her ears change shape and messed with her mind. In addition to the elf stuff, she had started to forget things." He let his head rest against the back of the couch. "I was going to try to have her committed, and then she disappeared."

Poor Fia. No wonder she had run away. I was afraid to look at Mark.

Josh stood. "I want to show you something."

We followed him upstairs, past a messy bedroom, also with drawn curtains, and into the last room down the hall. Large windows and a skylight brought in a flood of light.

Tacked-up drawings, each almost a yard square, covered most of the wall space. Every drawing was of birds. I studied the dark, evocative lines—swooping, fluttering, hovering—and thought of Fia sitting by the creek, watching ducks paddle. "What did she use to draw these?"

"Charcoal."

As a child, had Fia picked up the charred twigs from forest fires and lightning strikes? "Are you an artist, too?"

"No. I own a bike shop." Josh leaned against the wall, then slid down it and sat on the floor, as if standing were too tiring.

It would be kindest to let Josh know Fia was gone. "I have to tell you, it doesn't look good. I'm sorry." I turned and walked out of the room, wanting to get away from this man and his heartbreak.

When we got downstairs, I went in the kitchen and opened cupboards and drawers until I found a package of CLIF Bars, and handed two to Mark. "Eat these if you don't want to pass out."

Once outside the house, Mark took hold of my arm and stopped me. "Adlia. You have to talk to me."

"Let's go in the backyard. There's no reason to stand out here like a bunch of targets."

We walked to the side of the house and opened a rickety gate that led to the backyard. The late-afternoon light slanted across uncut grass, topped with seed heads. A couple of lawn chairs clustered around a rusty cast-iron table.

I directed Faith to sit down almost without thinking about it, then saw Mark look at me narrowly. He sat down in one of the other chairs. "What's going on?"

"What do you think is going on?" I countered wearily. Could I come up with a believable excuse for the last hour, or would he leave me now?

"I hardly know." He rested his arms on his knees and rubbed his hands together in a nervous gesture. "If I had to guess, based on the available evidence and giving up any preconceptions, I'd say you were an elf."

I stared at him dumbly for a moment. "When Fia told Josh she was an elf, he thought she was crazy. He wanted to put her away."

"Josh hasn't seen what I've seen." He tore open the wrapper of a CLIF Bar, took a bite, and swallowed, grimacing in discomfort.

"What do you think you've seen?" I asked cautiously.

"I think I've seen you put Faith into a trance instantly, and make her do things through some kind of mental telepathy." He leaned over and snapped his fingers in front of Faith's face, with no result. "I think I've seen you shoot electricity out of your fingertips. Your friend Galan did one of the best magic tricks I've ever seen, and I don't think there were any wires." He stood and came to stand in front of me, then reached out with one hand.

I stiffened, gripping the plastic arms of the chair.

Mark pushed back my hair and bent to look at me more closely, gently exploring the tip of my ear. "I don't think you could get these results with surgery." He squatted, putting his hands on my knees. "And finally, you're a little too spectacular to be real, especially during sex."

I looked into his golden-brown eyes, so serious and kind. "I'm as real as you are," I whispered.

One corner of his mouth lifted. "But you're not human."

The silence stretched between us. Whatever I said now, I couldn't glamour him to forget it. Dagovar would say that Mark would exploit me or turn me over to the government, but Dagovar didn't know Mark.

"No," I said. "I'm not human."

He pulled one of my hands loose, then the other, and cradled them in his. "And you're in trouble."

"You have no idea." I leaned forward into his embrace, and he rolled backward onto the grass with me on top of him, the sweet smell of broken greenery rising around us. My lips were wet with tears as I kissed him, and I blocked out every thought but one—that if this miracle could happen, maybe a few more things would be all right.

Faith's voice came from above us. "Guys, you seriously need to get a room. Hey . . . Where the hell are we?"

Chapter Nineteen

We went straight from Josh Temple's house to the Outlook Hotel, where Erin was staying. On the way there, I did two things—called Lenny and told him to meet us there, and explained Dagovar's betrayal of Elf Ops to Mark. I was okay with having Faith know the truth as well, but Mark wasn't, saying that if Faith knew Dagovar was an elf, she was likely to run straight into his arms. So I glamoured her during that part.

When we got to Erin's room, Lenny opened the door. As usual, he looked like one of Michelangelo's models—dressed as a skateboarder. His black muscle shirt barely met the waist of his low-slung jeans, and he wore a knit cap to cover his ears, his black hair spilling beneath it in glossy waves. Faith gave him an appreciative look.

I ushered the others in front of me, saying, "This is Mark and Faith. I have bad news about Fia, but the good news is that Mark wants to help us."

Erin sat at the small table with the jewelry-making

supplies Lily had brought her, Galan in a chair by her side. "Welcome to the club, Mark. It's very small."

"And getting smaller all the time," Lenny said.

Erin held up a hand. "Guys, I have some tremendous, fantastic news. Are you ready?"

I looked at Lenny.

He shrugged. "Don't ask me. I just got here."

"Before Erin tells us anything, I think Faith needs a *nap*," I said meaningfully.

"I'm not sleepy," Faith said, then went over to the bed and conked out.

"I know who Mark is," Lenny said, "but who exactly is Faith?"

"Mark's cousin. And up until a few hours ago, she was Dagovar's girlfriend."

"You're kidding!"

Erin stood up. "Nothing you have to say is more interesting than my fantastic news!"

"All right," Lenny said. "What is your fantastic news, Erin?"

"I'll *show* you. Watch this." She had been holding a pair of jewelry pliers, but now she put them down and pushed her chair back from the table.

Galan put a hand on her arm, looking anxious. "Don't stop."

"He's talking again!" Did this mean the forgetting disease was temporary?

Erin picked up the pliers again. "Earlier he actually said, *Don't stop, makes me feel better.*"

I stared at the small pile of completed jewelry in front of her. "*Earrings* make Galan feel better?" I turned to Mark. "Did that make sense to you?"

He shook his head. "Not even a little."

"I think I understand," Lenny said. "Metalworking is Galan's talent. Erin, are you saying that when you practice Galan's skill, it somehow helps him?"

She grinned hugely. "*Bingo*. This explains why it took him so long to get sick! I used to make jewelry all the time, but then I got busy with store management. Galan's jewelry is incredible, so eventually I stopped altogether. And shortly afterward, he got sick."

My brief moment of hope made this disappointment even worse. "You're telling me it was *coincidence* that he started losing his memory shortly after Fia showed up?"

Erin nodded. "So Mark just needs to learn your talent and you'll get better!" She laughed delightedly.

Lenny cleared his throat and looked at me. "Um . . ."

"I don't have a talent," I said.

Erin's smile disappeared as if switched off. "What? I thought all elves had one."

"I'm the only one I know of that doesn't. It's kind of a birth defect."

"So then, what—" Erin broke off and looked to Lenny as though for help.

"What am I going to do?" I finished for her. "My plan is still to kill Dagovar. That hasn't changed."

Mark lifted a hand. "Could someone explain this to me? I know Galan's been unwell, but Adlia, are you saying you have the same thing?"

I nodded slowly. "Bonding to humans causes it.

I was going to stay away from you—that's why I said I was leaving the country—but then Dagovar injured me and you were the only person I could reach. You don't remember, but you saved my life that night."

"But you have plenty of talent! You take great photographs, and—"

Lenny cut him off. "She doesn't have an elven talent. It's different."

I was glad he'd spoken for me, because my throat was tight with the effort of not crying. Then Mark's hand took mine and I gave up, turning into his chest and sobbing while he rocked me back and forth.

"Why is she crying?" Galan asked.

"Shhh . . . honey," Erin murmured soothingly. "Adlia's had some bad news."

Eventually I got hold of myself.

"All right." I came back from the bathroom, where I had splashed cold water on my face. "Let's make a plan. I've got to do something." I sat on the bed and made Faith roll to one side to give me more room.

Lenny sat on the floor. "You can have the armchair, Mark. What's the news on Fia, and what is this about Faith being Dagovar's girlfriend?"

Mark and I explained.

"I'm sorry to hear about Fia," Lenny said. "As for Dagovar, you're saying you actually hit him?"

"Gave him the hot foot." The memory made me briefly happy.

"That's great. Tracking I'm good at, but the first time I tried shooting something, my father almost lost an ear."

I gave him a humorless grin. "There's nothing like the risk of death to make you get good fast."

He smiled briefly. "The problem is, I'm not sure how we're going to lay a trap for Dagovar now. It wouldn't make sense for us to say, *Okay, you win, come and get the passwords,* when you've just beaten him. You still have the passwords, right?"

My messenger bag lay against the wall by the door, which was maybe not the best place for it. I got it and dumped the contents on the floor, then picked up the folded piece of paper. "Right here." I glanced at the rest of the contents. Something was missing. "Oh, shit."

"What?" Lenny asked sharply.

"My phone! It's not here!"

"What's that green thing?" Erin asked.

"Kutara's phone." I felt around inside my bag. "I was crawling and jumping around when I fought Dagovar. My phone must have fallen out." I looked at Mark, stricken. "If he found it, he knows who you are."

"Out of all the names and numbers on your phone, how would he know my name is anything special?" Mark asked.

I couldn't help rolling my eyes. "I'm not exactly Ms. Social. The only numbers on that phone are people at Elf Ops, Erin, and you. I think he'll be able to work it out."

"I'm afraid you're stuck with us, Mark," Lenny said. "Your house isn't safe now."

"My house . . ." Mark pointed at me. "Adlia, didn't I see your phone plugged into a charger at my house? In the bedroom?"

"Yes! Did I put it back in my bag before we went to Faith's house?" I thought hard but drew a blank. "I can't remember." My voice tightened on the last word. "I can't *remember!*"

"Don't panic, Adlia," Lenny said. "We have good memories, but they're not perfect."

"Why don't you call the phone?" Erin asked. "If Dagovar answers, you'll know where it is."

Lenny cocked his head. "Can't argue with that." He took his phone out of his jeans pocket and dialed. We all watched as he listened for a while and then disconnected. "No answer. It could still be under a car."

The thought that Dagovar might have listened to my phone ring was creepy. "So we don't know. He could have it or not."

"Is it worth going to my house to see if it's there?" Mark asked.

Lenny thought for a moment. "Probably not. We want to lie in wait for *him,* not the other way around. We'll assume your house isn't safe, and Adlia can use Kutara's phone." He held out his hand. "Give it to me and I'll make sure it's charged."

I tossed it to him. "So my fighting Dagovar has actually made things worse."

Mark gave me a look. "Except for the part where you saved my bacon and got Faith away from him. And he's injured."

Lenny shook his head. "By now, he's found someone to have sex with and is back to normal."

"Isn't *he* worried about bonding to a human?" Mark asked.

"It doesn't happen that easily," Erin said. "As far as I can tell, the elf has to either have deep affection for the human or be in danger of dying."

It was getting darker. Lenny got up and turned on some lights, then closed the drapes. "You know," he said thoughtfully, "there is something we might use to lure Dagovar—Faith."

Mark held up both hands. "We're not putting Faith in any danger."

"She wouldn't be." Lenny got up and paced a few steps. "We glamour Faith to call Dagovar." He looked at Mark. "What name does she know him by?"

"Daniel."

"Okay. She calls him." He held a pretend phone to his ear and made his voice higher. *"Daniel, Mark and his weird friends won't let me go home, and they won't tell me what's going on. Will you come get me?"*

Mark nodded. "That's not bad. But where is Faith when he comes here and we fight it out?"

"We wouldn't have him come here and involve even more humans," I said. "It's bad enough you, Erin, and Faith are involved. I don't think I could stand it if Mr. and Mrs. Paloosi of Iowa got in Dagovar's way."

Lenny sat down on the floor and smiled. "I think

they're staying at the Ramada, but you're right. How about this—we'll wait until it's really dark, and then Faith will call and say we're all at the park, and you and I seem to be looking for something around our old office."

"I like it! He might think we're looking for the passwords."

Mark nodded. "That sounds plausible, and Faith can stay here with Erin and Galan."

"And you," I said firmly.

He raised his eyebrows. "I don't think so. Did I ever mention that I studied kung fu for seven years?"

I gave him the eyebrows right back. "And that's going to work against an elf blast *how*?"

Erin got up. "He can take my Taser." She stepped over Lenny's outstretched legs and picked up the box from the dresser. "It shoots little darts up to fifteen feet."

"Sweet!" As Mark reached across Lenny to take it from her, his stomach gave a loud growl. "I really need to eat something."

"Yes." I put an arm around his waist. "And we should also take Faith's earlier advice."

"What advice was that?"

"To get a room."

Several hours later, I lay in bed, Mark's arms wrapped around me, listening to the faint hum of the air-conditioning. Mark nosed my hair aside and kissed the tip of my ear. "That was more than satisfactory."

"Some of my finest work, if you want to know the truth." I tilted my face back so I could look in his eyes. "You bring out the best in me, in all ways."

"Same here." He smiled wistfully, then pulled me close, burying his face in my hair. "There has to be a way to break this bond. Or maybe the fact that you don't have a talent means you won't get sick."

I rubbed a hand over his back, trying to comfort him. "Maybe so." The truth was, I had felt a little foggy for the past hour or so. It was more noticeable because of the energy we had raised during lovemaking, resulting in a strange combination of physical liveliness and mental fatigue.

We heard a knock and Lenny's voice. "We're ready when you are."

"Be right over," I called, and kissed Mark. "Come on. First one to kill Dagovar gets a prize."

We got dressed and went next door to Erin's room. Erin and Galan lounged on the bed, while Lenny and Faith sat at the table, talking in low voices. Lenny looked surprisingly fresh, considering how long he'd been out of *Ma'Nah*. Then I saw Faith run her knuckles over his arm where the muscle bulged below the black strap of his shirt.

I gave him a questioning look and tipped my head toward Faith.

He winked at me before clapping his hands to get everyone's attention. "Okay. You'll be happy to know that I've drilled Faith—"

I smothered a laugh.

"On any questions Dagovar might ask," he went on, giving me a warning look. "She came up with good answers every time and sounded completely natural."

Faith nudged his arm and smiled. "That's only because you're such a good teacher."

"I bet," Mark said, so quietly that only I heard him.

"Where are we going to be in the park?" I asked.

"I thought Faith could tell Dagovar we're down by that cement area below the library flyover, right beside the creek."

"That place where people do tai chi?" Mark asked.

"Exactly. We can stake out spots around it. Once he gets on that concrete, he won't be able to disappear into the earth."

Since it was Friday night, we waited until almost one o'clock, to avoid as many late partiers as possible.

The temperature dropped noticeably as we walked across the library's parking lot to the creek path and from there to the area below the flyover. Occasionally a car drove by on nearby Arapahoe Avenue, but mostly it was quiet, and the creek sounded loud in the relative silence.

Lenny had given instructions for Mark to lie flat on the weedy patch between the concrete area and the creek, since Dagovar was least likely to emerge close to the water. I crouched in the undergrowth to the west, and Lenny stayed partially merged on the less-covered east side, only his head above ground.

When we were all positioned, I phoned Erin. "Okay. Have Faith call him now."

We waited. Insects were no respecter of elves, and more than once I resisted the urge to slap at something. The minutes ticked by. We must have been there for half an hour. Had something gone wrong? Erin had been told to call me if the conversation with Dagovar didn't go well. Kutara's phone, set to vibrate, stayed reassuringly still in my pocket.

Loud voices neared, arguing in slurred tones, but they passed by on the other side of the creek. Still we waited. I began to think about finding Lenny, to ask what we should do.

And then I heard it—the gentle movement of someone coming *through* the water. I didn't dare twist my body and risk the sound of crackling. All I could do was slowly thread my arm through the shrubs around me, until it pointed toward the approaching sounds, where Mark lay in position.

Someone crept up the bank, between my spot and Mark's. The sound of dripping water patted against leaves as the figure came into view.

I flexed my fingers. Would it be better to shoot for his head or his chest?

Mark shot first. There was a loud *pop,* and the man went down.

"Got him!" Mark shouted.

I crashed through the undergrowth and heard Lenny run across the concrete behind me. We converged about five feet from where Dagovar lay.

"Should we shoot him while he's helpless?" Lenny asked.

My arm was up and ready. "That's the best time, as far as I'm concerned."

Dagovar lay on his face in the weeds, a humped shape in the dark. Lenny and I took up positions on either side of him, arms ready.

Mark was trying to turn him over.

"Get back, Mark," Lenny said, looking grim. "We want to do this before he comes to."

"Wait a minute," Mark said. "Do you smell that?"

I sniffed the air. *The tang of creek energy, crushed leaves, and . . . body odor?*

Crashing sounds came from the thicket beyond where I had hidden, and a woman's rough voice shouted, "You leave him alone!"

There were four of them, no problem for Lenny and me to glamour, except that none of them stopped. They continued to charge forward, trailed more slowly by the third, a slender figure.

The woman who had yelled grabbed me around the shoulders, smelling strongly of cigarette smoke. "You leave Big Jim alone!" she howled.

I bent forward, dragging her off her feet and then tipping her to the ground.

Lenny's elf blast, pale blue, hit the ground in front of his attacker, bringing him to a halt.

"Hey, now. You stop that," the man said mildly. His voice was very deep.

Mark had the other man in a headlock while the fourth person wandered in the dark nearby, looking at the ground.

At our feet, the Tasered man gave a groan and rolled over, revealing a bearded face.

"Big Jim!" My attacker let go of my legs and crawled over to the prostrate figure.

"Oh, shit," Mark said, letting go of the man he held. "I'm sorry. We thought he was someone else."

We knelt in a circle around the man. The light was dim, but I could see now that he had a deeply weathered face and shaggy hair. His wet clothes were a mishmash of layers, too warm for most people to wear in the summer, but typical for vagrants.

That's why they'd kept coming at us. Glamouring the homeless was hit-or-miss. A lot of them had mental issues, which made their thoughts impenetrable. It was also possible that their habit of living outdoors returned them to a state of wildness more similar to animals—or elves.

The man's eyelids flickered, then opened. "Fuck, man. I hate that Taser shit."

"I'm really sorry." Mark helped him sit up. "We were waiting for someone to come, someone who's been trying to kill us, and I thought you were him."

"I guess I'm lucky you didn't have a gun." He rubbed one shoulder. "Are you cops?"

"They're not the cops," the man with the deep voice said. He pointed to Lenny. "He shot lightning at me."

"Where's Sissy?" Big Jim asked sharply. "Don't let her wander off."

The woman got up and went over to the last member of their group, who still wandered aimlessly among the plants. "Sissy, come back here." She caught the sleeve of Sissy's overlarge shirt and pulled her over to join us. "Here she is. Sissy shoots lightning, too."

Sissy still stared at the ground. I caught her face in my hands and turned it toward the light that came from across the creek. It couldn't be. It *was*. "Kutara!"

"You know her?" the woman asked. Her short hair was as rough as dry grass, and deep lines creased her face.

"I do." Dirt smudged Kutara's face, and new wrinkles showed that she wasn't getting enough energy, but she was *alive*. She looked at me for a moment, unresponsive, and then stared at the ground again.

Lenny came over and gripped Kutara's arm, as if to make sure she was real. "We thought she was dead."

Big Jim pushed himself to his feet with a series of groans. "She would have been, if it weren't for us." He glanced around warily. "Are you one of them?"

He was missing a front tooth, I saw. "One of who?"

In answer, he raised a hand and pulled Kutara's hair back, showing her ear. The others stared, mesmerized, then turned and looked at us.

Lenny and I nodded.

"Let's see." This challenge was from the shortest man in the group. He had long, gray hair and stood with one foot turned at an awkward angle.

Lenny pulled off his cap, and I pushed back my hair.

The man holding Kutara nodded. "Let's go somewhere we can talk."

I took out my phone and looked at the time. "It's been an *hour*. Do you think Dagovar is going to come?"

Lenny shook his head. "I'll call Erin, but first let's get away from here, just in case."

"Hold on a minute." Big Jim walked toward the far side of the plaza and crawled among the plants of a landscaped area that butted up against the base of the library. When he came back, I saw he held a bottle. "All right, let's go," he said.

He took Kutara's hand and led us all back across the creek and west down the creek path.

Lenny took out his phone and called Erin.

Mark and I listened as he asked a few questions and then hung up.

"What'd she say?" Mark asked.

"Faith called, and Dagovar said he'd come. He didn't phone back or anything. All I can think is that, for some reason, he suspected it was a trap. Or maybe he did come, but he didn't see us and we didn't see him, and then he left. That seems unlikely, though."

"It does," I agreed. "You don't suppose it was something stupid, like he doesn't know where they do tai chi and thought we were in that area between the front of the library and the parking lot?"

"I have no idea," Lenny said. "Anyway, I hadn't given Faith instructions to call and say, *Hey, where are you?* so she didn't. I didn't mention Kutara to Erin.

She sounded really tired, and I didn't want her to stay awake."

I nodded. "We'll let her know when we get back."

We had walked perhaps half a mile before Big Jim scrambled down the bank and waded through the water to the other side. The bushes were thick here, with only a rabbit-trail of a path.

Mark stopped in the dark, and I bumped into his back. "I can't see a damn thing," he muttered.

Light flickered ahead, then steadied. "C'mon in," Big Jim called. We found our way into a domed clearing beneath the tangled branches—sort of a wicker igloo. Two battered tea lights cast a dim, wavering light in the center. Empty cigarette packs and other litter mixed with the trampled dirt.

The vagrants milled around, dumping possessions and getting comfortable on one side of the rough circle. Mark, Lenny, and I sat cross-legged, facing them.

Big Jim pulled Kutara down next to him, then opened the bottle and took a swig. He offered it to Mark next.

"No thanks, I'm driving."

Lenny and I shook our heads when Big Jim offered it to us. He passed it to the woman, who sat on his other side.

Kutara was dressed in a man's button-down shirt and what looked like the bottom half of pale-blue pajamas. Tennis shoes with holes in the toes peeked from underneath.

"Where did you find her?" Lenny asked.

"She was hard to miss, being in a knock-down-drag-out fight with some big bastard. We was on our way back from Liquor Mart when we came up on 'em, breakin' windows and fighting to beat the band."

"That's when we saw the lightning."

The deep voice made me turn. The third man looked the youngest, maybe thirty. Tiny brown moles speckled his coffee-and-cream skin and broad nose. His eyes were large and beautiful. He looked away as soon as I met his gaze.

Big Jim reclaimed the conversation. "She was losing, but he looked pretty tired, so we jumped him."

"You *jumped* Dagovar?"

He grinned, revealing the missing tooth. "There was one of him and four of us, so it seemed like pretty good odds."

I grinned at Lenny. "I bet Dagovar wasn't happy when he couldn't glamour them."

"What's that mean? Glamour?" the woman asked.

"He couldn't take control of your thoughts."

Big Jim shrugged. "Not that I noticed, anyway."

"I was drunk," the gray-haired man volunteered.

The woman gave him a disapproving look. "I told you not to drink leftovers on tables."

"They were outside tables!"

"You'll get arrested that way."

The gray-haired man grinned. "I don't mind getting arrested."

The woman cuffed him on the shoulder. "Next time you do, don't count on getting your stuff back. You leave it all for me to carry one more time, it's mine."

He looked at the ground. "I don't mean to get arrested. It just happens sometimes."

I steered the conversation back on course. "So you fought Dagovar."

"After that kid hit him with his bicycle," the woman said.

Big Jim nodded. "The kid came whizzing up, got off his bike, picked it up, and hit this *Dagovar*—is that how you say it?"

Lenny nodded.

"He hit him pretty good, but the big sonofabitch picked the kid up and tossed him." He poked his tongue through the gap in his teeth, a thoughtful gesture. "I kinda wanted to change my mind about fighting then, but we'd already run up behind him." He snugged Kutara against his shoulder. "And then there was this poor thing, naked as the day she was born."

Lenny and I exchanged a glance. Kutara must have been close to death.

Big Jim went on. "I got in a couple good hits on the side of his head before he could turn around. He was lookin' pretty dazed when we heard the sirens coming. One minute we was all on top of him, the next he had kind of melted into the ground." He squinted at me. "What are you people, anyway?"

I waited to see if Lenny would answer.

"Elves," he said.

"Ha!" Big Jim pointed at the freckled man. "You owe me three ciggies!"

"What did you think we were?" I asked the freckled man.

He smiled shyly. "Demons."

I looked around. "Didn't anyone choose aliens?"

The woman gave me an amused look. "No space-ship, honey. I figured you for demons, too, but I don't gamble. The Lord don't like it."

"So what happened after Dagovar left?" Lenny asked.

"We had to carry Sissy." Big Jim grinned suddenly. "She took a big shine to me right off the bat."

"She sure did," the freckled man said.

The others chortled.

I wasn't surprised. Kutara would have needed all the energy she could get. It was a miracle she hadn't eaten anything. "How long has it been since she stopped talking?"

The freckled man shook his head. "She's never talked."

"*Never?*" Had fighting with Dagovar somehow accelerated Kutara's condition? "Did she at least *act* sane when you first met her?"

Big Jim bristled. "What do you mean, *sane?* She's fine."

I raised my hands. "Of course. It's just that this woman used to be our boss. She ran an entire organization."

They didn't look particularly surprised at this revelation.

"Lots of people wind up on the streets," the gray-haired man said. "I was foreman on a construction site until a piece of culvert fell on my leg. I started drinking 'cause of the pain." He took a swig from the bottle.

"Maybe she can't talk because that lightning fried her brain," the freckled man suggested.

Lenny shook his head. "It's a kind of disease that elves get. But we just found a way to fix it."

Big Jim looked at Kutara's blank face. "I guess she should go with you, then. I'll miss her."

Mark struggled into a crouch in the confined space and took out his wallet. "Here's all the cash I have." He handed it over. "Thanks for taking care of her. And again, I'm sorry about the Taser."

Big Jim passed bills around to the others. "Don't mention it."

Chapter Twenty

I sat in the backseat with Kutara on the way to the hotel. She stared out the window as we drove down the darkened streets, apparently fascinated by the movement. Once I touched her arm. She ignored me.

"Lenny, what's Kutara's talent?" I managed to keep my voice casual, although this was a piece of information I should know.

Lenny, in the front passenger seat, turned and looked at me, headlights from passing cars sliding across the side of his face.

I met his gaze steadily.

"Ice carving." He moved his hand, as if to reach back and touch me, but didn't, apparently realizing it would be my undoing.

"Thanks." I hoped Mark didn't hear the thickness in my voice.

Lenny was quiet for a few minutes. "I'm not sure how Guy is going to manage that skill, with all his injuries."

I smiled in the dark. "If Guy has to learn with an

ice cube and a magnifying glass, he'll do it. What I wonder is whether Kutara has to be near him for it to work."

"I wouldn't think so. Their bond still exists at a distance. I guess we'll find out. He's not in a position to have her with him, what with being in the hospital."

"I guess we should wait until morning to call him."

"Definitely," Mark said. "Morning is the time to talk about Kutara, and Dagovar, and everything else. Right now I just want to eat something from the minibar and then go to bed."

"Lenny, I guess you could have gone home from the library," I said.

"That's okay. I'll say goodnight to Faith if she's still up."

We had just entered the hotel lobby when we were hailed by the desk clerk, one of the many laid-back young men who staffed the hotel. "Excuse me, but there's a message for you." He held up a piece of paper.

Lenny looked at me, his brows raised. Not only had we registered under fake names and glamoured the clerks to forget what we looked like, but Erin had paid in cash. We approached the hotel desk cautiously.

"Who left this message?" Lenny asked.

"Big guy. Long blond hair."

Lenny almost snatched the note.

"I offered to let him leave a phone message," the

clerk said, "but he said you'd be in later and told me what you looked like. My name's Eric. I'll be happy to book rooms for you."

I glamoured him to be quiet and tried to read the note in Lenny's hands. "What's it say?"

"Sorry I missed our appointment," he read. "You can be sure I'll make the next one. Dagovar."

"Come on." Mark took off running.

Mark and Lenny pelted through the silent pool area and up the stairs. I followed more slowly, towing Kutara behind me.

Erin had given Mark and me one of her key cards, and vice versa. By the time I got to our floor, Mark and Lenny were already coming out of Erin's room.

"Erin and Galan are here," Mark said. "Erin says Faith went to sleep in our room."

I already had the key card in my hand. The lock's green light blinked on and I shoved open the door, then switched on the light. One of the beds was unmade, the covers turned back. "Faith!" I ran into the bathroom. It was empty.

I came back out, shaking my head.

"How did he know we were here?" Lenny asked.

Erin appeared in the doorway, pulling a shirt down around her waist. "She's gone?"

"Yes," Mark said heavily.

"Come back to my room," she said. "I don't want to leave Galan in there alone." She caught sight of Kutara and her mouth fell open. A moment later, she was hugging her. "*Kutara!*"

Kutara fidgeted uneasily as Erin held her, shoulders pressed back and fingers wriggling.

"Am I glad to see you," Erin said, pulling Kutara into her room. "Look, Galan!"

Galan sat up in bed, brow furrowed as if he knew Kutara was someone he should remember.

Erin patted Kutara on the back. "You'll both be really happy later."

"Should we call Dagovar?" Mark asked.

Lenny shook his head wearily. "The more we let on how much Faith means to us, the stronger his bargaining position."

I plopped into a chair at the table. There were a few more chairs around it—Erin must have asked someone to bring extras. "I agree. I'm sure he means to exchange her for the passwords."

Erin hugged herself. "But how did he know we were here? Could it have been our cell phones? I know there's supposed to be some feature that allows emergency people to trace you, but I never turned it on."

Mark shook his head. "I think it's automatic now. But only the police would have access to that information."

"All Dagovar had to do was walk into the police station and glamour someone," I said gently.

"Right." Mark looked angry. "I should have thought of that."

"Don't feel too bad," Lenny said. "Dagovar could just as easily have gone to every hotel and wandered around glamouring people to come out of their rooms."

"Which would explain why he didn't find Galan and me," Erin said. "After Faith made the call, we waited a little bit, and then she went to your room. She was going to try to get some sleep, and said she didn't want you guys to come back without telling us what had happened." She gestured to Kutara. "Where did you find her?"

"She was with a bunch of homeless people at the park," I said. "If Dagovar *had* shown up, we might never have found her." I gave Erin a brief account of what had happened.

"That's something, anyway," Erin said. "And once Guy learns how to do ice carving, you'll have one more elf to fight him with."

"That's true," Lenny said thoughtfully. "Dagovar doesn't know we've found a cure for the forgetting disease, and he doesn't know we have Kutara. We might be able to surprise him a little."

"So are we going to stay here tonight?" I looked at the clock radio on the nightstand, which showed that it was past three in the morning. "We can't expect Guy to do anything right now."

"I think we should stay here," Lenny said. "It's probably not what Dagovar would expect, and I don't really think he'll come back. He got what he wanted."

"What about you?" I asked him. "You must be tired."

He looked at Erin. "Could you meditate and raise some energy for me?"

"If it means having you stay with us for the night, you bet."

Mark and I left and went next door. He walked to the middle of our room and stared at the floor. *"Shit."*

I raised my hand to touch him, but let it drop. He might not be fond of elves at the moment. "If it's any comfort to you, Faith probably has no idea that anything is wrong."

"You don't think he'll hurt her?"

"That would only make us more unwilling to co-operate. No, I imagine he'll call us tomorrow and arrange for a trade, after he's given us some time to stew." Now I did touch his arm, lightly. "I'm so sorry I got you involved."

He turned and pulled me into his arms. "Don't be stupid. Faith had clammed up about her *new boyfriend* before you and I got together."

I struggled to remember. "Had she?" I was hardly aware that I spoke out loud, but Mark drew back and studied me.

"Are you having trouble? Has it started?" he asked, gripping my upper arms.

I shrugged nonchalantly. "Eh, you forget things when you've been around a couple hundred years."

"Adlia?" His face suddenly looked older. "Don't hide things from me. It doesn't help."

"No, I suppose it doesn't. You might have to keep me from making mistakes." I nodded. "It has started."

He wrapped his arms around me again, more gently this time. "I have to believe there's a way to fix this memory problem, but if you need someone to take care of you while your friends work on a solution, I want to be the one to do that."

I lifted my face and kissed him, although my lips trembled. "Why is it that some humans are so generous?"

"My parents taught me to give back." He rested his forehead against mine and smiled, although his eyes were wet. "And they always said, *If you're lucky enough to have an elven girlfriend, don't let her get away.*"

I managed to smile for him, then took his hand and led him to the bed. "You're the first person to make me feel like I'm not alone in the world." I pulled back the covers and sat on the edge of the mattress.

He climbed on the bed and knelt behind me to kiss my neck. "I promise you'll never feel alone while I can prevent it. Now I want you to promise me something."

I turned my head and kissed him softly. "What?"

"Promise me you'll fight this forgetting thing. Don't take care of Dagovar and then give in."

I wasn't counting on surviving my encounter with Dagovar, but my words didn't have to say that. "I promise I'll fight. For you."

He pulled me down and lay above me, stroking my cheek with his fingers. "For us."

I woke to the sound of knocking and froze for a moment, unable to remember where I was.

Then Mark sat up next to me and knocked on the wall above our heads. "All right, we're awake," he groaned, before flopping back down. His lashes were ridiculously long, his face stubbled.

I smoothed his hair where it spilled untidily over his cheekbone, willing myself to remember his features, then trailed my finger down his neck to his collarbone, which looked more pronounced. "You're losing weight."

He captured my hand and kissed it sleepily. "I'll start drinking milkshakes."

"See that you do. I need my big, strong man to protect me."

He gave a snort of laughter, his closed eyes crinkling at the corners.

The knocking came again. "Right. Gotta get Faith back," Mark said, and rolled out of bed.

Next door, Erin sat on the bed, Galan seated on the floor between her legs as she brushed his hair. Kutara wandered the room.

Lenny sat at the table with a phone book open in front of him.

"Have you called Guy?" I asked him.

"I called Boulder Community Hospital, then realized I don't know his last name. And I don't have his number on my phone."

I took out Kutara's phone and scrolled through the contact list. "Do you want to call, or should I?"

"He's talked to you before, so go ahead. Call him on the hotel phone, though."

I sat down on the bed and dialed Guy's cell number. It rang and rang, and then the voice mail picked up. I left a brief message for him to call me at the hotel, along with Erin's room number. "Now what do we do?" I asked, after hanging up. "Go to the hospital and look for him?"

"If we have to." Lenny looked tired as well as dejected. His dark hair had lost its gloss, and lavender shadows darkened the skin below his eyes. "I can't believe we don't know his last name."

Erin chewed on her lip. "I think it began with an *E*."

The room phone rang. I snatched it up. "Hello?"

"Adlia, it's Guy! I'm sorry I missed your call. I was on the phone, trying to find a home-health aide. I'm going to get out of here as soon as possible."

"That's great! I have more good news for you. We've found Kutara."

For a moment he was silent. Then, "Thank God. You have no idea how I prayed for this." His voice trembled with emotion. "Is she all right?"

"She will be, with some help from you." Lenny made motions for me to give him the phone. "Hold on. Lenny wants to talk to you. He's in charge of things."

I gave the phone to Lenny and joined Mark at the table. "Lenny is doing a great job, but it'll be good to have Kutara back."

Mark and I watched Kutara as she drifted around the room. She looked cleaner—Erin had apparently washed her face and pulled back her hair with a rubber band.

"What's Kutara like?" Mark asked.

I blew a breath through my pursed lips, wondering how to sum her up. "Hideously smart, brutally honest, and viciously practical."

He looked at me with raised brows. "Those are quite the adjectives."

"She's your basic tyrant, but she gets the job done and she cares in her own way. It took me a while to realize that. If you had asked me a week ago if I would miss her, I'd have said I'd pay to have her gone."

"What changed?"

"I did. I hope we'll understand each other a little better, once this is over." Unfortunately, thinking of the future made me remember how short mine was likely to be.

Lenny hung up. "Guy says he'll be home from the hospital this afternoon, and he wants us to stay at his house."

"What do we do until then?" Erin asked. "Besides eat."

"I'm up for eating," Mark said.

"You guys eat. We'll plan," Lenny said.

The smell of French toast filled the room. Erin and Mark sat at the table, wolfing down slices. Galan watched, then reached for a slice on Erin's plate.

She grabbed his wrist and pushed it away. "Uh-uh. None for you."

Lenny and I sat on the floor, our backs against the side of the bed.

Lenny dragged off his cap and ruffled his hair. "The question is, if Dagovar offers to trade Faith for the passwords, do we just do it and not try for anything more? After all, he'd have no reason to bother us again, right?"

"I want to kill him."

He rolled his head and looked at me. "Yeah, I'm

getting that. What if trying to kill him means additional risk to other people?"

"Dagovar presents a risk to other people just by existing. I still like your idea of meeting on concrete or something where he can't merge."

"But Faith would be there. It would put her at risk to start blasting away."

I thought for a moment. "What if I give him a fake list of passwords? Then we send everyone else away and let Dagovar come after me when he realizes what we've done."

"Do you *want* to die?" Lenny asked.

"What's this about dying?" Mark asked, coming over.

"Lenny's exaggerating," I said. "All I'm saying is that I'm the logical person to take the most risk."

"We don't need to take risks," Lenny said. "Let's just hand over the passwords and get Faith. I don't want Dagovar to have any reason to come back."

"I agree," Mark said. "And anyway, Galan and Kutara are recovering. It doesn't have to be just you and Lenny."

"Maybe Galan will be recovered enough to be involved," I said. "But Kutara? Look at her." I gestured to where she stood by the window, staring blankly out at the sky. "I guess it depends on how long we have until Dagovar calls."

Lenny's phone rang, and he got to his feet. "Not long, is my guess." He picked up his phone from the table and looked at the display. "It's him. Everyone be quiet." He put the phone to his ear. "This is Lenny." A pause. "You were there when Kutara put me in charge, Dagovar." A longer pause. "Fine." He held the phone out to me. "He insists on talking to you."

I put the phone on speaker and pasted a smile on my face so I would sound confident. "Hello, Dagovar. Done any dancing lately?"

"You should have killed me when you had the chance. Now I know how much your human friends mean to you."

Mark's eyes met mine, and I gave him a reassuring smile. "Yes, well, loyalty among elves isn't what it used to be."

"That's certainly true." He sounded angry. "As for me, I only want what's mine."

I had hit a nerve, but I wasn't sure which one. "I assume you're talking about the money, but how do figure it's yours?"

"Fellseth was my father."

The inexplicable aspects of Dagovar's betrayal rearranged themselves in my head, like a scrambled puzzle that now made sense.

"That money is my inheritance," he said, "but this is also about justice. Knowing that my father's killers took his fortune for themselves—it's wrong."

"Dagovar, your father's *killers*, as you put it, acted in self-defense. He was trying to murder them, like he murdered other people."

"He might have killed some humans, but they're killing us all the time with their development of *Ma'Nah*."

"He killed elves, too, and with less excuse than humans, who don't *know* they're doing it!"

"Humans know they're killing other things. What's the difference?" he asked.

Lenny made a circling gesture, signaling me to get to the point.

I took a calming breath. "As fascinating as this discussion is, I don't think it's why you called."

"I suppose not, although I always enjoyed our conversations. All right—I'm willing to give your friend back to you, unharmed, in exchange for a few things."

A *few* things? What else did we have that Dagovar wanted? "I assume you're talking about the passwords."

"And Kutara."

Erin gave a tiny gasp, then clapped her hand over her mouth.

I took the phone off speaker and looked at Lenny.

"He must have seen that Kutara's phone was in use," he said. "Tell him you found it."

I nodded and pushed the speaker button again. "We can't bring Kutara," I told Dagovar. "She disappeared after you attacked her. I found her phone, but that's all."

"Bring Kutara, or I'll put Faith's head in Mark's mailbox," Dagovar growled. "Then I'll pick off your other human friends, one by one, until you give me what I want."

"Why this sudden obsession with Kutara?"

"She killed my father."

Erin opened her mouth to contradict this, but I shook my hand to stop her.

Dagovar went on. "In addition to revenge, she'll

be useful to me once I make her mortal. It's hard to travel without a human slave to raise energy with. And I'll never have to worry about bonding, considering how I feel about her."

I closed my eyes, as if that could block out the image this presented. "Like father, like son," I said, "but none of that changes the fact that we don't have Kutara. What makes you think she's still alive?"

"I'm looking at her."

I spun toward Kutara, who still stared out at the sky. Behind me, the door opened, then closed on the sound of running footsteps—Lenny giving chase. I walked to the window.

Two stories below, Dagovar stood beneath a solitary tree, planted in the median between the hotel and parking lot.

I needed to keep him talking until Lenny reached him. "Let's say we agree with your demands. How would this work?"

He looked up at me, mouth moving in sync with the voice in my ear. "Meet me in Central Park tonight, between the band shell area and the creek. Two hours after midnight. And I want *you* to make the exchange. No one else."

"Why me?"

He smiled faintly. "I want you where I can see you."

His head turned, as if at a sudden noise, and then he dissolved into the ground.

Lenny ran into view, not slowing down, and I realized he planned to follow, tracking Dagovar through *Ma'Nah*. I banged on the window with both fists.

Lenny stopped and looked up.

"No!" I shouted.

He looked toward the tree, then at me, a rueful expression on his face. Finally he nodded and turned back toward the hotel.

I let out a breath, my hands sliding down the glass.

Erin and Mark came to the window and looked down.

"What happened?" Erin asked. Galan came to stand beside her, and she put her arm around him.

"Lenny is the only elf I know who could track Dagovar through *Ma'Nah*," I said. "For a minute, it looked like he was going to do it."

Mark nodded in understanding. "But what would happen when he emerged and found Dagovar waiting?"

"Exactly."

Kutara, apparently tired of the view outside, turned and bumped into me.

I gripped her arm and looked in her face. "I won't let him take you. Do you understand?"

For a moment, I thought she focused on me. Then her eyes skated away, and she pulled out of my grasp

Chapter Twenty-One

Lenny's face was grim as he talked to the Kansas elves about help in dealing with Dagovar.

Erin stood with her hands on Kutara's shoulders, raising energy for her by meditating. Galan lay on the bed and watched.

Mark and I sat at the table and listened as Lenny paced the room with his cell phone to his ear.

"Uh-huh," he said. "And there's nothing I can say that will change your mind? Well, I don't think that's an option, but I'll let you know. Good-bye." He hung up. "They won't help us."

"Mark has offered to buy their plane tickets," I said, "but they can't be bothered to help their own kind?"

"Until Galan recovers completely, they're still not convinced that the illness isn't contagious. They said that if we want to go there, they'll mount a watch for Dagovar outside wherever we stay, at a safe distance."

"Right," Mark said. "I'm sure Dagovar will be happy to bring Faith to Kansas for the exchange."

"I suppose I can understand where they're coming from," I said reluctantly. "They have to look out for themselves, and Dagovar doesn't seem to be much of a threat to anyone but us."

Mark chewed a peanut-butter cracker from the minibar and swallowed thickly. "Without their help, we're not in a very good position."

"We're not," I agreed. Now that Dagovar wanted Kutara, there was no more talk of a simple exchange. "I'll be surprised if Galan and Kutara will be able to fight. Lenny, there might be some place for you to hide."

"And me," Mark said. "There's still a cartridge left for Erin's Taser."

I squeezed his hand in thanks. How would this work? Dagovar must know that Kutara could no longer merge. He couldn't take her into *Ma'Nah* with him—he'd need a vehicle. Assuming he didn't drive off with Kutara in his lap, would I be able to shoot him when he got in the car?

Fighting Dagovar in the parking lot, I had had one opportunity as Mark drove away, but excitement made me shoot high. If I'd been calm, I might have got him. I saw myself there again, elf fire shooting from my fingertips.

Elf fire . . . I'd never heard anyone call it that, but it seemed to fit. Mine was green and seemed to have a slight upward arc as it shot across the blackness . . .

"Adlia?"

It felt like I had to swim to find the voice calling me.

"Adlia!" Someone was shaking my shoulder.

"What?" I demanded, blinking the world back into focus.

Mark looked into my face, his brow creased with worry. Across the table, Lenny and Erin had the same expression. Even Galan was staring at me.

"What's the last thing you remember talking about?" Mark asked.

"I don't know." Panic was a luxury I couldn't afford. I thought hard instead. "You wanted to hide somewhere with the Taser."

Lenny shook his head. "That was probably five minutes ago. Did you black out?"

"No, I was thinking!"

"About what?" Mark asked.

But I couldn't remember. It flickered at the edge of my consciousness and was gone. "Stuff. I don't know. I guess my concentration isn't as good as it could be."

Lenny glanced at Mark.

I sighed. "Maybe we should talk about what sacrifices we're prepared to make, in case things go wrong."

"What do you mean by *sacrifices*?" Lenny asked. "I know you're not suggesting we hand Kutara over to Dagovar."

"Actually, I was talking about me. I want to make something perfectly clear. If it's a choice between killing Dagovar or saving me, I want you to kill Dagovar. I need you both to agree on that." I looked from one to another of them.

They stared at me stonily.

I crossed my arms over my chest. "Oh, I see. I'm

probably going to become a mental vegetable, but you want to keep me from going out in a blaze of glory."

"What about Kutara's idea that becoming mortal might cure the forgetting disease?" Lenny asked.

"What?" Mark glared at me. "Why haven't I heard about this before?"

I shook my head. "Because there's no reason to think it would work. Everything I've ever heard suggests that when an elf turns mortal, only three things change. They don't have pointed ears anymore, they don't have any magic, and they start to age."

Mark started to say something, but I raised my hands. "Kutara will get better. We need to kill Dagovar in order to save her. If I have the chance, I'm asking that you not get in my way. Can you both do that?"

They finally nodded, but they didn't look happy about it.

Mark and I went back to our room to wait until we could go to Guy's house.

I lay on the bed while he ordered a milkshake, fighting the tendency for my mind to wander.

After putting the empty glass in the hall outside, Mark sat next to me and stroked my hair. "You've changed since this has all happened, you know that?"

I nodded glumly. "Exactly how stupid am I?"

"I don't mean that. You're no more absent-minded than the average human, at the moment."

I propped myself on my elbows. "Then how have I changed?"

"You're more determined. You were always funny, and smart, and kind of warped." He smiled, then looked thoughtful. "But this is the first time I've seen you completely confident that you can do something."

"I'm not *completely* confident, but it definitely feels possible."

"I agree. And while it goes against my nature to let you risk yourself, when you told us to stay out of your way, I found myself agreeing."

I pushed myself up farther and grasped Mark's shoulder. "If something happens and you wind up facing him, remember that he shoots a little to the side, assuming you'll dodge right. So always dodge left."

"That's a hit-man trick." Mark rubbed his chin on my hand where it lay on his shoulder. "What does elf energy do to humans? Does Erin know?"

I shook my head. "I don't know of any human who's been hit. It's so much easier to glamour them."

"But Dagovar can't glamour me." Mark leaned closer in his excitement. "What if elf energy doesn't do *anything* to humans?"

"Huh." I thought for a moment. "Guy couldn't be glamoured either. I assumed Dagovar hit Guy physically because he was angry, but maybe that's not the case."

"If I can fight him like a regular human, that would make a big difference."

"He's a little bigger than you," I pointed out.

"Remember that I used to practice kung fu. It's been a while, but the principles stay with you. That would give me an edge."

"I wouldn't want you to try unless we knew for sure that elf fire wouldn't hurt you," I said.

Mark got off the bed and stood, spreading his arms. "Go ahead and fire off a little blast. We need to know."

"Really? Okay, but get back on the bed." I scrambled off. "Sit on the edge, so if something happens, you won't fall on the floor."

He did so, then spread his arms again and grinned. "Go for it."

"I'm going to shoot for your hand."

He let both arms fall. "What will *that* tell us?"

"For starters, it'll tell us if your skin melts or catches on fire."

He made a face. "Okay, go for my hand."

I aimed carefully at his outstretched hand and fired a small shot. To my eyes, the crackling green light seemed to come out slowly, almost in a trickle.

Mark gave a yip and whipped back his hand.

"Are you okay?" I ran over and peered at his hand as he examined it.

"It's fine." He rubbed his fingers over the palm. "Not even red."

I was vaguely disappointed. "But you felt it, right?"

"Oh, yeah. Feels like a pretty good shock, but it's not disabling or anything. I think I could fight through it. Do it again, and this time give me a body shot."

I went to the middle of the room and positioned myself. "Did it look like it came at you kind of slow?"

He frowned. "I didn't get a sense of speed. I barely saw something, and then it was over."

I raised my arm. *Too close.* "I'm going to go to the far corner of the room. Turn sideways a little so you're facing me."

He turned, then spread his arms and grinned at me. "You're short, and your ears are funny."

"Ha-ha." I leaned against the wall and fired, holding back. Again it seemed slow, but it hit Mark full in the chest. His shoulders pulled forward, arms shaking like they were made of rubber, and his eyes rolled up in his head.

"Mark!" I ran over as he slumped sideways and slid from the bed to the floor with a thump.

Someone banged on the wall, and then I heard Erin yell, "Are you okay in there?"

I knelt on the floor and put my ear to Mark's mouth. He was breathing huskily.

A moment later, someone pounded on the door. "Adlia!" Lenny called from outside.

I scrambled to my feet and let him in. "Mark asked me to shoot him, to see what elf fire does to humans." I ran back to Mark's side and went down on my knees again.

Lenny knelt next to me and put a hand on Mark's chest. "His heart's going like a rabbit, but that's better than not at all, I guess."

Mark's lips moved feebly, and his eyes came down from under his lids. *"Ahgl . . ."*

"Can you hear me?" I asked loudly.

"Mah," Mark said.

"He thinks I'm his mother," I wailed.

Mark swallowed, and his eyes focused on me. "My God, that was embarrassing."

"You scared me to death!" I took his wrist and tried to pull him to his feet.

He shook his head limply, not even trying to help. "I'm not in standing condition yet."

"What'd it feel like?" Lenny asked.

"Like she used Erin's Taser on me." He wet his lips. "Did you dial it down even a *little?*"

I looked up and fired a blast at the air-conditioning vent. Pale green fire blossomed on the metal, and wisps of smoke curled at the edges where it met the ceiling.

Mark grimaced. "Okay, so you barely touched me." He held out his hands, and Lenny and I each took one and pulled him to his feet.

Mark sank heavily onto the bed and shook his head gingerly, as if to clear it. "I guess I won't be much help against Dagovar, unless I can sneak something in by surprise."

"That might be what turns the tide," Lenny said, patting him on the shoulder. He went to the door. "Don't forget to bolt the door." He gave Mark a significant look. "And I'll expect Adlia to be fully energized when we go to Guy's house." He left.

Mark groaned, subsiding onto the patterned

bedspread. "Maybe I should have thought of that before I had you scramble my neurons."

I pulled off my shirt and jeans. "Your neurons are welcome to take a little break," I said, crawling onto the bed astride Mark's prone figure. "I'll do all the work."

His face brightened as my breasts came into view. "Pretty." He raised his mouth to first one nipple and then the other, sucking gently, his whiskers rough against my skin.

I hummed in pleasure, my eyes closed, then pulled free and sat on his thighs to unfasten his shirt and jeans. "Raise your hips."

He put his feet on the bed, bumping me forward, and took the opportunity to suckle my breasts again while he pushed down his jeans and boxers. Something large and warm bounced up and hit my bare bottom.

I giggled. "Don't need neurons for that."

His arm snaked down between us.

I felt him guide himself through my curls and between my folds. "Nice," I whispered, closing my eyes.

He rubbed himself back and forth, moistening us and making me tingle before surprising me with a push that took him halfway inside.

"I see you're recovering," I groaned.

He gripped my thighs and pulled me down on him, slowly, until he was completely sheathed.

I collapsed against his chest, panting slightly as he rocked back and forth beneath me.

"Kiss me," he said, gripping my wrists where they rested on either side of his head.

I raised myself enough to meet his mouth. He guided one of my forearms beneath his neck and put his free hand at the back of my head, trapping me and plundering my mouth with his tongue.

His hips rose, and I bent my knees to meet him closer, tighter, until something in me broke loose and I shuddered around him. He hooked his hands behind my thighs and pulled me hard onto him as he thrusted. Our mouths broke apart as we gasped and shook together.

I collapsed on top of him, my hair in a nimbus around my head. A strand tickled the back of my neck and I gave a whole-body shiver.

"Stop moving," he groaned, putting his hands on my hips to keep me still.

"How about I get off?"

"No." He patted my back absently. "Just . . . nap."

His mouth opened on a little snuffling breath, and he was asleep.

Chapter Twenty-Two

"Adlia."

Sound. A . . . name.

"Adlia!"

Movement. Something moves me. Light.

"Adlia, say something!"

Face. Face I know. "Mark?" Rational thought swam back, but slowly, as though it were unfamiliar.

Mark, who knelt above me, gathered me in his arms. "Thank God. I thought you were gone."

It was work to think of something to say. "I'm still here."

He kissed me. "You're sure? Okay, good. Get your clothes on. It's time to go to Guy's house."

I lay back down. It was soft.

"Adlia!" He sat on the bed next to me.

"You're sad," I said.

"Oh, God. I didn't want to believe this could happen. Look. Here are your clothes. Put them on."

He handed me things. Clothes. I lay them on top of me.

Mark came back with someone. She was pretty. I thought for a moment. "Erin."

"Let's get you dressed, honey."

Eventually I realized that my vagueness was making everybody unhappy. If I paid attention to *everything,* I was able to push away the fog.

We were in a van with Lenny driving, Erin in the passenger seat next to him. I had no memory of getting there. Mark sat next to me, holding my hand.

"Where are we going?" I asked, looking past Galan to see out the window. The glass was a funny gray color.

"Adlia?" Mark tugged on my hand.

I turned to face him. "What?" He looked so worried.

"Can you understand what I'm saying?"

Erin turned in the front seat. "Did she say something?"

"She asked where we were going."

I was getting better at paying attention, but it was a lot of work. I turned in my seat. Kutara sat behind us, staring out the window. Did it make sense for her to be there? *Yes,* I decided, although I wasn't sure how I'd figured it out.

Mark kissed me, which made me feel better. "You've been out of it for a little while. We're going to Guy's house. He's out of the hospital . . ."

"Guy was in the *hospital?*" Something bad tugged at my memory. "Wait. I remember now. Dagovar attacked him. Go on."

Mark glanced at Erin, who still watched us. "One
of the doctors is a friend of Guy's, or apparently
they wouldn't have let him go. He has a nurse staying with him."

"And tonight I'm going to fight Dagovar," I
remembered.

Mark looked at Erin. Erin glanced at Lenny.

"Look at *me!*" I insisted. "Tonight I fight Dagovar." Just saying the words made me feel better.

"We'll see," Mark said.

We got out of the van at someone's house. Lenny
wanted us to hurry and get inside.

A plump woman opened the door for us. "He's
waiting downstairs for you. Have you known Guy
long?"

"I've never met him," Mark said.

She smiled, but it didn't look real. "He's quite a
character."

We all went downstairs. It was cold, and noisy
with machines. Plastic sheets hung from the ceiling
to the floor, making a little room.

I found that if I connected the things I looked at,
my thoughts stayed together better. Guy. The man
doing something behind those clear plastic walls
was Guy, Kutara's lover.

One section of the plastic walls had been cut
into strips, which waved gently in the cold air.
Inside, Guy sat in a chair, wearing a puffy coat with
a fur-trimmed hood. One leg stuck straight out in
front of him, propped on a box. It was wrapped
in blankets.

A piece of ice sat on a table in front of him, and

he was holding a little whirring machine and doing something to the ice. The arm with which Guy held the machine rested in a loop of stretchy cord, which hung from the ceiling.

Erin looked at Lenny. "I guess you told him about Kutara's talent."

Guy looked up. "You're here!" His voice wasn't very strong. "This jacket is rated for Arctic conditions, but with this hood, I can't see much of anything except what's in front of me." He looked eagerly past me. "Where is she? Did you bring her?"

Guy struggled to stand up as Erin led Kutara past the rest of us and took her through the plastic strips. Finally he made it, his arm still hanging in the stretchy sling, the other bracing himself on the table. "Hi, honey," he said.

Kutara stood and looked at him for a moment. Then she walked straight to him and put her arms around his waist, resting her head on his shoulder.

"Get my arm out of this thing," Guy said to Erin, his voice husky.

Erin turned off the whirring machine, put it on the table, and gently removed Guy's arm from the hanging sling. Guy wrapped it around Kutara and pulled her close, his hand fisting in her shirt.

Something tickled my cheek. I brushed at it and my fingers came away wet.

"Adlia." Mark turned me toward him and kissed me. He looked so sad. "I'm going to the backyard for just a minute."

"Why?" I wanted him to stay with me.

"I just . . ." His cheeks were wet, too. "I'll be back in a few minutes, okay?" He went up the stairs.

Erin had come out of the plastic room. "Maybe we should all go upstairs for bit."

"Don't leave," Guy called to us. "Just don't come inside here. It heats up the room too much." He still held on to Kutara, though.

Lenny, Erin, Galan, and I got up next to one of the clear walls and looked inside.

"What is all this?" Lenny asked.

Guy pointed to some big white boxes with open lids. "Two chest freezers and a Dremel tool with carving attachments." He waved at a space between the two white chests, where a silver cylinder stood, tubes coming out of the top. "Oh, and an oxygen tank. I did have a little lung puncture, so sitting up is actually a good thing. It's hard to sleep, with all my busted parts, so I've been up since two, carving away."

"Is your arm broken, too?" Lenny asked.

"Oh, you mean the sling? No, that's just to keep me from getting too tired. It's bungee cord—lets me move around without having to hold my arm up all by myself." He kissed Kutara, then kissed her again and let go of her. "Erin, you want to come and get her? I'm not really supposed to stand."

"Of course." Erin went inside and pulled Kutara gently away.

"Guy," Kutara said, sounding a little angry.

Erin patted her arm. "That's the first word I've heard her say since we got her back."

Guy gestured toward a corner. "You can sit

right outside, honey, and watch. Lenny, there's a desk chair over there, if you could bring that over for her."

"Sure." Lenny rolled a chair over, and Erin got Kutara to sit in it.

Guy smiled happily at her.

After a moment, Kutara smiled back.

"What are you making?" I asked Guy.

"St. Paul's Cathedral." He picked up the Dremel tool and put his arm back in the sling. "I thought about carving a duck. Then I thought, *I'm an architect. I'm used to making models of buildings.* So I decided to play to my strengths. The dome is coming along nicely, don't you think?"

"It's almost lifelike." Erin looked like she wanted to laugh, for some reason. "I'm sure it'll go even quicker now that Kutara is here with you. How did you get this set up so quickly?"

"I called in some favors."

Lenny breathed on the plastic and watched it fog up. "Is there anything you need us to do for you?"

"No, I'm all set. Erin, if you and Mark want a late lunch, the nurse will make you something. Her name is Carol."

We went upstairs. The room was large and open, with books everywhere except in the kitchen. While the nurse made sandwiches, Galan and I sat at the dining table. Big windows looked out on a deck and a large backyard.

Outside, Mark stood on the grass, doing some kind of exercise.

One of the windows was a door. Lenny opened it. "Mark! Food!"

A minute later, Mark came inside and joined us. His eyes looked pink.

I got up and hugged him. "What were you doing?"

"I was trying to remember my old kung fu warm-up. Thought it might come in handy."

Lenny shrugged. "You never know."

Erin leaned on the counter that defined the kitchen area. "Mark, you must want something to eat."

"Yeah, I guess so."

"You *guess?* Aren't you starving?"

The nurse gave Erin a curious look.

"I mean," Erin said, "What with your new *diet,* and all." She inclined her head toward me.

Mark smiled. "I'm definitely hungrier, but it's not a huge thing."

"Do you want mustard?" the nurse asked Erin.

"And mayo. Lots of mayo." Erin came around the counter and took Mark's arm. "Show me the deck."

"I'm coming, too," I said.

"That's a good idea, sweetie." Erin opened the door for us. When we were all outside with the door shut beside us, she leaned on the railing. "I'm hungry most of the time with Galan, unless we're having sex like crazy." She rolled her eyes. "Sorry about the *too much information,* but you know what I mean."

"We did—you know—this morning," Mark said.

"How did you feel when Adlia fought Dago-var?" Erin asked. "I forgot to ask before, but when

Galan fought Fellseth, it drained me so much, I was in real trouble."

Mark shook his head. "I didn't get anything like that—just a stomach cramp. Maybe it's because of the size difference. I'm big and she's little."

"Maybe." Erin nodded. "There could be some gender thing going on, too. Maybe male elves are more wasteful than females when they fight."

"Right," Mark said dryly.

She rolled her eyes. "Or maybe it's because they're so much more *powerful.*"

"I don't know about that. Did Lenny tell you I had Adlia give me a little blast, to see how it affects humans? It was not pretty."

Erin brightened. "I heard."

"I'm going to fight Dagovar tonight," I said. That was the important thing, and I didn't want them to forget it.

After Mark and Erin had sandwiches, Erin disappeared with Galan.

"I wonder where your friends got to?" Carol asked.

"I wouldn't look for them, if I were you," Lenny said. "They'll turn up."

Her lips thinned. "Excuse me. I'm going to speak to Mr. Eddy."

Carol came back with her lips even thinner. "You know, Mr. Eddy's family could hardly believe he left the hospital so soon. I don't know what they'll think about him having all this excitement." She picked up her purse from the kitchen counter and went outside.

Lenny took the chair opposite Mark. "Do you get the feeling she disapproves of us?"

"Probably gone to call Guy's relatives and tell them the house is full of moochers and sex addicts." Mark leaned forward. "What are we going to do about tonight, now that Adlia is having problems?"

"Unless she's completely incapacitated, she still has to make the trade. I can't exactly call Dagovar and say, *We need you to let someone else kill you.*"

"But you could tell him that someone needs to bring her there," Mark said.

"That's true. It's an excuse for one of us to be present. That's not really a plus, though, because I wanted to be there but hidden."

"Then tell Dagovar I insist on driving Adlia there because Faith is my cousin."

"He might believe that," Lenny said. "I wonder if Kutara will be recovered enough to get in a shot. Otherwise, it's just me against Dagovar, and I don't know how close I'll be able to get."

Why did people keep saying stuff like that? "*I'm* fighting Dagovar."

"I don't think that's a good idea, Adlia." Mark checked to make sure the nurse was still outside. "Don't you think Dagovar will have a hard time handling Kutara *and* getting away from us?"

"He doesn't have to handle her. He just has to threaten to kill her. She'll probably be recovered enough to understand that," Lenny said. "Although she would prefer death to what he has planned."

Mark nodded. "Then threatening to kill her isn't much of a threat, is it?"

Lenny looked thoughtful. "You've got a point."

"Any way you look at it, he's going to have a lot of distractions," Mark said. "You blast him when you get a chance, and if you don't kill him outright, maybe I can sneak up on him. It's been a long time since I did any fighting, but I assume a rock to the head is always effective?"

"That would probably do it." Lenny smiled. "Normally I wouldn't feel comfortable having a human there at all, but you're okay. Although I don't understand why you're willing to risk your life to try to save Kutara."

"You're risking yours for my cousin."

"We need to get rid of Dagovar anyway, and this is probably our last, best chance."

"I have a vested interest, and not just because of Faith." Mark glanced at me. "Lenny, I wanted to ask—did Kutara raise Adlia or something?"

"Or something." Lenny smiled. "You wouldn't know it to see Adlia mooning over Kutara, but those two seemed to really hate each other when they were in their right minds."

Mark looked at me. "Adlia, did you hate Kutara?"

I looked at Lenny. "Did I?"

He laughed. "Pretty much."

"Oh," I said. "I hate Dagovar worse."

Carol came back in. "I'm going to check on Mr. Eddy again. He's on oxygen, you know."

We all watched her go. Mark let out a snort of laughter when she was gone. "Poor thing."

Lenny got up. "I'm going to the park and see where I can hide tonight."

Mark pushed back his chair. "All right, let's go."

Lenny shook his head. "Not you. Maybe later. Right now, I'm going to travel through *Ma'Nah*. It'll be quicker and safer. After I check out the park, I'll find a phone somewhere else and call you on the house phone. But then I have to spend some time at home, so I'm ready for tonight."

"All right." Mark sighed. "I hate that everything is so up in the air."

I didn't like to see him sad. "It'll be okay."

He squeezed my hand. "As soon as this is over, we're going to see about breaking our bond. There has to be a way."

Lenny walked to the glass door and looked into the backyard. "That's a pretty high fence. I don't think anyone will see me leave from here. Tell Erin and Galan where I am when they come up for air, will you?"

"Sure," Mark said. "Hey, Lenny . . ."

Lenny paused with his hand on the door. "Yeah?"

Mark grinned. "Can I watch you disappear?"

Lenny lowered his chin and gave Mark a look. "You want to see me merge?"

"Unless it's some kind of forbidden thing."

"It's not forbidden," I said. "I'll come, too." I pushed past Mark to get to the door.

"I don't see what the big deal is." Lenny opened the door and we all went outside.

The deck was made of some gray, plastic-looking

wood. A large blue umbrella shaded a metal table and chairs, and a big grill sat beyond them.

Lenny led the way down the stairs to the yard. "This is a little weird, just so you know." He glanced back at Mark.

As Lenny turned to look at Mark, elf fire came from behind a large tree at the back of Guy's yard, forking through the air like a silver-gray snake. When Lenny turned back, the blast hit him full in the face. He dropped like a stone.

"Down!" I screamed. In that moment, my brain achieved perfect clarity. I saw Dagovar lean out from behind the tree and take a second shot. I could have dodged it easily, but Mark was somewhere behind me, so I shifted my aim and met Dagovar's bolt with one of my own. They met a few yards from my face in an explosion that heated the air enough to make me squint.

Then I was running toward him, firing bolt after bolt. Dagovar returned only one, and his shot went wide. I heard him shout, as though in pain, and then I reached the tree. He was already gone.

"Adlia!" Mark yelled from behind me.

"Pick Lenny up and get him inside," I called, without looking back.

I walked backward, keeping my firing arm up and scanning the yard as I went, then ran up the stairs. Mark stood at the top of the deck, Lenny hanging limply in his arms. We were most vulnerable up here.

"Someone open the door!" I banged on the glass, still watching the yard.

Running footsteps vibrated through the deck's surface, and then the door opened.

"Get in here," Erin said, and pulled me backward into the house.

Mark started to lay Lenny on the floor.

I shook my head. "Behind the couch. Erin, lock that door."

In a few moments, we all knelt around Lenny, who breathed harshly, his eyes closed.

"I don't suppose getting the nurse would do any good," Mark said.

The nurse. "Mark, check that the rest of the doors are locked, and make sure the nurse doesn't let anyone in."

"Got it."

Erin looked around wildly. "Where's Galan?"

"Here. What's happening?" Galan looked backward as Mark thundered down the stairs past him. "I heard noises."

"Galan's doing better," I remarked.

"You're not doing so bad yourself." Erin rested both hands on Lenny's chest, palms down, and closed her eyes.

When the sound of thumping came from downstairs, I stood and turned in one movement, my arm already raised.

Mark ducked his head below the landing. "It's me!"

The thumping continued. "What's that noise?"

"The nurse." He came up to meet me. "I shut her in the downstairs bathroom, with a chair under the doorknob. I figured you could glamour her afterwards."

"Good thinking."

He took hold of my shoulders and kissed me, hard and quick. "How's Lenny?"

"Hurt," Lenny said, his voice faint.

We knelt by him again. Erin still had her hands on him, her eyes closed.

"How much of you hurts?" I asked.

"Everything from my rib cage up." He gave a few quick, panting breaths, his eyes squeezed shut.

"Is this helping at all?" Erin asked.

"I think so." Another gasp. "I need to get home." He lifted his head but fell back immediately, moaning, *"Yee'ahmin trose."*

"What does that mean?" Mark whispered.

"Ma'Nah, help me," I whispered back. "It's a cry to the mother of all."

"Can he travel through the earth in this condition?" Erin asked, looking at me.

I shook my head. "I think it's too far." The fog was closing in again. I heard the hesitation in my speech as I searched for words.

"What if we drove him there?" Mark said. "Adlia, you know where he lives, right?"

Was it north of here? "I don't . . ." My thoughts dodged and faded. I could seem to hold on only to the here and now. "I don't think I can." I began to cry. "I'm sorry, Lenny."

Galan, who knelt beside me, took my hand.

"Adlia, don't feel bad." Lenny opened his eyes,

blinking painfully. "Oh, no," he said, the words no more than a sigh.

"What?" Erin's fingers tensed on his chest. "Lenny?!"

"I can't see." He blinked again. "The bastard blinded me." His eyes fluttered shut. "Just make me stronger, Erin. I don't need to see to find my way home through *Ma'Nah*."

Erin moved one hand to his face, stroking the hair back from his forehead. "I'll do my best." She looked up at us. "If everyone could go somewhere else, that'll help me concentrate."

Galan headed downstairs.

"Let's keep an eye on the backyard," Mark said.

We went behind the counter in the kitchen, where we could raise our heads just enough to look outside. I had to stoop, but Mark was tall enough that he could kneel on the floor.

He rested his hand in the curve of my waist. "That second shot was headed right for me. I couldn't believe you stopped it."

"I wish I could have done more."

"You were *amazing*. I'm sure he never expected you to go after him like that."

I nodded. "Dagovar counts too much on . . . What do you call it?" I squinted in an effort to think of the word. "Strategy. But sometimes you just have to *go*. You have to . . ." Words failed me. "I can't think of it."

He lifted the hem of my shirt and kissed the bare skin beneath. "You're doing great, honey."

Chapter Twenty-Three

The nurse's banging had stopped. Mark checked to make sure her cell phone was in her purse, which she had put on the counter after coming in. We had left all *our* phones in the hotel, so Dagovar couldn't trace us through them.

"Could Dagovar have glamoured her to call him when we arrived?" Mark asked me.

I shrugged. It was too hard for me to work out.

Finally Erin called us over. Lenny sat hunched on the couch, eyes still closed, arms wrapped around himself.

"How're you doing, man?" Mark asked.

"I'm not in as much pain."

"That's good."

"Can you see?" I asked.

Lenny shook his head.

Erin chewed on her lip a moment. "I have no idea if it's permanent. His eyes don't look different, but he says everything is gray. He can't even make out shapes."

"I'm sorry I didn't shoot him first, Lenny."

"None of us saw it coming, Adlia." He stretched a hand toward me.

I took it. His felt a little cold, so I put my other one on top.

"Adlia fought Dagovar off, Lenny," Mark said. "He almost got me, but she stopped his shot with one of her own and then ran toward him like a damn greyhound, firing the whole way."

"Are you serious?" Erin asked.

I didn't think she needed to sound so surprised.

"I think she hit him once," Mark said.

I nodded, showing my teeth. "He yelled."

Erin leaned forward and kissed my cheek. "Maybe you *can* fight him."

"I *told* you." I frowned to let her know I was serious. "Don't try to stop me."

Lenny gave my hand a squeeze before letting go. "Well, I'm out of the picture, so you're going to have to let Adlia try unless you want to give him Kutara."

"Adlia will fight," Kutara said from behind us.

We all turned. She wore a red shirt and black pants.

"Kutara!" Lenny seemed happiest of all, even though he couldn't see her. "You're well!"

She stared at him for a while, until I thought she wasn't going to say anything. Then she said, "Not well."

Erin's shoulders slumped. "But you're *better*."

"Yes."

"I'm wondering if we should think things through some more," Mark said. "I really don't like this."

"There's a lot not to like," Erin said. "What, specifically, don't you like?"

"It was one thing to talk about risking Kutara when she was sitting around like a vegetable, but now she's talking." He spread his hands. "What if we didn't bring her? What if we told Dagovar that he could have the passwords in exchange for Faith, but that was it? What would he do?"

Erin tilted her head. "As I recall, he said he'd put Faith's head in your mailbox and then he'd pick off us humans one by one."

"Do you really think he'd do it?" Mark asked.

Lenny pointed to his closed eyes. "What do *you* think?"

Kutara took hold of Mark's arm. "I am going tonight."

"And I'm going to fight Dagovar," I said.

Mark rubbed his forehead with his fingers. "It's like the blind leading the blind. Sorry, Lenny."

It turned out that Guy didn't have any relatives who knew he was in the hospital. Before Lenny went home, he glamoured the nurse and found out that Dagovar was the *family* she had called. So he made her think we were Guy's only family and Dagovar was the person who had hit Guy. That last part was true.

After that, I led Lenny into the backyard, checking for Dagovar the whole time.

He sat down on the lawn, breathing heavily. "Let me rest for a minute before I go."

"Okay."

"Adlia, I want to tell you something."

"What?" I didn't look at him. I had to keep watching.

"Remember when we had sex?"

I thought for a moment. "No."

He gave a weak chuckle. "Well, we did, and I thought about asking you to be my mate. But I couldn't tell if you were really interested in me, so I didn't. I just want to say that I wish I had asked, and not only because it might have saved you from this whole mess, but because you're pretty incredible."

I smiled. "Thanks, Lenny."

"You're welcome." His hand found my calf and patted it. "Take care of yourself. I hope we see each other again."

"Me, too." I felt his hand dissolve. When I looked down, he was gone.

When I went back inside, the nurse had made Guy quit carving because his teeth were chattering. She made dinner for everyone.

We didn't talk about Dagovar while Guy and the nurse were at the table. I didn't know if anyone had told Guy that Dagovar wanted Kutara. It didn't matter, because I wasn't going to let him have her.

Finally Guy put down his fork. "That was delicious. I think I might need to rest for a while."

The nurse got up. "I'll get you settled."

As soon as they left, Mark reached for the tuna casserole. "She didn't make much of this."

Erin grabbed the other side of the dish. "Leave some for me!"

"You don't need it like I do."

"We're going, too, Mark . . . What's your last name?"

"Speranzi."

"We're going, too, Mark Speranzi!" she said.

He let go of the dish. "How do you figure that?"

"The van has tinted windows—Dagovar's not going to be able to see who's in there." She looked at Galan. "We might be able to help, you never know."

Kutara stirred. "No."

"Don't you start," Erin said.

One corner of Kutara's mouth raised slightly. "Galan might be next leader. Stay here."

Erin twisted her napkin, then threw it on the table. "I'm not happy about this."

After a moment, Kutara shrugged.

Mark had been tapping his fingers on the table. "So I'll drive Adlia and Kutara to the park."

Erin nodded. "Between the band shell area and the creek. Are you going to let Dagovar know you're there?"

"No. I'm going to try to sneak around behind him."

"Don't get in the way when I shoot him," I said.

Kutara nodded. "I'll try to shoot, too. For surprise."

Mark looked around the table, his mouth twisted unhappily. "I guess that's all the plan we have."

We got up at midnight and met in the basement so we wouldn't wake Guy or the nurse.

Erin looked at me, then raised her eyebrows at Mark. "Her hair is standing on end."

"Let's just say she's as ready as I can make her," he said.

Erin had found a fresh shirt for Mark, and some of Kutara's clothes for me. She knelt to roll up the cuffs of the pants. "All black is a good look for you, Adlia. Like an elven ninja." She got to her feet. "How do you feel?"

"Fine. I'm going to kill Dagovar."

She patted me on the shoulder. "Hold that thought."

"She's going to do fine," Mark said, then hugged me to his side and kissed the side of my face.

Galan hugged me, too. "Good luck," he whispered.

Erin hugged Mark and me, then wiped her hands under her eyes before turning to Kutara. "Call me superstitious, but I'm glad you changed out of that red shirt. The blue is much better." She gave a little sob and put her arms around Kutara.

Kutara's hand came up and rubbed Erin's back. "Don't worry."

Erin cried harder. "I'll see you soon." She pulled away and ran up the stairs.

Galan gave us a parting wave and followed her.

We went outside and got in the van.

Mark was backing out of the drive when Erin ran up and yelled, "Wait!"

He slammed on the brakes and lowered his window. "What?"

I had both arms up and was looking around for Dagovar.

Erin handed my messenger bag through the window. "You might want the passwords."

"It's a good thing I've taken so many pictures along the creek path," Mark said, as he drove. "I have a pretty clear image of where we're meeting. There's the band shell next to Arapahoe, and then the seating for the band shell, and then the chain-link fence that used to keep people from climbing on the old train engine before they took it away. Do you remember the train, Adlia?"

I thought for a little. He had put me in the front seat, next to him, and it was harder to think with stuff rushing by. "No."

"That's okay. Concentrate on Dagovar."

When we reached the meeting place, Mark parked across from the fancy teahouse. "Not much in the way of streetlights, and it's easy to get to Canyon and away. I can see why he picked it." He leaned over the stick thing and kissed me. "How do you feel?"

"Nice. That was a good kiss." I leaned toward him.

He smiled and kissed me again. "That's all we have time for. Do you feel pretty clear in your head?"

"I wish I was better."

"You're going to do fine. Don't be nervous."

"I'm not nervous. I just wish I was better."

I looked toward the meeting place. Another van sat in the middle of the grass, its nose pointed toward the street. "I think he's already here."

We peered out the windows. Nothing happened.

The other van was some dark color. No light came from inside.

"Two can play at that game," Mark said, starting the van. "Hold on." He drove over the curb and onto the grass, making us bounce. Then he made a circle and parked on the other side of the grassy area, nose pointed toward the street, just like Dagovar's van. "I'll get out on the side he can't see," he whispered.

"That's so smart!" I whispered back.

"Thanks. I just hope that's not a drug dealer over there, and Dagovar's hiding somewhere in the bushes."

I unbuckled my seat belt. "I'm going out."

"Wait a minute. Let me turn the interior lights off." He switched some things and then turned to look in the back. "How you doin', Kutara?"

"Dandy."

He laughed softly. "Adlia, go back there with her. When I say so, I want you to open the side door. Stay in front of Kutara as you walk over there."

Now that it was quiet and dark, it seemed easier to think, and I understood what he meant. "Okay." I climbed into the back between the two seats and held out my hand. "Give me the passwords."

Mark took the folded paper out of my bag and handed it to me. "Break a leg. Preferably his."

"Kutara, stay right behind me," I told her.

"Ready?" Mark asked. "Go."

I slid open the side door and felt the driver's door open as Mark slipped out. It was very quiet. Across the way, a little light went on inside the other van, but I couldn't see anyone in the front.

Kutara grasped the back of my shirt.

"I'm ready," she said.

"Then let's go." The other van was maybe thirty feet away. Kutara kept hold of my shirt as I walked about a third of the way. I stopped and waited. The other van was shaking a little, as if people were moving around inside, and then I heard a metal *clonk*. The door slid open.

Faith stepped out, with Dagovar behind her. It had been a while since I had seen him while both of us were standing still, and he was bigger than I remembered.

A little breeze blew past, and I wrinkled my nose at the smell it brought—something sharp and unnatural. I took a step back and bumped into Kutara. "What's that smell?"

"Not gasoline," she whispered, "but something close."

Faith's hair and clothes clung wetly to her body, and she held a little light in front of her—a lighter, I realized. She walked slowly toward us, raising her other hand to shield the flame. Her mouth was open, her eyes squeezed shut. In the light of the little flame, I saw moisture run down her neck.

The lighter was chunky, with a silver cap tilted back. If I could just glamour her to flip it closed . . . I sent the thought as hard as I could, only to feel that Faith's mind was closed tight against me.

"I'm better at it than you are," Dagovar said, as he walked behind her. "You should also know that her lighter is very resistant to wind. If you don't do exactly as I say, she'll set herself on fire. I've also found that elf energy ignites turpentine just fine. Give me what I want, and I'll leave her behind when I go."

Dagovar had always been better at thinking ahead, even when my thoughts weren't slowed to a trickle. *Would he really burn Faith?* He had tried to kill me, and had blinded Lenny.

Faith stopped about ten feet from me.

Dagovar stood hunched behind her, so I couldn't get a clear shot at his head. "Do you have the passwords?"

"Here they are." I held out my hand, the paper between finger and thumb.

"Put it on the ground."

I dropped it on the grass. "What would you have done if it was windy?"

"I had other plans. Now walk over there." He waved his hand to one side.

My eyes followed his gesture like a cat watching a bird. I wanted to fight, *now,* but I walked sideways, keeping Kutara behind me.

Faith walked past the paper. Dagovar stooped and picked it up, still keeping her between us. A breeze blew her hair over the lighter, and a few strands blazed like glowing threads before Dagovar quickly patted them with his hand. The smell of burnt hair blew past me.

"If you want her alive, I think we should finish this quickly," he said.

Was Mark somewhere nearby? Could he see what was happening? "I've given you the passwords," I said. "Send Faith over."

"Not until I get Kutara."

"Put the lighter out and I'll send her over."

"No." He had straightened slightly. My arm must have given away my intention, because he hunched over again, taking away my chance for a shot. "Send Kutara over now, or I'll set Faith on fire. Mark will be next."

Faith moved the lighter closer to her face. Somehow, her blank expression made it even scarier. At what point would she know she was burning?

"We'll move away," I said. "You'll never find us." The lighter was only inches from Faith's chin.

"And what about Galan and Erin? And Erin's and Mark's families? I'll kill all of them, just as I did Lenny."

Kutara stepped out from behind me. "I'll go with you."

Faith moved the lighter away with the same, slow, deliberate movement.

"That's better," Dagovar said. "Come here, Kutara. Adlia, you stay where you are."

Kutara edged slowly toward Dagovar. She looked afraid.

"Kutara didn't kill your father," I said. "Someone else did." Should I not have told him that? It seemed as though that might be a secret. "So there's no reason for you to hate her."

"I don't believe you," Dagovar said. "And now that she's barely functioning, she'll make an ideal slave."

I took a step toward him, and Faith jerked the lighter toward herself.

"Stay *back*. I'm not going to tell you again." He raised his arm and fired.

I dodged to one side and heard a scream come from behind me. By the time I had righted myself and turned, gray sparks crackled around Kutara. She sank to her knees, her arms crossed in front of her.

Dagovar glanced at me. "She's tough, I'll give her that."

I raised my arm, but Faith had moved to stay between us, still holding the lighter.

Dagovar shot Kutara again. Some of the blast bounced off her crossed arms, but not all. She didn't scream this time, but slipped sideways onto one hip, her head drooping.

The air tasted of sadness and pain, and something brushed against me. I looked down and couldn't see anything, but I knew what it was—dark energy, released from all living things as they died. I looked up in time to see Kutara fall onto her side.

The need to fight swelled in me like a bubble, and I raised my arm higher, sighting along it. My vision seemed to narrow on Dagovar as I watched for my chance, so I almost missed the dark blur that came from behind Dagovar's van—Mark, head lowered and fists pumping as he ran.

Dagovar heard him in time to swing round, and Faith brought the lighter to her chest. Flames swept across her shirt, blue in the dark, and then Mark hit her and they were down and rolling across the grass.

It could only have been an instant that Dagovar

and I stared at each other across the field. The dark cloud of Kutara's energy floated around us like murky water—powerful energy for anyone willing to use it.

I sucked it in as my arm lifted.

Dagovar's eyes widened in shock.

Elf fire left my fingertips in a thick, green blaze tinged with black. It met Dagovar's silver fire in midair and paused only long enough to engulf it and continue on, shattering against his chest like a cloud of thrown knives.

He fell backward, his form expanding like a brighter shadow in the darkness before winking out.

Dagovar's death energy surged into me, following Kutara's. I couldn't seem to stop taking it in, and my hand shook, wanting to shoot something else. I lifted my face and screamed until I fought down the impulse, then staggered to where Kutara lay on the ground, glad to see she hadn't dissolved. I could still say good-bye. Where were Mark and Faith? My head swung sluggishly to find them.

Mark was helping Faith get her clothes off. One side of her hair was burned short, and she vomited as I watched.

I slumped onto the ground next to Kutara, feeling sick and bloated. Black specks floated in front of my eyes like a cloud of gnats. I lay down and watched them until all thought left me and I was free.

Chapter Twenty-Four

Voices.

"You say it looked different than the other times she fought?"

"It came roaring out of her like she was a cannon. I *knew* she could do it."

I opened my eyes.

"Adlia!" Mark held my hand in both of his. "You did it!"

He kissed me, and I closed my eyes again. So restful, not to have to think.

"Adlia, we think you should stay awake." Galan's voice.

I sighed and opened my eyes again. I couldn't remember how we'd gotten here. All I remembered was my fight with Dagovar. "Where are we?"

"At Guy's house," Mark said.

"Kutara? Is she—"

"With Erin and Guy," he said. "Erin thought it might help her to be close to him."

I looked at his eyes, so beautiful and kind. "I took dark energy."

Behind Mark, Galan made a noise, but Mark shook his head. "I'm sorry, I don't understand. What is that?"

"Death energy. I took Kutara's death energy to help me beat Dagovar."

Galan took a step back, a look of shock and distaste on his face.

Mark squeezed my hands. "Good for you, honey. That's called using the enemy's energy against him."

"It's not the same thing *at all*," Galan said. "She's benefited from the dying spirit of another creature. You've heard us talk about dark elves. Adlia is tainted now."

The look Mark gave him was not friendly. "She is *not*. *Dagovar* released that energy, it was part of the battle, and Adlia only took it to beat him. Would you rather Dagovar had used it and killed us all?"

They had put me on a bed. I squirmed, feeling cold and sick. "Dagovar wasn't going to use the dark energy, Mark."

"You don't know that." He gave my hand a little shake. "Faith is going to be fine and Kutara has a good chance, all because of you."

Behind him, Galan left the room.

I smiled at Mark, because I knew it would make him happy. "You got Faith out of the way."

"Lucky for me I was wet from the creek, or we might both have been burned. I ran halfway around the damn block to get there."

"And you were so smart, to roll."

"The roll is the first thing you learn in martial arts. It keeps you from getting really hurt. Not that I don't hurt. I think Faith has extra elbows." He flexed his back and winced. "We're both going to be black and blue tomorrow."

"Tomorrow." I breathed the word out. Tomorrow all my worries might be gone, because I might not remember them.

Mark leaned forward suddenly and gathered me in his arms. "You're the bravest, strongest person I know," he whispered into my hair. "I love you."

A tear leaked out. "Love you, too."

Mark slept with me. I woke several times during the night, feeling darkness twist inside me. Once when I woke up I couldn't remember his name.

In the morning, I opened my eyes to see him putting a chair next to the bed. He smiled when he saw I was awake. "I have a surprise for you."

Culan came into the room, carrying Kutara. He placed her on the chair.

"I can walk," she said, "but I wanted to save my strength to examine you."

I looked at her in surprise. "Hair."

She touched the white streak at the side of her face. "Guy says it's exotic." She moved her hand to my chest, below the bone.

Something twisted inside me.

She took her hand away. "Adlia, are you paying attention to me?"

"Trying."

"Taking my dark energy was the right thing to do. In fact, it saved my life. I would have willingly given it to you if I could have, so let go of any guilt you feel."

I nodded. *Guilt.* What did that word mean? Trees moved outside the window. I looked at them.

"She's not talking much today," the man said.

"I wish I could say I'm surprised. I think it was sheer willpower that got her through the fight."

Dark. Light. Faces. Voices.

"Do that again. I think she's paying attention to it, for some reason."

Grass. Trees. Warm on face.
Man moving.

Wind blowing the grass and trees. Sun on my face.
Man fighting the air.

The man stood on one leg. Then he jumped. I knew him.

He came over. "Adlia?"

I thought hard. "Mark."

He smiled. "That's my girl."

* * *

Mark leaned on his back leg, one hand raised. It was like a dance, but not.

I wanted to know more. "What are you doing?"

"Cat stance. Come here and I'll show you."

I got up. My legs were stiff and didn't move well.

"Straighten your arm like you're going to punch me or throw elf fire at me." He grinned. "But don't, okay?"

I straightened my arm.

"Okay, I've just grabbed it, to stop you."

"That wouldn't stop me firing."

"I know. Kung fu doesn't take elves into account, as far as I know. Now look—with my weight on my back leg, I'm free to kick with this one." He straightened his forward leg toward my waist. "Low kick." This time his foot moved toward my neck. "Midsection, and, um . . ." Mark wobbled, dragging me forward a step, then lowered his leg to the ground. "There's a higher one, but I need more practice."

Still holding my arm, he tugged me toward him. "Come here."

I pressed against him, feeling my hair stir as he kissed me.

"Oh, you don't know how I've missed you," he whispered in my ear.

"I couldn't remember anything." I pulled back so I could look at him. "Am I better?"

"Yes. You're much better."

I looked around Guy's yard, tensing when I saw the tree that had hidden Dagovar. But Dagovar wouldn't be bothering us again. "*Why* am I better?" I turned at the sound of steps behind me.

Kutara came down the stairs from the deck, wearing gray slacks and a pink shirt. A wing of white hair framed the left side of her face. "You're better because we have discovered your talent."

I closed my mouth, which had fallen open in astonishment. "But I thought I'd tried everything!" I turned back to Mark. "Is it something cool? Can I show it off at bars?"

He laughed. "Not unless you want everyone to run screaming for the door."

"What are you talking about?"

"You're a warrior," Kutara said.

A warrior elf? "I've never heard of such a thing."

"Fighting is not a talent with which I was familiar either," Kutara said, "but when the only thing that seemed to pique your interest was Mark's kung fu exercises—"

"I was pretty stiff after rolling across the ground," Mark said. "Plus, I kept thinking that if I'd been in training, I could have taken Dagovar's head right off."

"Very unlikely," Kutara said. "As I was saying, I did some research. No hard information existed, but some elders remembered legends of elves who had a facility for fighting. Oddly, the words *elf fire* surfaced once or twice. It is apparently an archaic term."

"I'm a *warrior*." It was a strange thought, and a strange talent. "But I'm so small!"

"That's just less of you to hit," Mark said, sounding excited. "We also think you're more energy efficient, since I didn't pass out or get sick after you and Dagovar fought."

"Is that why my hair is short compared to other elves?" I wondered. "So it takes less energy to grow?"

"That, or so your enemy can't grab it as easily."

"Huh." I shook my head, still trying to come to grips with everything. "How long have I been out of it?"

"Almost two weeks," Kutara said. "I think the dark energy delayed your recovery, since it was not in your nature to take it."

I took quick stock of my body. "I don't feel anything weird inside anymore."

Mark hugged me with his arm. "You probably kicked its ass."

Kutara smiled. "Your recovery today is quite spectacular."

"And how about you?" I asked her. "Guy must be pretty good at the ice-sculpting by now."

Kutara's face softened. "He has started a replica of Notre Dame. It's quite challenging, but he says the beauty lies in its complexity and sharp edges."

I turned to Mark. "And Faith? What about her?"

"She should be fine. After we cleaned the turpentine off her, Kutara glamoured her to think she'd had a car wreck and been in a coma for a couple of days. She's back in Boston with her parents, recovering."

I had saved my next question for last, afraid of what I'd hear. "And Lenny?"

"He can see shapes now," Kutara said. "I have hope that he'll recover completely."

I heaved a sigh of pure relief. "That's everyone, isn't it?"

"Except for Fia." Kutara frowned. "We failed her."

I reached forward and gripped her hand for a moment. "I'm so sorry."

"It was not your fault." Her eyes narrowed. "It was Erin's fault."

I looked at Mark. "Could I talk to Kutara alone for a minute?"

"Sure." He ran his hand along my back as he left, as if reluctant to lose contact.

When he was inside Guy's house, Kutara raised her brows expectantly.

"I want to apologize for how difficult I was, back when we were working at Elf Ops," I said.

She lifted one shoulder. "It's in the past. And I have been told that I can be slightly demanding."

I fought down a smile. "Who had the nerve to tell you that?"

"Everyone I have ever worked with."

I couldn't help laughing this time, and she smiled in response. "So what happens to Elf Ops, now that we've lost all of Fellseth's money?" I asked.

"You'll be happy to know that we have located the laptops with the international-account information. I visited a few shipping companies in Boulder. *Daniel Kelly* paid for five boxes to be sent to a Swiss Post warehouse." She clasped her hands behind her back and walked toward the steps to the deck, and I fell into step with her. "As for the Kansas elves," she said, "they expressed no interest in working with the money and have given it all back. That group seems to have stronger than usual anti-human sentiment."

"That brings up one more thing I want to ask you," I said, "and I'll understand if you don't want to answer it."

She stopped at the foot of the stairs. "This sounds serious."

"I only ask because I have a lot of respect for the way you think," I began nervously. "I just wondered why you were willing to sacrifice yourself for Faith. It always seemed to me that you put a little more value on elves, what with humans outnumbering us so much, and you're pretty important. Was it from a sense of honor—because an elf put Faith in danger?"

She laughed. "You have a high opinion of my ideals, but in my mind, honor is not as important as practicality." She put a hand on my shoulder. "No, Adlia. I was willing to take that risk because I was confident you would save me."

Mark was waiting for me inside. "I called Erin. She and Galan are coming over to see you, and Guy is downstairs. I figured you'd want to catch up with everyone." He took my hands and swung them back and forth lightly. "Will you save this evening for me? We have things to talk about."

"Yeah, we do." Such as what the future held for an elf bonded to a man with a big Italian family.

"If you call, I'll pick you up," Mark said.

"No, I can get there. What time?"

"Six?"

"Okay." I stepped closer and linked my arms behind his neck. "Before I start this social whirl, do you think we could find an empty bedroom?"

He bent his head and rubbed his lips gently across mine—once, twice. "You know, human gals sometimes say they're too tired to make love."

"Funny. I have the opposite problem."

Chapter Twenty-Five

I took a cab to Mark's place. It felt strange to hand over money and be treated like anyone else. Strange, but not bad. I went up the walk and pressed the bell.

A moment later, Mark opened the door, wearing a dark blue shirt with the sleeves rolled up and black dress slacks.

"Oh, you look so nice!" I said regretfully. I wore my habitual jeans, and a T-shirt Erin had given me as a present. It had a picture of a bulldog and the slogan, CONSIDER YOURSELF WARNED.

Mark stretched out a hand and pulled me inside. "Would you *like* to wear something else? Because I have some gifts for you. We could start now."

I grinned. "Yes, please."

With Mark helping, it took a while to put on my new dress. It was red, with matching bra, panties, and shoes. By the time I had everything on, I felt very energetic.

I followed Mark out of the bedroom and toward the kitchen, flexing my shoulders. "I've never worn one of these bra things before."

"I had noticed, believe me." He pulled out a chair at the dining table for me. "And I'm definitely not complaining, but there are occasions when you might want one, such as when you meet my family."

His family. We had gotten to that subject so soon. Instead of tackling it, I sat down and gestured to the lovely table setting in front of me. "Have you forgotten that elves don't eat?"

"I got the memo, don't worry. Your plate is strictly for dessert, although not the food kind. And that's spring water in your glass, by the way. Galan said you could have that." He took his plate into the kitchen and came back with pasta and a side salad.

I pushed at the edge of my plate. "There are other things you should know about elves."

Mark poured wine into his glass from a bottle on the table. "Tell me."

I took a sip of my water. "Well, we don't age. I mean, we show age when we're really low on energy, but we don't get older over time. We don't die, unless someone kills us."

He swallowed a bite of his salad. "Uh-huh. Go on."

"As far as the bond between you and me goes, it will last until one of us dies."

He pointed his fork at his chest. "That would be me, in all likelihood."

I nodded.

"Let me ask you something." He speared a ravioli. "To your knowledge, does Kutara have any plans to kill me so we won't be bonded?"

"No! God, no."

"Just checking. Now that Kutara has her wits about her, she's kind of scary."

"Not *that* scary."

He lay his fork on his plate. "Is there anything else I need to know about elves?"

I got up and came around the table. "Just that this one loves you." I framed his face in my hands and kissed him. "And wants you to be happy."

He scooted his chair back and settled me on his lap. "You know what would make me happy?"

"Adding a nice human wife and some kids to your big Italian family?" I dropped my gaze to his chest.

"Look at me, Adlia."

I raised my gaze to his, so kind beneath his dark brows. He hadn't gotten a haircut, and his hair was shaggier than ever. "I'm looking."

"Then believe me when I say that what would make me happiest is to see you get the family and love you never had—*my* family, and *my* love. Leaving everything else aside, do you want that?"

My gaze dropped again, and my lip trembled. "It's just that elves aren't supposed to have children with humans, and you should have—"

"That's not what I asked." He tipped my chin up. "Would it make *you*, Adlia, happy to live with me and be part of my family?"

"Yes." I burst into tears.

He cradled my face, kissing me over and over. "I hope those are tears of joy."

"They are, but don't you want children? Half-elven kids can't be glamoured. It puts us in danger, not only because elves can't hide from them later

on, but because *I* couldn't hide from them. I can't
have my four-year-old going to school and talking
about her mommy the elf. She'd get sent to the
principal for lying, if nothing else."

Mark laughed. "Honey, haven't you ever heard of
adoption?"

Sheer surprise stopped my crying. "You'd do that?"
I wiped tears from my cheeks. "I don't know why I'm
surprised. You seem to really like helping people."

"Oh, I'm not completely selfless." He put his cheek
to mine and murmured in my ear. "Think of it—one
shot of mama's glamour and they'd spill all their
secrets. We'd have the best-behaved kids in the *world.*"
He lowered his voice to a whisper. "My mother would
think the sun shines out of your backside."

I was laughing when he pulled away. "You'd still
have a wife who looked more and more younger
than you," I warned.

He made a mock sad face. "Oh, imagine my
heartbreak. No, as long as you're willing to glamour
my family to ignore some things when we're visiting, I don't think that's a problem."

"Or I could let myself get tired and develop a few
temporary wrinkles," I said.

He nodded solemnly. "My family can be very
tiring. Now go sit in your own chair. I have another
present for you."

I went back to my chair and waited while he got
something from a drawer in the kitchen.

He came back with a small box and put it in the
middle of my plate. "Here's your dessert."

I had seen this happen in dozens of movies, but

my breath had never quickened while I watched. It did now, and my hands trembled as I carefully opened the hinged lid. Four diamonds sparkled on a white band of metal. "It's beautiful."

"What we have is beautiful." He took it from me and slipped it on the ring finger of my left hand, then pointed to the stones, his head next to mine. "Those two diamonds are us, and the smaller ones can be our kids. I thought we'd order one of each."

I moved my hand to watch the sparkle. "It fits perfectly. That must be a sign."

He kissed the top of my head. "It's a sign I measured your finger while you were a moron. Now take it off."

I looked up. "*Already?* Why?"

He laughed. "I want to show you something. Your name means *unknown,* right?"

I took off the ring. "That's right."

"Well, my last name, Speranzi, means *hope.* Both our rings will be engraved. Mine will say, *My future is Unknown.*"

I read the tiny script in my ring. "But I have Hope."

Mark and I were married in Boston. Kutara and Guy flew up for the wedding and met Mark's family for the first time at the rehearsal dinner.

Kutara offered her hand to Lucy Speranzi, Mark's mother. "It's a pleasure to meet you."

Lucy pulled Kutara into a full-body hug and rocked her back and forth. "So you're the one who brought up our Adlia! Aunt Kootie!"

Kutara glared at me over Lucy's shoulder. "*Not* Aunt Kootie. You may call me Kutara."

Lucy finally let go, rubbing her hands up and down Kutara's arms a few times before breaking contact. "I know *exactly* how you feel. When my daughter Amy was little, she started calling me *Maw* for some reason. Drove me crazy. *Maw.* Finally I told her, every time you call me *Maw,* I'm taking a Care Bear away. That fixed her."

"A wise strategy," Kutara said. "Unfortunately for me, Adlia never had anything that really meant something to her until Mark came along."

"Oh, my God." Lucy's eyes overflowed, and she hugged Kutara again.

I owe you, I mouthed at Kutara.

She absently patted Lucy's back. *Yes,* she mouthed back. *You do.*

Nonno Nino, who was slightly deaf, leaned toward Mark. "They're a little *WASPy,* but *nice,*" he whispered loudly.

Our wedding was beautiful. Guy and Kutara flew back afterward, but Mark and I stayed in Boston a while longer. I was finally having the family experience I had missed—and then some.

"Show me another one!" Mark's nephew yelled.

I put my hands on my hips. "Tommy, I have showed you every move I know. There's only so much kung fu in the world, okay?"

"Show me another one, Adlia, pleeeeease!"

I squatted so I was eye level with him. "Buh-bye."

"Mark!" I shouted, as I left the family room and went through the kitchen. Shouting was the only way to communicate with so many people around.

Mark's sister and mother sat at the kitchen table, having coffee. Amy grabbed my sleeve as I went by. "You don't cook?"

Her mother shushed her. "I told you, it's not a big deal. Adlia, honey, Amy could give you some of her cookbooks. I know for a fact that she has some she never uses."

Amy let go of my sleeve. "Mom, I use every cookbook you have ever given me, I swear to God."

I smiled at both of them. "Nonno Nino pinched my ass today, did I tell you that?"

Lucy shoved back her chair, bellowing, "Nino!"

I looked toward the ceiling as rapid footsteps shuffled across the floor above us. "Sounds like he's upstairs."

They took off in pursuit.

I almost ran into Mark as he came out of the downstairs bathroom. I pushed him back inside and shut the door behind us. "If I don't get some peace and quiet, I'm going to glamour your entire family to think they've gone mute."

He took my hands, his fingers still damp from washing them. "Give me a minute to round them up for you."

I fell against his chest and felt his arms come around me. "They're a wonderful family. Exhausting, but wonderful."

"Have I told you"—he pulled up my shirt and slid

his hands around my bare lower back—"what my mother said just before the wedding?"

"What'd she say?" I opened the middle button on his shirt and kissed his skin there.

"She said, *This one's tough. I think she can handle us.* Then she smacked my arm and told me to be a good husband."

"Did she cry when she said it?"

"She cried the whole time she was talking."

"I love your mother."

He lifted my chin so he could see my expression. "I don't see any wrinkles. Can you take two more days?"

"Absolutely." I bared my teeth and gave a little growl. "Like Mom says, I'm tough."

"There's one more thing."

I pursed my mouth and lifted it for a kiss. "Yesh?"

"Tommy told me who hid Nonno Nino's teeth."

"That little traitor!" I lunged for the door. "I'll show him kung fu!"

Mark pulled me back, laughing. "If I had *designed* a woman to make me as happy as possible *and* fit in with my family, I never would have come up with someone as good as you." He kissed me softly. "I know we're going to have occasional difficulties, but promise me you'll always remember something."

"What?"

"I love you most."

I pushed a lock of Mark's hair off his forehead and smiled. "I will always remember that."

Someone pounded on the door. From outside, Nonno Nino yelled, "Yo! I got an old man's bladder out here!"

Epilogue

Two months later, Kutara and Guy attended an auction to benefit a Denver homeless shelter. Several huge drawings of birds received a lot of attention and the highest bids. Kutara bought all of them, then arranged to meet the artist. She asked me to go with her.

The administrator of the shelter had set up a meeting at the Cottage Inn Coffee Shop.

We walked in, and Kutara scanned the tables. "There she is!" She took a few steps and halted. "She's changed."

I followed Kutara's gaze. Fia was tan and a little thinner. Her short, spiky haircut revealed rounded ears with multiple piercings.

Kutara gave a tiny sigh before she put her small purse under her arm and walked briskly forward. "Mr. Rodriguez?" she asked the man sitting across from Fia. He was about forty, with grizzled hair and brown skin. "We spoke on the phone. I'm Kutara."

They shook hands, and then Kutara turned. "And you must be the artist I admired so much."

Fia shook hands with both of us. "It's nice to meet you. I'm Sue."

Sue told us she was an amnesiac. She couldn't remember a thing before her first good meal at the shelter.

As far as I could tell, her transition to human had left her with all knowledge that wasn't strictly elven, such as language—and drawing. She still had her talent.

"What are your plans?" Kutara asked.

Sue toyed with her straw. "I'm still in the missing persons database, so my family might find me someday."

"Somebody contacted us a month ago," Rodriguez said, "Josh Temple. He claimed to be Sue's exboyfriend, but he didn't have any hard information and the name he knew her by wasn't on record anywhere."

"Seeing him didn't trigger any memories," Sue said. "I don't think he was sure I was the same person."

"What about work?" Kutara asked.

Sue looked at Rodriguez. "Hector is teaching me administration work at the shelter. Typing and stuff. I'm hoping to make my own living eventually."

"You don't want a career in art?" Kutara asked.

Sue laughed. "Doesn't every artist? But that's not exactly a sure way to make money." She gave us a look of chagrin. "I'm not saying the drawings you bought are worthless. I'm sure they'll turn out to be an awesome investment." She looked at Rodriguez. "I'm smooth, aren't I?"

Kutara opened her purse and took out a business card. "I would like to sponsor you." She put the card on the table and slid it toward Sue. "If you'll contact this attorney, he'll provide you with a place to live, a car, and an allowance. I hope that you will use your opportunities to make a career for yourself as an artist." She stood. "And now, I have to go."

I untangled my foot from the table legs as Kutara walked away. "Um, it was nice meeting you both."

"Wait!" Sue picked up Kutara's card, then looked at me. "Is she *serious*? Why would she do that?" She pushed herself to her feet. "Does she *know* me?"

"No." I shook my head firmly. "You just remind her of someone."